CRITICAL PRAISE FOR
The Last Policeman
by Ben H. Winters
An Edgar Award Finalist

"[The] plotting is sure-footed and surprising. . . . Ben H. Winters reveals himself as a novelist with an eye for the well-drawn detail."

—*Slate*

"Ben H. Winters makes noir mystery even darker: *The Last Policeman* sets a despondent detective on a suspicious suicide case— while an asteroid hurtles toward earth."

—*Wired*

"I love this book. I stayed up until seven in the morning reading because I could not stop. Full of compelling twists, likable characters, and a sad beauty, *The Last Policeman* is a gem. It's the first in a trilogy, and I am already excited for book two."

—Audrey Curtis, *San Francisco Book Review*

"I'm eager to read the other books, and expect that they'll keep me as enthralled as the first one did."

—Mark Frauenfelder, *Boing Boing*

"I haven't had to defend my love for science fiction in quite a while, but when I do, I point to books like *The Last Policeman*. [It] explores human emotions and relationships through situations that would be impossible (or worse yet, metaphorical) in literary fiction. This is a book that asks big questions about civilization, community, desperation and hope. But it doesn't provide big, pat answers."

—Michael Ann Dobbs, *io9*

"I've rarely been more surprised by a mystery novel than I was by this one—it's an unlikely cross-genre mashup that coheres for two reasons: the glum, relentless, and implausibly charming detective Hank Palace; and, most importantly, Ben H. Winters's clean, clever, thoughtful, and gently comic prose."

—J. Robert Lennon

"A solidly plotted whodunit with strong characters and excellent dialogue ... the impending apocalypse isn't merely window dressing, either: it's a key piece of the puzzle Hank is trying to solve."

—*Booklist*

"This thought-provoking mystery should appeal to crime fiction aficionados who like an unusual setting and readers looking for a fresh take on apocalypse stories."

—*Library Journal*

"A promising kickoff to a planned trilogy. For Winters, the beauty is in the details rather than the plot's grim main thrust."

—Kirkus Reviews (starred review)

"Ben H. Winters spins a wonderful tale while creating unique characters that fit in perfectly with the ever-changing societal pressures. . . . [This] well-written mystery will have readers eagerly awaiting the second installment."

—*The New York Journal of Books*

"Extraordinary—as well as brilliant, surprising, and, considering the circumstances, oddly uplifting."

—*Mystery Scene Magazine*

"Exhilarating. . . . do not wait for the movie!"

—*E! Online*

COUNTDOWN

CITY

COUNTDOWN

CITY

The Last Policeman Book II

By Ben H. Winters

QUIRK BOOKS
PHILADELPHIA

Library of Congress Cataloging in Publication Number: 2013930159

ISBN: 978-1-59474-626-0

Printed in Canada
Typeset in Bembo and OCRA

Designed by Doogie Horner
Cover photographs: (diner scene) © Jonathan Pushnik;
(rioting crowd) © Nameer Galal/Demotix/Corbis
Cover model: Thom Gallen
Special thanks to Silk City
Production management by John J. McGurk

Quirk Books
215 Church St.
Philadelphia, PA 19106
quirkbooks.com
10 9 8 7 6 5 4 3 2 1

For Adele and Sherman Winters
(43 years)
and
Alma and Irwin Hyman
(44 years)

"*Nahui Olin* was not the first sun. According to the Aztecs and their neighbors, there have been four previous suns. Each of them presided over a world that was destroyed in a cosmic catastrophe. These catastrophes did not always result in mass extinction; the results were sometimes transformative, i.e., of humans into animals."

—*Meteors and Comets in Ancient Mexico* (Ulrich Köhler, in the Geological Society of America Special Paper 356: *Catastrophic Events and Mass Extinctions*)

━━━━━━

"Forever doesn't mean forever anymore
I said 'forever'
but it doesn't look like I'm gonna be around
much anymore."

—Elvis Costello, "Riot Act"

PART ONE

....

A Man with a Woman on His Mind

....

Wednesday, July 18

Right Ascension 20 08 05.1
Declination -59 27 39
Elongation 141.5
Delta 0.873 AU

1.

"It's just that he *promised*," says Martha Milano, pale eyes flashing, cheeks flushed with anxiety. Grieving, bewildered, desperate. "We both did. We promised each other like a million times."

"Right," I say. "Of course."

I pluck a tissue from the box on her kitchen table and Martha takes it, smiles weakly, blows her nose. "I'm sorry," she says, and honks again, and then she gathers herself, just a little, sits up straight and takes a breath. "But so Henry, you're a policeman."

"I was."

"Right. You were. But, I mean, is there . . ."

She can't finish, but she doesn't need to. I understand the question and it floats there in the air between us and slowly revolves: *Is there anything you can do?* And of course I'm dying to help her, but frankly I'm not sure whether there *is* anything that I can do, and it's hard, it's impossible, really, to know what to say. For the last hour I've just been sitting here and listening, taking down the information in my slim blue exam-taker's notebook. Martha's missing husband is Brett Cavatone; age thirty-three; last seen at a restaurant called Rocky's Rock 'n' Bowl, on Old Loudon Road, out by the Steeplegate Mall. It's her father's place, Martha explained, a family-friendly pizza-joint-slash-bowling-alley, still open despite everything, though with a drastically reduced menu. Brett has worked there, her father's right-hand man, for two years. Yesterday morning, about 8:45, he left to do some errands and never came back.

I read over these scant notes one more time in the worried silence of Martha's neat and sunlit kitchen. Officially her name is Martha Cavatone, but to me she will always be Martha Milano, the fifteen-year-old kid who watched my sister Nico and me after school, five days a week, until my mom got home, gave her ten bucks in an envelope, and asked after her folks. It's unmooring to see her as an adult, let alone one overturned by the emotional catastrophe of having been abandoned by her husband. How much stranger it must be for her to be turning to me, of all people, whom she last laid eyes on when I was twelve. She blows her nose again, and I give her a small gentle smile. Martha Milano with the overstuffed purple JanSport backpack, the Pearl Jam T-shirt. Cherry-pink bubblegum and cinnamon lip gloss.

She wears no makeup now. Her hair is an unruly brown pile; her eyes are red rimmed from crying; she's gnawing vigorously on the nail of her thumb.

"Disgusting, right?" she says, catching me looking. "But I've been smoking like crazy since April, and Brett never says anything even though I know it grosses him out. I have this stupid feeling, like, if I stop now, it'll bring him home. I'm sorry, Henry, did you—" She stands abruptly. "Do you want tea or something?"

"No, thank you."

"Water?"

"No. It's okay, Martha. Sit down."

She falls back into the chair, stares at the ceiling. What I want of course is coffee, but thanks to whatever byzantine chain of infrastructural disintegration is determining the relative availability of various perishable items, coffee cannot be found. I close my notebook and look Martha in the eye.

"It's tough," I say slowly, "it really is. There are just a lot of reasons why a missing-persons investigation is especially challenging in the current environment."

"Yeah. No." She blinks her eyes, closed and then open again. "I mean, of course. I know."

Dozens of reasons, really. Hundreds. There is no way to put out a description on the wires, to issue an APB or post to the FBI Kidnappings and Missing Persons List. Witnesses who might know the location of a missing individual have very little interest or incentive to divulge that information, if they haven't gone missing themselves. There is no way to access federal or local databases. As of last Friday, in fact, southern New Hampshire appears to have no electricity whatsoever. Plus of course I'm not a policeman anymore, and even if I was, the CPD as a matter of policy is no longer pursuing such cases. All of which makes finding one particular individual a long shot, is what I tell Martha. Especially—and here I pause, load my voice with as much care and sensitivity as I can—especially since many such people left on purpose.

"Yeah," she says flatly. "Of course."

Martha knows all of this. Everybody knows. The world is on the move. Plenty still leaving in droves on their Bucket List adventures, going off to snorkel or skydive or make love to strangers in public parks. And now, more recently, whole new forms of abrupt departure, new species of madness as we approach the end. Religious sects wandering New England in robes, competing for converts: the Doomsday Mormons, the Satellites of God. The mercy cruisers, traveling the deserted highways in buses with converted engines running on wood gas or coal, seeking opportunities for Samaritanship. And of course the preppers, down in their basements, hoarding what they can, building piles for the aftermath, as if any amount of preparation will suffice.

I stand up, close my notebook. Change the subject. "How is your block?"

"It's fine," says Martha. "I guess."

"There's an active residents association?"

"Yes." She nods blankly, not interested in the line of questioning, not ready to contemplate how things will be for her alone.

"And let me ask, hypothetically, if there were a firearm in the home . . ."

"There is," she begins. "Brett left his—"

I hold up one hand, cut her off. "Hypothetically. Would you know how to use it?"

"Yes," she says. "I can shoot. Yes."

I nod. Fine. All I needed to hear. Private ownership or sale of firearms is technically forbidden, although the brief wave of house-to-house searches ended months ago. Obviously I'm not going to bike over to School Street and report that Martha Cavatone has her husband's service piece under the bed—get her sent away for the duration—but neither do I need to hear any details.

Martha murmurs "excuse me" and gets up, jerks open the pantry door and reaches for a tottering pile of cigarette cartons. But then she stops herself, slams the door, and spins around to press her fingers into her eyes. It's almost comical, it's such a teenage set of gestures: the impetuous grab for comfort, the immediate and disgusted self-abnegation. I remember standing in our front hallway, at seven or eight years old, just after Martha went home in the evenings, trying to catch one last sniff of cinnamon and bubblegum.

"Okay, so, Martha, what I can do is go by the restaurant," I say—I hear myself saying—"and ask a few questions." And as soon as the words are out she's across the room, hugging me around the neck, grinning into my chest, like it's a done deal, like I've already brought her husband home and he's out there on the stoop, ready to come in.

"Oh, thank you," she says. "*Thank you*, Henry."

"Listen, wait—wait, Martha."

I gently pry her arms from around my neck, step back and plant her in front of me, summon the stern hardheaded spirit of my grand-father, level Martha with his severe stare. "I will do what I can to find your husband, okay?"

"Okay," she says, breathless. "You promise?"

"Yes." I nod. "I can't promise that I will find him, and I definitely can't promise that I will bring him home. But I'll do what I can."

"Of course," she says, "I understand," and she's beaming, hugging me again, my notes of caution sliding unheard off her cheeks. I can't help it, I'm smiling, too, Martha Milano is hugging me and I'm smiling.

"I'll pay you, of course," she says.

"No, you won't."

"No, I know, not with *money* money, but we can figure out something . . ."

"Martha, no. I won't take anything from you. Let's have a look around, okay?"

"Okay," she says, wiping the last of the tears from her eyes.

* * *

Martha finds me a recent picture of her husband, a nice full-body snapshot from a fishing trip a couple years back. I study him, Brett Cavatone, a short man with a broad powerful frame, standing at the bank of a stream in the classic pose, holding aloft a dripping wide-mouth bass, man and fish staring into the camera with the same skeptical and somber expression. Brett has a black beard, thick and untrimmed, but the hair on his head is neat and short, a crew cut only slightly grown out.

"Was your husband in the military, Martha?"

"No," she says, "he was a cop. Like you. But not Concord. The state force."

"A trooper?"

"Yes." Martha takes the picture from me, gazes at it proudly.

"Why did he leave the force?"

"Oh, you know. Tired of it. Ready for a change. And my dad was starting this restaurant. So, I don't know."

She murmurs these fragments—*tired of it, ready for a change*—as if they require no further explanation, like the idea of leaving law enforcement voluntarily makes self-evident sense. I take the photograph back and slip it into my pocket, thinking of my own brief career: patrolman for fifteen months, detective on Adult Crimes for four months, forcibly retired along with my colleagues on March twenty-eighth of this year.

We walk around the house together. I'm peering into the closets, opening Brett's drawers, finding nothing interesting, nothing remarkable: a flashlight, some paperbacks, a dozen ounces of gold. Brett's closet and dresser drawers are still full of clothes, which in normal circumstances would suggest foul play rather than intentional abandonment, but there is no longer any such thing as normal circumstances. At lunch yesterday, McGully told us a story he heard, where the husband and wife were out for a walk in White Park, and the woman just runs, literally runs, leaps over a hedge and disappears into the distance.

"She said, 'Can you hold my ice cream a sec?'" McGully said, laughing, bellowing, pounding the table. "Poor dummy standing there with two ice creams."

The Cavatones' bedroom furniture is handsome and sturdy and plain. On Martha's night table is a hot-pink journal with a small brass lock, like a child's diary, and when I lift it I get just the lightest scent of cinnamon. Perfect. I smile. On the opposite night table, Brett's, is a miniature chess board, pieces arranged midgame; her husband, Martha tells me with another fond smile, plays against himself. Hung above the dresser is a small tasteful painting of Christ crucified. On the wall of the bathroom, next to the mirror, is a slogan in neat all-capital block letters: IF YOU ARE WHAT YOU SHOULD BE, YOU WILL SET THE WORLD ABLAZE!

"Saint Catherine," says Martha, appearing beside me in the mirror, tracing the words with her forefinger. "Isn't it beautiful?"

We go back downstairs and sit facing each other on a tidy brown sofa in the living room. There's a column of dead bolts along the front door and rows of iron bars on the windows. I flip open my notebook and gather a few more details: what time her husband left for work yesterday, what time her father came by, said "have you seen Brett?" and they realized that he was gone.

"This may seem like an obvious question," I say, when I'm done writing down her answers. "But what do you think he might be doing?"

Martha worries at the nail of her pinky. "I've thought about it so much, believe me. I mean, it sounds silly, but something *good*. He wouldn't be off bungee jumping or shooting heroin or whatever." My mind flashes on Peter Zell, the last poor soul I went in search of, while Martha continues. "If he really left, if he's not . . ."

I nod. If he's not dead. Because that possibility, too, hovers over us. A lot of missing people are missing because they're dead.

"He'd be doing something, like, *noble*," Martha concludes. "Something he thought was noble."

I smooth the edges of my mustache. Something noble. A powerful thing to think about one's husband, especially one who's just disappeared without explanation. A pink bead of blood has appeared at the edge of her fingernail.

"And you don't feel it's possible—"

"No," says Martha. "No women. No way." She shakes her head, adamant. "Not Brett."

I don't press it; I move on. She tells me that he was getting around on a black ten-speed bicycle; she tells me no, he didn't have any regular activities outside of work and home. I ask her if there's anything else she needs to tell me about her husband or her marriage, and she says no: He was here, they had a plan, and then he went away.

Now all that's left is the million-dollar question. Because even if I do track him down—which I almost certainly will not be able to do—it remains the case that abandoning one's spouse is not illegal and never has been, and of course I have no power at this point to compel anyone to do anything. I'm unsure exactly how to explain any of this to Martha Milano, and I suspect she knows it anyway, so I just go ahead and say it:

"What do you want me to do if I find him?"

She doesn't answer at first, but leans across the sofa and stares deeply, almost romantically, into my eyes. "Tell him he has to come home. Tell him his salvation depends on it."

"His . . . salvation?"

"Will you tell him that, Henry? His salvation."

I murmur something, I don't know what, and look down at my notebook, vaguely embarrassed. The faith and fervency are new; they weren't an aspect of Martha Milano when we were young. It's not just that she loves this man and misses him; she believes that he has sinned by abandoning her and will suffer for it in the world to come. Which is coming, of course, a lot sooner than it used to be.

I tell Martha I'll be back soon if I have any news and where she can find me, in the meantime, if she needs to.

As we stand up, her expression changes.

"Jeez, I'm sorry, I'm such a—I'm sorry. Henry, how's your sister doing?"

"I don't know," I say.

I'm already at the door, I'm working my way through the series of dead bolts and chains.

"You don't know?"

"I'll be in touch, Martha. I'll let you know what I can find."

* * *

The current environment. That's what I said to Martha: *A missing-person investigation is especially challenging in the current environment.* I sigh, now, at the pale inadequacy of the euphemism. Even now, fourteen months since the first scattered disbelieving sightings, seven months after the odds of impact rose to one hundred percent, nobody knows what to call it. "The situation," some people say, or "what's going on." "This craziness." On October third, seventy-seven days from today, the asteroid $2011GV_1$, 6.5 kilometers in diameter, will plow into planet Earth and destroy us all. *The current environment.*

I trot briskly down the stairs of the Cavatones' porch in the sunlight and unchain my bike from their charming cement birdbath. Their lawn is the only one mowed on the street. It's a beautiful day today, hot but not too hot, clear blue sky, drifting white clouds. Pure uncomplicated summertime. On the street there are no cars, no sound of cars.

I snap on my helmet and take my bike slowly down the street, right on Bradley, east toward Loudon Bridge, heading in the direction of Steeplegate Mall. A police car is parked at the end of Church with an officer in the driver's seat, a young man sitting upright in black wraparound shades. I nod hello and he nods back, slow, impassive. There's a second cop car at Main and Pearl, this one with a driver I slightly recognize, although his wave in return to mine is cursory at best, quick and unsmiling. He's one of the legions of inexperienced young patrol officers who swelled the ranks of the CPD in the weeks before its abrupt reorganization under the federal Department of Justice—the same reorganization that dissolved the Adult Crimes Unit and the rest of the detective divisions. I don't get the memos any-more, of course, but the current operating strategy appears to be one of overwhelming presence: no investigations, no neighborhood polic-ing, just a cop on every corner, rapid response to any whiff of public disturbance, as with the recent events on Independence Day.

If I *were* still on the force, it would be General Order 44-2 that would be relevant to Martha's case. I can call up the form in my mind, practically see it: Part I, procedures; Part VI, Unusual Circum-stances. Additional investigative steps.

There's a guy at Main and Court, dirty beard and no shirt, whirling in circles and punching the air, earbuds in place, though I'd be willing to bet there's no music coming out of them. I raise my hand from my handlebars and the bearded man waves back then pauses, looks down, adjusting the nonexistent volume. Once I'm over the bridge I make a small detour, weave over to Quincy Street and the elementary school. I chain my bike to the fence surrounding the playing field, take off my helmet and scan the recess yard. It's the height of summer but there's a small army of kids hanging out here, as there has been all day, every day, playing four-square and hop-scotch, chasing one another across the weeds of the soccer field, uri-nating against the wall of the deserted brick schoolhouse. Many spend the night here too, camping out on their beach towels and *Star Wars: The Clone Wars* bed sheets.

Micah Rose is sitting on a bench on the outskirts of the play-ground, his legs drawn up and hugged to his chest. He's eight. His sister Alyssa is six, and she's pacing back and forth in front of him. I take the pair of eyeglasses I've been carrying in my coat pocket and hand them to Alyssa, who claps her hands delightedly.

"You fixed them."

"Not me personally," I say, eyeing Micah, who is looking stonily at the ground. "I know a guy." I tilt my head toward the bench. "What's wrong with my man?"

Micah looks up and scowls warningly at his sister. Alyssa looks away. She's wearing a sleeveless jean jacket I gave her a couple weeks ago, two sizes too big, with a Social Distortion patch sewn on the back. It belonged to Nico, my own sister, many years ago.

"Come on, guys," I say, and Alyssa glances one last time at Micah and launches in: "Some big kids from St. Alban's were here and they were being all crazy and pushing and stuff, and they took things."

"Shut *up*," says Micah. Alyssa looks back and forth from him to me and almost cries, but then keeps it together. "They took Micah's sword."

"Sword?" I say. "Huh."

Their father is a feckless character named Johnson Rose, whom I went to high school with, and who I happen to know went Bucket List very early on. The mother, unless I got the story wrong, subsequently overdosed on vodka and pain pills. A lot of the kids spending their days out here have similar stories. There's one, Andy Blackstone—I see him right now, bouncing a big rubber medicine ball against the school—who was being raised, for one reason or another, by an uncle. When the odds rose to a hundred percent, the uncle apparently just told him to get the fuck out.

A little more gentle prodding of Alyssa and Micah, and it emerges, to my relief, that what has been lost is a toy—a plastic samurai sword that once upon a time came with a ninja costume, but which Micah had been wearing at his belt for some weeks.

"Okay," I say, squeezing Alyssa's shoulder and turning to look at Micah in the eye. "It's not a big deal."

"It just sucks," says Micah emphatically. "It sucks."

"I know that."

I flip past the details on Brett Cavatone to the back of my notebook, where I've got certain small tasks laid out for myself. I cross out *A's glasses* and pencil in *samurai sword* with a couple of question marks beside it. As I straighten awkwardly out of my squat, Andy Blackstone bounces the medicine ball my way, and I turn just in time for it to sproing up off the pavement and hit my outstretched palms with a satisfying, stinging *whap*.

"Hey, Palace," hollers Blackstone. "Play some kickball?"

"Rain check," I say, winking at Alyssa and clipping my helmet back on. "I've got a case I'm working on."

2.

Rocky's Rock 'n' Bowl turns out to be a great big brick building with black-glass windows and a hokey sign above the door—
musical notes and a smiling cartoon family munching on pizza.
Rocky's sits just past the abandoned husk of Steeplegate Mall, and to
get there you've got to go through the vast mall parking lot, through
a small obstacle course of garbage cans, overturned and spilling out,
and abandoned vehicles, their hoods popped by thieves to dig out
the engines. In front of the doors of the restaurant, sitting atop an
empty newspaper box like statuary, is a young guy, twenty maybe,
twenty-one, a stubbly uneven teenager's beard and a short ponytail,
who calls out "how you doin'?" as I approach.

"Just fine," I say, mopping my sweaty brow with a handkerchief.
The kid hops down from the newspaper box and sidles up to meet
me, nice and easy, his hands jammed in the pockets of his light jacket.

A criminal's trick—you don't know if he's got a gun or not.

"Nice suit, man," he says. "Help you find something?"

"I'm looking for the pizza place," I say, pointing behind him.

"Sure. Sorry, what's your name?"

"Henry," I say. "Palace."

"How'd you hear about us?"

Lots of questions, rat-a-tat, not to get the answers but to get a read: *How nervous is this guy? What does he want?* But he's nervous himself, eyes slipping warily side to side, and I talk slow and calm, keep my hands where he can see them.

"I know the owner's daughter."

"Oh, no kidding?" he says. "And what's her name again?"

"Martha."

"Martha," he says, like he'd forgotten it and needed reminding. "Totally."

Satisfied, the kid takes an exaggerated step backward to push open the door. "Heya, Rocky," he calls. A blast of music and warm smells from the darkness within. "A friend of Martha's." And then, to me, as I walk past, "Sorry about the hassle. Can't be too cautious these days, know what I'm saying?"

I nod politely, wondering what he's got hidden up in the jacket, what means are tucked away to welcome a visitor without the right answers: a switchblade, a crowbar, a snub-nose pistol. *Can't be too cautious these days.*

The music playing inside is early rock and roll, tinny but loud; there must be a battery-operated boom box tucked away somewhere, turned up to ten. Rocky's is just one big room, wide as an airplane hangar, high ceilinged and noisy and echoey. At one end is an open kitchen with a massive wood-burning pizza oven, a couple of cooks back there with rolled-up sleeves and aprons, drinking beers, bustling around, laughing. The dining area has the classic cheap red-and-white checked tablecloths, fat little barrels of red pepper flakes, vinyl records and cardboard cutout guitars displayed along the upper moldings. There's a sign shaped like a Wurlitzer jukebox advertising specials, all named after girls from classic-rock songs: the Layla, the Hazel, the Sally Simpson, the Julia.

A big man in a stained white apron shambles over from the kitchen, raising a bear paw of a hand in friendly greeting.

"How you doin'?" he says, just like the kid outside, same practiced geniality. Old Saint Nick belly, fading anchor tattoos on his forearms, sauce stains down his front like cartoon blood. "You wanna shoot, or you wanna eat?"

"Shoot?"

He points. Behind me are six bowling alleys that have been repurposed as firing ranges, with rifle stands at one end and paper human targets at the other. As I watch, a young woman in noise-canceling headphones narrows her eyes and squeezes off a round from a paintball gun, blasting a yellow splotch onto the upper arm of the target. She shouts happily and her husband, boyfriend maybe, claps and says "nice." At the next alley over, a hunched and white-haired man, one of a cluster of seniors, is hobbling slowly up to the rifle stand to take his turn.

I turn back to the big man. "You're Mr. Milano?"

"Rocky," he says, the easy relaxed smile freezing and hardening. "Can I help you with something?"

"I hope so."

He crosses his thick arms, narrows his eyes, and waits. It's "Ooby Dooby"—the song playing from the boom box—vintage Roy Orbison. Love this song.

"My name is Henry Palace," I say. "We've met, actually."

"Oh, yeah?" He smiles, pleasant but disinterested: a restaurateur, a man who meets a lot of people.

"I was a kid. I've had a growth spurt. "

"Oh, okay." He looks me up and down. "Looks like you've had a couple of those."

I smile. "Martha has asked me to try and locate your son-in-law."

"Whoa, whoa," says Rocky, eyes suddenly sharpening, taking me in more carefully. "What, you're a cop? She called the *cops*?"

"No, sir," I say. "I'm not a policeman. I used to be. Not anymore."

"Well, whatever you are, let me save you some time," he says. "That asshole said he'd be with my daughter till boomsday, and then he changed his mind and made a run for it." He grunts, refolds his arms across his chest. "Any questions?"

"A couple," I say. Behind us the dull dead thud of the paintball rounds smashing into their targets. This sort of thing is going on all over the city, to varying degrees, people getting "aftermath ready" in various ways. Learning to shoot, learning karate, building water-conservation devices. Last month there was a free class at the public library called "Eat Less and Live."

Rocky Milano leads me through the restaurant to a small cluttered alcove off the kitchen. There were always rumors about Martha's dad, silly little-kid rumors, discussed in confidential tones by those of us she babysat for: he was "connected," he had "done time," he had a rap sheet a mile long. Once I think I asked my mother, who worked at the police station, if she could run his file for me, a request she treated as dismissively as is appropriate for any such request coming from a ten-year-old.

Now here's Rocky, apologizing with a good-natured grin as he pushes a pile of paper plates off a chair for me, settling himself behind a battered metal desk. He essentially confirms everything that Martha said. Brett Cavatone married his daughter about six years ago, when still an active-duty state trooper. They didn't have a ton in common, Brett and Rocky, but they got along just fine. The older man respected his new son-in-law and liked the way he treated his daughter: "Like a princess—like an absolute princess." When Rocky decided to open this place, Brett left the force to work for him, to be the right-hand man.

"Okay," I say, nodding, writing it all down. "Why?"

"Why what?"

"Why come work here?"

"Oh, what? You wouldn't want to come work for me?"

I look up sharply but Rocky's easy smile is still in place. "I meant, why would he leave the force?"

"Yeah, I know what you meant," he says, and now the smile widens—broadens, more like, taking up more real estate on his round face. "You'll have to ask him."

He's joking, of course, goofing on me, but I don't mind. The truth is I'm enjoying the company of Martha's father. I'm impressed by his ramshackle restaurant and his defiant insistence on keeping it open, providing some measure of normalcy and comfort until "boomsday."

"Thing about Brett," says Rocky, comfortable now, leaning back with his hands laced behind his head, "is that the guy was terrific. Hardworking. An ox. He was here more than I was. He built the chair you're sitting on. He named the house specials, for Pete's sake." Rocky chuckles, points absently out at the dining room, where the husband and wife from the target range sit at one of the tables now, sharing a pizza. "That's a plain they're enjoying, by the way. This week's special is called Good Luck Finding Any Fucking Meat."

He chortles, coughs.

"Anyway, the plan was, we'd get the place going together, then when I died or went soft in the head, he'd take over. Obviously that isn't happening, thank you very much Mr. Goddamn Asteroid, but when I said I'm staying open till October, Brett said 'sure thing.' No sweat. He's in."

I nod, okay, I'm writing all of this down: *hardworking—built the chairs—open till October.* Filling a fresh page of the blue book.

"He promised," Milano says acidly. "But the kid made a lot of promises. As you've heard."

I lower my pencil, unsure what to ask next, abruptly seized by the absurdity of my mission. As if any amount of information will prepare me to go out in the vast chaotic wilderness that the world has become and bring Martha Milano's husband back to his promises. In the kitchen, the small cluster of cooks crack up riotously about something and slap each other five. Taped up behind Rocky in the cluttered office is one of the target forms from the bowling alleys, a silhouetted human figure, blue paint splattered all over the face: bull's-eye.

"What about friends? Did Brett have a lot of friends?"

"Ah, not really," says Milano. He sniffs, scratches his cheek. "Not that I know of."

"Hobbies?"

He shrugs. I'm grasping at straws. The real question is not whether he had hobbies but vices, or maybe a new vice he wanted to take for a test drive, now that the world has slipped into count-down mode. A girlfriend, maybe? But these are not the sorts of things a father-in-law is likely to know. The boom box is playing Buddy Holly, "A Man with a Woman on His Mind." Another great one. I'm not listening to enough music these days—no car radio, no iPod, no stereo. At home I listen to ham radio on a police scanner, jockeying between the federal emergency band and an energetic rumormonger who calls himself Dan Dan the Radio Man.

"Can you give me an idea, sir, of where your son-in-law was supposed to be going when he left here yesterday morning?"

"Yeah," he says. "Just running errands. Milk, cheese, flour. Toilet paper. Canned tomatoes if anybody has 'em. Most days, he'd come in and open up with me, then go out first thing on the ten-speed, find what he could find, come back for lunch."

"And where would he have gone to find those things?"

Rocky laughs. "Next question."

"Right," I say. "Sure."

I turn the page of my notebook. It was worth a shot. Wherever Brett was headed yesterday morning to shop, it probably wasn't an establishment operating within the rigorous strictures on food markets as spelled out in IPSS-3, the revised titles of the impact-preparation law governing resource allocation: rationing, barter limits, water-usage restrictions. Rocky Milano isn't about to tell all the details to an inquisitive visitor, particularly one with ties to the police force. I wonder in passing how Brett Cavatone felt about these small negotiations of current law: a former policeman, a man with a painting of Jesus on the wall above his bed.

"Can I just ask you, sir, whether there was anything unusual in yesterday's list? Anything out of the ordinary?"

"Ah, let's see," he says, and he closes his eyes for a second, checking some internal log. "Yeah. Actually. Yesterday he was supposed to go down to Suncook."

"Why Suncook?"

"Place called Butler's Warehouse down there, a furniture place. A gal came in for dinner over the weekend, said this place was still piled with old wood tables. We thought we'd scoop 'em up, see if we could use 'em."

"Okay," I say, then pause. "He was on a bicycle, you said?"

"Yup," says Milano, after a brief pause of his own. "We got a trailer hitch on the thing. Like I said, the kid's an ox."

He looks at me evenly, eyebrows slightly raised, and I can't help but read a cheerful defiance in that expression: Am I supposed to believe it? I picture the short powerful man with the wooly beard from Martha's photograph, picture him on a ten-speed bike with a trailer hitch on a hot July morning, leaning forward, muscles straining, muling a stack of round wooden tables all the way back from Suncook.

Rocky stands abruptly and I look behind me, following his gaze. It's the kid from outside, the one with the stubbly adolescent beard and the ponytail.

"Heya, Jeremy," says Rocky, offers the kid a mock salute. "How's the world outside?"

"Not bad. Mr. Norman is here."

"No kidding?" says Milano, standing up. "Already?"

"Should I—"

"No, I'm coming." My host stretches like a bear and reties his apron. "Hey, our friend here wants to know about Brett," he says to Jeremy. "You got anything to say about Brett?"

Jeremy smiles, blushes almost. He's wiry, this kid, small, with delicate features and thoughtful eyes. "Brett's awesome."

"Yeah," says Rocky Milano, striding out of the alcove and into the kitchen proper, on to the next order of business. "He used to be."

* * *

Outside Rocky's Rock 'n' Bowl a mangy tabby has insinuated itself under the back wheel of my bike, mewling in terror at the shrill insistent alarm sounding off one of the abandoned cars at Steeplegate Mall. A low-altitude fighter jet whooshes past overhead, fast and loud, leaving a bright white contrail against the gleaming blue of the sky. *He's pretty far inland*, I think, extricating the cat and depositing her in a warm patch of sidewalk. Most of the Air Force sorties are closer to the coast, where they've been providing support to the Coast Guard cutters tasked with intercepting the catastrophe immigrants. There are more and more of these every day, at least according to Dan Dan the Radio Man: big cargo ships and rickety rafts, pleasure boats and stolen naval vessels, an unceasing tide of refugees from all over the Eastern Hemisphere, desperate to make their way to the part of the earth not in Maia's direct path, where there is some slim chance of surviving, at least for a little while. The government's policy is interdiction and containment, meaning the cutters turn back those ships that can safely be turned back, intercept the rest and shepherd them to shore. There the immigrants are processed en masse, moved to one of the secure facilities that have been constructed, or are being constructed, up and down the seaboard.

A certain percentage of the CI's inevitably escape or are overlooked by these patrols, and manage to evade even the anti-immigrant militias who stalk them along the coasts and in the woods. I've only seen a handful here in Concord: a Chinese family, threadbare and emaciated, begging politely for food a couple weeks ago outside the ERAS site at Waugh's Bakery on South Street. Inside I waited in line for three large rolls and I tore off bits, handed them to the family like they were pigeons or ducks.

* * *

On my way back I stop on the broad overgrown lawn of the New Hampshire statehouse, which is ringing right now with hoots and laughter, a small cheering crowd, spread out in groups of two and three. Small families, young couples, card tables pushed together and surrounded by smartly dressed elderly people. Picnic baskets, bottles of wine. A speaker is up on a crate, a middle-aged man, bald, his hands formed into a megaphone.

"The Boston Patriots," bellows the guy. "The US Open. Outback Steakhouse." Appreciative laughter; a few cheers. This has been going on for a few weeks now, someone's bright idea that caught on: people taking turns, waiting patiently, a nonstop recitation of the things that we will miss about the world. There are two policemen, anonymous as robots in their black riot gear, machine guns strapped across their backs, keeping silent watch over the scene.

"Ping-pong. Starbucks," the speaker says. People hoot, clap, and nudge one another. A skinny young mother with a toddler balanced on her arm stands behind him, waiting to say her piece. "Those big tins of popcorn you get for the holidays."

I am aware of a sarcastic counterdemonstration being held on and off in a basement bar on Phenix Street, organized by a guy who used to be an assistant manager at the Capital Arts Center. There, people announce in mock solemnity all the things they will *not* miss: Customer-service representatives. Income taxes. The Internet.

I get back on the bike and go north and then west, toward my lunch date, thinking about Brett Cavatone—the man who got to marry Martha Milano, and then left her behind. A picture is forming in my mind: a tough man, smart, strong. And—what was Martha's word?—noble. *He must be doing something noble.* One thing I know, they don't let just anybody become a state trooper. And I've never met one who left to work in food service.

3.

"So this lady's at the doctor, she's got this strange pain, the doctor does all the tests, says, 'I'm sorry, but you got cancer.'" Detective McGully is gesticulating like a vaudeville comedian, his bald head flushed with red, his throaty voice rumbling with anticipatory laughter. "And the thing is, there's nothing they can do about it. Nothing! No radiation, no chemo. They don't have the pills and the drip-drip machines don't work right on the generators. It's a mess. Doctor says, 'Listen, lady, I'm sorry, but you got six months to live.'" Culverson rolls his eyes. McGully goes in for the kill. "And the lady looks at him and goes, 'Six months? Terrific! That's three months longer than everybody else!'"

McGully does a big freeze-frame comedy face on his punch line, waves his hands, *wakka-wakka*. I smile politely. Culverson scrapes honey into his tea from along the rim of the jar.

"Screw you both." McGully dismisses us with a wave of his thick hands. "That's funny."

Detective Culverson grunts and sips his tea and I go back to my notebook, which is flipped open on the table beside our pile of unread menus. Ruth-Ann, the waitress here at the Somerset Diner, has kept the menus meticulously updated, editing them week by week, scrawling in changes, crossing out unavailable items with a thick black marker. McGully, still chortling at his own joke, takes out two cigars and rolls one across the table to Culverson, who lights them both and hands one back. My friends, chomping on their cigars in virtual unison: Middle-aged bald white man, middle-aged paunchy black man, peas in a pod, at their ease in a diner booth. Men in the lap of forced retirement, enjoying their leisure like octogenarians.

What I'm doing is reviewing my notes from this morning, re-membering Martha, chewing on her fingernails, staring into the corners of the room.

"That's a true story, by the way," says McGully. "Not the bit where she says about the six months. But Beth has got a friend, just diagnosed, forty years old, not a goddamn thing they can do for her. True story."

"How is Beth?"

"She's fine," says McGully. "She's knitting sweaters. I tell her it's summer, and she says it's going to be cold. I tell her, what, you mean, when the sun is swallowed by ash?"

McGully says this like it's supposed to be another joke, but nobody laughs, not even him.

"Hey, you guys hear about Dotseth?" says Culverson.

"Yeah," says McGully. "You hear about the lieutenant governor?"

"Yeah. Nuts."

I've heard all these stories already. I study the pages of my notebook. How the heck am I going to get ahold of a plastic samurai sword?

Ruth-Ann, ancient and gray headed and sturdy, stops by to clear our dishes and slide ashtrays under the cigars, and everybody nods thanks. Besides the oatmeal and the cheese, the main refreshment she can offer is tea, because its chief ingredient is water, which for now is still coming out of the taps. Estimates vary on how long the public water supply will last now that the electricity is down for good. It depends on how much is in the reserve tanks; it depends on whether the Department of Energy has prioritized our city generators over other sections of the Northeast—it depends, it depends, it depends . . .

"Hey, so, Palace," says Culverson all of sudden, with practiced nonchalance, like something just occurred to him. My spine stiffens with irritation—I know what he's going to ask. "Any word on your sister?"

"Nope."

"Nothing?"

"Nope."

He's asked before. He keeps asking.

"You haven't heard from her?"

"Not a thing."

McGully chimes in: "You're not gonna try and find her?"

"Nope," I say. "I'm not."

They look at each other: *Such a shame*. I change the subject.

"Let me ask you guys a question. How many miles would you say it is from here to Suncook?"

Culverson tilts his head. "I don't know. Six?"

"Nah," says McGully. "Eight. And change." He blows out a thick cluster of smoke, which I fan away with the flat of my hand. The ceiling fan used to carry away some of the smoke, but now the fan is stilled and the thick gray cloud hangs low over the booth.

"Why?" says Culverson.

"A man I'm looking for, he was supposed to bike down to Suncook and pick up some chairs."

"On a bike? With a trailer?"

"What man are you looking for?" says McGully.

"A missing person."

"Bike them back from Suncook?" says Culverson. "What is he, a bull elephant?"

"Wait. Hold on." McGully cocks his head at me, his cigar burning in the V of two fingers. "A missing person? You working on a case, detective?"

I give it to them briefly: my old babysitter, her runaway husband, the pizza restaurant by the Steeplegate Mall.

"Guy's a trooper?" says Culverson.

"Was. He quit to work at the pizza place."

Culverson makes a face. McGully interrupts: "What's this chick paying you? To find her runaway man?"

"I said, she's an old friend."

"That's not a kind of money."

Culverson chuckles absently. I can tell he's turning over the other thing, the trooper-turns-pizza-man element. McGully's not done: "You told this chick it's useless, right?"

"I told her it's a long shot."

"A *long shot*?" McGully, animated, thumping the table with a closed fist. "That's one way to put it. You know what you should tell her, Ichabod Crane? You should tell her that her man is gone. He's dead or he's in a whorehouse or he's smoking crack in New Orleans or Belize or some goddamn place. And that if he left her, it's 'cause he wanted to, and the smart thing to do is to forget all about him. Pull up a chair and get ready to watch the sun go down."

"Sure," I say. "Yeah."

I turn away from the conversation, look down at my hands, at the redacted menus. Dirty yellow sunbeams glow through the murk of the window glass, spreading across the tabletop like wavering prison bars. When I look back, McGully is shaking his head. "Listen, you like this chick? Then don't give her false hope. Don't waste her time. Don't waste yours."

Now I look to Culverson, who smiles mildly, tapping his forehead with his fingertips. "Hey, I ever tell you guys that my next-door neighbor is Sergeant Thunder?" he says.

"What?" says McGully.

"The weatherman?" I say.

"Channel Four at six and ten. My own personal celebrity." Culverson starts patting his jacket pockets, looking for something.

Culverson and I still wear blazers, most of the time; most of the time I put a tie on, too. McGully's in a polo shirt with his name stitched across the breast pocket.

"We never used to talk that much," Culverson explains, "just to say hi, except now it's just him and me on the block, so I pop in on the guy every now and then, just knock on the door, how you doing, you know? He's pretty old."

McGully puffs on his cigar, getting bored.

"Anyway, yesterday Sergeant Thunder comes by to show me something. Says he really isn't supposed to, but he can't resist."

Culverson finds what he was looking for in the right-inside pocket of his blazer and slides it across the table to me. It's a brochure, slim and elegant, a glossy all-color trifold with pictures of smiling elderly people in a wood-paneled lounge, sconce lit and pleasant. There are photos of heroic-jawed security men in helmets striding sterile hallways. A young couple beaming over a meal: linen table-cloth, pasta and salad. And in a tasteful and understated font, *The World of Tomorrow Awaits You* . . .

"The World of Tomorrow?" I ask, and McGully grabs the brochure. "Bull hockey," he snorts, turning it this way and that. "A dump truck full of bull hockey."

He tosses it back across the table and I read the pitch on the reverse side. The World of Tomorrow offers berths in a "meticulously appointed, securely constructed, permanent facility in an undisclosed location in the White Mountains of New Hampshire." The word "permanent" is in italics. There are three levels of accommodation on offer: standard, premium, and luxury.

I lay it back on the table. "Here," says McGully. "Take a napkin. Dab off some of the bull hockey."

There is, I note, no admission price listed for this marvelous "World of Tomorrow." I ask Culverson and he says drily that from what Sergeant Thunder said, it varies from customer to customer. In other words, the price is whatever you've got.

"Last night I watched them come and take Sergeant Thunder's riding lawnmower, his little wine refrigerator, and his microwave," says Culverson. "This morning they dismantled his brick shed, knocked it apart with those big masonry hammers and carted away the bricks. They wear jumpsuits, these guys. I think jumpsuits are a nice touch, if you're looking to swindle someone out of everything they own."

"You didn't try and stop them?" says McGully, and Culverson rears back, gives him an *are-you-crazy?*

"Yeah," he says. "I put up my dukes. You think these guys aren't carrying?"

I turn the brochure over in my hands. State-of-the-art medical facilities. Gourmet meals. Craps tables.

"Besides," says Culverson. "You should have seen the smile on the Sergeant's face." He leans back and gives us the look, fox in a henhouse. "Grinning like a sex fiend. I've never seen an old man look so happy."

McGully looks agitated. He taps ash into his teacup and says, "What's the point?" but he already knows the point, and I do, too.

Culverson gives it to us anyway. "Maybe it's false hope you're giving this girl, your old babysitter—but it's hope, right? Little spark in the darkness?" McGully makes an irritated sputter, and Culverson turns to him, says, "I'm serious, man. Maybe having Palace working on her case keeps this lady from going nuts."

"Exactly," I say. "That's—exactly."

Culverson takes a hard look at me, turns back to McGully. "Hell, maybe it keeps Palace from going nuts."

I bend back over my notebook, moving on. "If you wanted to make a pizza, where would you go for ingredients? This guy's boss sends him out yesterday morning for basics, and I presume he means at a rummage."

"No question," says Culverson. "No one's running a pizza restaurant with ERAS cheese." He doesn't say the letters, he pronounces it out like most people, sounds like *heiress*. The Emergency Resource Allocation System.

"Which rummage, though? Pirelli's?"

"Hey, don't ask me. I'm doing fine with my little garden and Ruth-Ann's hospitality. But my esteemed colleague is a married man and has different needs."

There's a long pause then, as Culverson stubs out his cigar in the ashtray and stares pointedly at McGully, who at last throws up his hands and sighs. "Fuck's sake," he says. "The old Elks Lodge building. On South Street, past Corvant."

"You sure?" I'm scrawling it in my notebook, tapping my feet on Ruth-Ann's floor. "I was just down that way to get some eyeglasses fixed at Paulie's. The lodge looked like it'd been looted clean."

"Not the basement," he says. "The guy was shopping for cheese, for canned tomatoes, olives? Elks Rummage. Dollars to donuts. Tell them I sent you."

"Thank you, McGully," I say, laying down my pencil, beaming.

"Don't forget, you got to bring something."

"Thank you so much."

"Yeah, well. Up yours."

"Deep down inside," says Culverson, gazing fondly at McGully, "you're a shining star."

"Up yours, too."

Ruth-Ann circles back around, swift and nimble in her orthopedic shoes. I smile at her and she winks. I've been coming to the Somerset since I was twelve years old. "How much do we owe you?" asks Culverson like always, and Ruth-Ann says, "A zillion trillion dollars," like always, and bustles away.

* * *

I get home and dump everybody's leftovers into a big plastic bowl and whistle for my dog, a puffy white bichon frisé named Houdini who used to belong to a drug dealer.

"Whoa, wait," I tell him, as he hurls his little body across the room at the food bowl. "Sit. Stay."

The dog ignores me; he woofs with delight and plunges his tiny happy face into the leftovers. Very briefly, when we first met, I was determined to train Houdini as a search-and-rescue dog, but I have long since abandoned that project. He has zero interest in obeying orders or instructions of any kind; he remains a pure untutored child of an animal. I settle into a wooden chair at my kitchen table to watch him eat.

I lied to Culverson and McGully, earlier, as I do every time they press me on the subject of my little sister. I know where she is and I know what she's doing. Nico has gotten herself involved with some kind of anti-asteroid conspiracy, one of the many small networks of fantasists and fools who believe they know how to avert what's coming, or prove that it's a massive government frame-up, like the moon landing or the Kennedy assassination. The details of her particular operation I do not know, and nor do I want to. And I certainly have no interest in discussing any of this with my colleagues. There are other things I'd prefer to think about.

"Sorry, boy," I tell Houdini, when he empties the bowl and turns up to me expectantly. "That's it."

I turn on my scanner and fiddle with the crystal till I get Dan Dan the Radio Man. He's talking about the Mayfair Commission, the joint House–Senate hearings on the failure of NASA and various agencies within the departments of Defense and Homeland Security "to provide adequate warning or protection against the looming threat, over a period of years and even decades." We had fun with that one, over at the Somerset, the other detectives and I, imagining old Senator Mayfair rooting out who knew what about $2011GV_1$, and when. "Why, it's an outrage!" McGully declaimed in character, jabbing a senatorial forefinger in the air. "Our own scientists, conspiring with the asteroid *the whole time!*"

Now Dan Dan the Radio Man reports with dismay that Eleanor Tollhouse, deputy director of NASA from 1981 to 1987 and now eighty-five years old, is being held on the floor of the Senate in a cage, "for her own protection."

I turn off the scanner. Houdini is still looking at me, sad eyed and earnest, so I sigh and pour out a quarter cup of dry kibble, exactly what I had hoped to avoid by bringing home the table scraps. There is now just a single serving left in this bag, and after this one I have sixteen bags with ten servings per bag. Houdini eats approximately two servings a day, so we should be just about okay for the seventy-seven days remaining. But who's counting?

I stand up and stretch and fill his water bowl. That's one of the big jokes: *Who's counting?* The answer, of course, is everyone—everyone is counting.

4.

The dog barks and I open my eyes and sit upright with my heart clenched like a fist.

"What, boy?" I say. "What is it?"

Houdini is barking at the front door, just a few feet from the dilapidated living-room sofa I've been sleeping on since April. Houdini keeps barking, loud and shrill and insistent, very much unlike himself. I roll off the sofa and push it aside and lift the four loose floorboards beneath. My hands fumbling in the darkness, I find the safe, find the dial, roll through the combination, pull up the door, and draw out a long serrated knife and a Ruger LCP handgun.

Houdini is still yelping and pacing, a short tight wire of anxiety, jerking one way and then the other. I order him uselessly to calm. Clutching my weapons I step past the dog, moving slowly and deliberately until my shoulder is pressed against the front door.

"It's okay, boy," I mutter, my heart hammering now, the handle of the knife sweating in my palm. "It's okay."

From out the door's small inset window I can see a slim shiver of light, a flashlight beam darting across the lawn. *And what if Palace is murdered in a home invasion before he can start looking,* I ask Detective Culverson silently. *Then what happens to my old babysitter and her spark in the darkness?*

You hear these stories now, people trade them in stunned whispers, the tales of home invasion and physical assault. Leon James, up on Thayer, a former banker, beaten unconscious, the house stripped for copper. The two middle-aged women, old friends who had moved in together after their husbands went Bucket List. For them it was a gang of teenagers in gorilla masks, both women sexually assaulted and beaten nearly to death. The gorillas took nothing and were neither drunk nor high, simply on a rampage. That one I reported, when I heard about it—I knocked on the driver's-side window of one of the Chevrolet Impalas planted on one of the corners, gave the house number and the woman's name as they had been described to me. The young officer in the cruiser stared back at me blankly, said he'd fill out a report, and slowly rolled up his window.

The flashlight beam is gone. I stare at the darkness, the overhanging trees, the summer-barren branches silhouetted against moonlight. My pulse galloping; Houdini's rapid troubled breaths.

And then a crash outside, somewhere on the lawn, the sound of breaking glass, followed a moment later by a man's voice, low but distinct: "Shit. Fuck. Balls."

I push open the door and rush out, screaming, gun in one hand and knife in the other, like a barbarian rushing a medieval camp.

I stop halfway across the lawn. There's nothing. I see no one. There's a row of streetlights along my stretch of West Clinton, but of course they're all dead now, dimly reflecting the starlight, hanging from their poles like fossilized glass fruits. More noise: a scrape and then a crunch, glass on glass, and then more muttered cursing.

The weight of the gun is unfamiliar; it's smaller and more compact than the SIG Sauer P229 service revolver I used to carry on patrol. My friend Trish McConnell provided me with the Ruger just last week, after I mentioned that I was adhering to IPSS firearm rules and had no gun in my home. McConnell, a former colleague still on the force, later left the gun in a small manila envelope between my screen door and front door with a note. *Take it,* said the note. *Please.*

Now I'm glad I've got it. I sweep the gun in a wide arc across the lawn, talking big in the darkness. "Stay where you are. Freeze and drop your weapon."

"I'm not—I don't have a weapon. Shit, man, I'm really sorry." That voice, croaking from my neighbor's lawn as I approach—it's familiar but I can't place it, like a voice from a dream. "Fuck, man, I'm really sorry."

I stop walking. "Who is that?"

"It's Jeremy."

Jeremy. The kid outside the restaurant, three-day's beard and a ponytail. I exhale. My pulse slows. For God's sake.

"I think I fell in, like, a trap or something," he says.

"Hang on," I say. "I'm coming."

Jeremy's in the ditch on Mr. Maron's lawn, in a puddle of shards and thick pieces of broken glass. My eyes blink in the moonlight and I focus and find him, disheveled and confused, a gash like a stab wound in his forehead.

"Hey," he says weakly. "Sorry."

"It's not a trap," I tell Jeremy. I peer down at him, and he gazes back at me bashfully like a wounded fawn. "It's a solar still."

"What's a solar still?" he says, and then looks around him at the mess of glass. "I think I broke it."

I laugh out loud, feeling along with my wash of relief a muddled affection for this kid who has injured himself wandering around outside my house in the middle of the night. As if the stupid thing actually *was* a trap, and I've caught myself some kind of hapless fairy.

"A solar still is a catchment system," I say, "for capturing water from the atmosphere. My neighbor built it."

"Oh. Tell him I'm sorry."

"He's dead," I say. "What are you doing here?"

Jeremy raises a hand to the cut on his head, winces, then inspects his blood-smeared fingertips. He looks much as he did at the restaurant: small guy, sensitive dark eyes, soft and unmasculine face. My neighbor, Mr. Moran, a jovial middle-aged bachelor shoe salesman, spent three weeks building the solar still before he was shot on July fourth by a group of vigilantes from an organization called American Soil. Mr. Moran was trying to pull them off a truck driver, who was leaving for the Cape Cod immigrant camp with food and first aid. The truck driver was murdered also.

"Yeah, I'm really sorry," says Jeremy again. "It's just, I didn't want Rocky to know I was coming to see you, and I couldn't think of any particularly buyable reason to leave the restaurant early, so I had to wait till we closed."

"Okay," I say.

"Then I had to get over to the library to look up your address."

"Okay."

"You weren't in the phone book, but there was another Palace—N. Palace?"

"My sister," I say. "She used to use my address for credit card applications."

"Oh."

He's still lying there in the glass, which is where I want him until I know exactly what's going on here. The main branch of the Concord Public Library is open twenty-four hours a day at this point, kept clean and lit by a skeleton crew of librarians and a cadre of volunteers.

"Jeremy," I say. "Why are you here?"

"I just wanted to say, don't do it. Don't bring Brett back, I mean. Leave the guy alone."

"Come on," I say, set down my knife and my gun and extend a hand down into the remains of the solar still. "Get up."

* * *

"This was stupid."

"It's okay."

"I feel like a dummy."

"It's okay."

Jeremy is sitting at my kitchen table now, a paper towel pressed to his forehead with blood seeping around the edges.

"Seriously," he says. "I feel like an idiot."

"Really," I say. "Don't worry about it."

I don't press Jeremy about Brett, not yet, don't ask him to expound on his purposes for trekking all the way across town to find me. I don't want him to run, and that's what it feels like: He's embarrassed and disconcerted, and if pushed he's going to say "forget the whole thing" and book it, off into the night.

I light candles, get my camp stove going, put up a kettle for tea, and ask him a couple easy and casual questions. Jeremy's last name, as it turns out, is Canliss, which sounds familiar, so I ask him to spell it.

"Huh," I say. "Are you from Concord?"

"No," he says. "Yes." Exhales, resettles himself on the chair, getting comfortable. "Well, not really."

He was born here, he says, but then moved at fifteen months old. It's a typical New England story: raised outside Montpelier; limped through high school; did some outdoorsy stuff; "drifted away from my family, kind of," ended up in Portsmouth and then went to UNH for a semester; dropped out, tried one more time, dropped out again; and then he ended up here in Concord, crashing with some friends in a "shitty little house." Then he got a gig at the pizza place, and then they announced the end of the world.

"And what about Brett?" I say at last, very casual, pouring the tea, speaking softly and over my shoulder from the far side of the room. "Why don't you want me to find him?"

"I mean, look, it's none of my business," he says, and then gets quiet, and I focus on the water and the cups. When I turn back he's rubbing his chin, and then he just goes, "Because, man, he's just *Brett*, you know?" I set down the teacups and sit, waiting.

"If he—" Jeremy raises his hands, as if literally groping for the words. "If he had to go, he had to go. You know what I mean?"

"Not really. I don't know him. Tell me about him."

"I don't know." He laughs uneasily, repeats himself: "He's just *Brett*."

In this unspecific and tautological compliment there is a respect and admiration so deep it changes the timbre of his voice. When he says "Brett" it's like how other people might say Elvis or Jesus. He's not just any person—he's *Brett*. Houdini is still trembling beneath the table, not yet convinced that the danger has passed. I get up and pour him out the last of the bag of kibble, a treat to calm his nerves. Sixteen bags left, now, ten servings per bag.

"I'm sure he had his reasons," Jeremy blurts out. "That's all I'm saying."

"What kind of reasons?"

"Man, come on," he says, ducking his head. "You know."

"I don't. I really don't. Were you close with him?"

"No." He peels the wadded paper towel from his forehead and

. bobbles it from hand to hand. "Not really."

"But he was a friend?"

"Well, like a, a work friend, you know? From the restaurant."

"You worked together often?"

"Yeah. Definitely. More before the stupid fucking asteroid."

I smile. A certain vividness absent from *our current environment*. Stupid fucking asteroid.

"At first I thought he was boring, you know? Kind of a goody-goody. He's religious, he's doesn't drink, he's the boss's son-in-law, all that."

I don't have a notebook down here. No pencil. I'm nodding slowly, registering details, demanding of my midnight mind that it pay attention, catalog and order these incoming facts.

"But hanging out with Brett, you'd suddenly go: oh. This guy's cool. He'd make these weird jokes all the time, like under his breath, when you're driving around. Smart jokes, like where you don't get it exactly but you know it's brilliant. He'd help you do shit you were bad at, without making you feel stupid."

I nod. I have known people like that, but for some reason the person who comes to mind is my grandfather Nathanael Palace, who raised Nico and me after the deaths of our parents, and who possessed the opposite sort of spirit: always ready to show you that you were bad at something, that you were doing it wrong.

"Me and Brett used to sit on my steps and watch them drive the—what do you call 'em, the trucks full of prisoners?—in and out of the jail."

"Transport vans," I say, shaking off the image of Grandfather, staying on target.

"Right, right. And Brett would point at the vans and say, 'There but for the grace of God, my friend. There but for His grace.' Like he cared about me, you know? Not just me, either. He cared about people in general."

"And . . ." I pause, turn this over. "Did Brett talk about leaving? Going Bucket List, I mean?"

Jeremy looks down. His cheeks color. "Shit, man. You ask a lot of questions."

"It's in my nature. Did he talk about it or not?"

"No," he says. "Not specifically. But he was ready to go. You know?"

"Did he have a girlfriend?"

"I don't know. No."

"You don't know, or no?"

"Maybe he did," says Jeremy. "I think so, maybe, yeah."

"What girl?" I lean forward, my heart racing now, galloping. "Where?"

"I don't know," he says, pulling back, recoiling from my eagerness. "I don't know."

"Was there a girl who came in to the pizza place?"

"No. I don't know."

He does know, though. He knows something. But he's not going to tell me, not now. I rub my eyes with my fingertips. There's something else that's been on my mind. "Brett was a solid goody-

goody, you said, religious. How did he feel about Rocky working off-ERAS?"

"What?" He looks puzzled, upset.

"I mean, sending him to the rummage, black-marketing?"

"Wait," says Jeremy suddenly, and slaps a flat hand on the table. "Stop. Look."

And then my anxious night visitor is talking so fast and so ardently that his mouth is like a blur in the darkness on the other side of the table. "If he *wanted* to go off and sow some wild oats or whatever, then he didn't have to, like, get anyone's permission."

"Not even his wife?"

"No, not even his wife. I don't know about you, man, but I don't have the balls to just go off and do what I want. Whether it's a chick, or parasailing, or I don't know—whatever. Even now, I don't have the courage." Jeremy shakes his head in bitter self-recrimination, as if this is the ultimate character flaw, this lack of apocalyptic bravery. "But it looks like Brett *did* have the balls, right? And like I said, he was—he was just a solid citizen. So he should get to do what he wants, is all I'm saying. And I don't think you or Martha or anyone should go off and try and drag him back."

He tosses the blood-soaked paper towel on the table and pushes back his chair.

"That's it, man. I'm sorry to bother you."

He stands up. I stand up. "I have more questions."

"Sorry about your neighbor's thing, too. On the lawn. I'm really sorry."

And that's it, he's out the door, and given that I am no longer vested with any powers by the city of Concord to make him stay, I just watch him go, stumbling away in the darkness, a flashlight beam bobbling unevenly through the dark shapes of the trees. I'm contemplating the force of personality that my missing man must have possessed, to inspire the intense, if peculiar, devotion I've just seen. This kid may feel that he lacks courage, but he took a not-insignificant cross-city walk just now, in the unprotected darkness, to argue his friend's case. Because he admires him. Because he wishes he had gone off somewhere, too.

I go into the living room, carrying a candle on a plate like a Dickens character, and when I find a pencil and my notebook I write down what I remember, write as swiftly and carefully as I can: *a chick? parasailing? Kind of a goody-goody*. I sketch the tale of Jeremy's childhood, write down his full name and stare at it. Such an old-fashioned term he used, *sow some wild oats*. "If he wanted to sow some wild oats or whatever . . ."

When I'm done writing I lay down the pencil and stare into the flickering candle flame. The big question remains the one I asked Martha, twelve hours ago or however long ago it was: What do I do if I find him? If Jeremy is right, if Brett is out there sowing oats, and if I do by some miracle manage to track down this formidable character, this former state trooper—what then? I stroll up to this adult man doing what he pleases with his remaining scraps and shards of time, and say what, exactly?

My name is Henry Palace, sir. Your wife would like you to please come home now.

I blow out the candle.

I tiptoe past my sleeping dog and hang my long legs over the edge of the sofa and close my eyes.

The memories well up as they always do, and I push them away.

These are the scenes that I have studiously blocked, and which I am aware that I have blocked. Not of my parents; my dead parents I have lived with for many years now, and I have integrated their absence and my grief deep into my character. But there is a more recent wound, a woman named Naomi whom I loved and who was torn from me, a loss as sudden and brutal as a gunshot in a darkened room. And I am aware that the appropriate thing to do, from a therapeutic perspective, would be to summon up the relevant memories, allow myself to face the trauma, expose it to the light and allow time to do its healing work.

But there is no time. Seventy-seven days—seventy-six now— less than three months—who's counting? There *is* no time.

I push away the memories, roll over, and think about my case.

PART TWO

....

The Long Way

....

Thursday, July 19

Right Ascension 20 06 33.0
Declination -59 53 12
Elongation 141.0
Delta 0.863 AU

1.

"Oh, sure, I know him. Serious man. Broad shoulders. Boots."

"That's right," I say, holding up the photograph, my missing man and his caught fish. "His name is Brett Cavatone."

"If you say so. I don't think we ever got so far as to names."

The dairyman is an old New England farmer from a storybook, John Deere cap pushed back, sunburned forehead, crags beneath his eyes like coastal cliffs. I'm in his stall in one crowded corner of the Elks rummage, him behind his rickety card table, handwritten signs, a couple of ice-packed travel coolers as big as steamer trunks.

"He was here frequently?" I ask.

"Most days, yes, I believe he was."

"Was he here on Tuesday?"

"Tuesday?" The slightest hesitation. He tilts his head. "No."

"I'm not asking about yesterday, you understand. Tuesday. Two days ago."

The old man pushes back his cap. "I know what day it is, young fella."

I smile tightly, peek in the old man's cooler. He's selling glass jars of milk and rough sticks of butter wrapped in wax paper. His chalk sign lists what he'd like in exchange: "chicken feed, in quantity." Fresh fruit and juices, "in quantity." "Underthings," with a list of sizes.

"I'm sorry to press, but it's important. Are you certain this man didn't come by on Tuesday morning?"

"Nothing is certain but the death and resurrection of our Lord Jesus Christ," says the farmer, glancing up at the ceiling of the Elks lodge basement and past it up to heaven—and then down to glower at Houdini, who is sniffing at his butter. "But no, I didn't see him yesterday."

The dairyman snaps the lid closed on his cooler, and my dog and I move on, navigating through the crowded chaotic aisles of the rummage. It's crowded in here but quiet, people picking their way alone or in small groups from table to table, stall to stall, murmuring hello, nodding, hushed. I watch a thin woman with freckles and sharp nervous eyes investigate the wares on one table: She lifts a block of soap, puts it down again, whispers something to the burly man operating the stall, who shakes his head.

We cut across the room, Houdini and I, weave through the big ungainly piles of take-what-you-want scattered and heaped on blankets in the middle of the room. Broken shells of computers and phones, empty buckets and deflated soccer balls, big picked-over piles of the kind of useless articles once found in pharmacies and big-box stores: greeting cards, reading glasses, celebrity magazines. The really valuable objects are in the manned stalls: dairy goods and smoked meats, cans and can openers, bottles of water and bottles of soda. It's all barter and exchange, though some stalls still have prices posted, dating from the peak of hyperinflation, before the dollar-economy collapsed: bar/soap, $14,500. Box/mac&cheese $240,000, then an arrow pointing to it, *no more mac&cheese*. One huge individual in a camouflage hunting jacket stands in the center of his uncluttered stall, silent and serious, under a sign reading simply GENERATORS.

"Bananas," says a slovenly man slouching past in a windbreaker and hunting cap, muttering under his breath. "You want?"

"No, thanks."

He moves on, addressing the room in general. "Real good bananas."

I work the room, making the rounds, flashing Brett's picture, tugging on the sleeves of the scavengers and tapping the shoulders of the ragged salesmen, meeting their grim and distrustful expressions with calm confidence, with my TV-detective cliché: "Pardon me, have you seen this man?" Everyone I ask gives the same story as the dairyman, with the same minimal level of detail: Yeah, they've seen him. Yeah, he was here a lot. One merchant, an earnest woman offering three kinds of jerky, as well as Bibles with laminated pages, remembers Brett fondly—she says he's one of her favorite customers.

"We never did business together?" she says, turning the statement into a question with a mild uplift at the end of the sentence.

"But some mornings we would pray?"

"For what, ma'am?"

"Peace," she says. "Just peace for everyone?"

I move on, booth after booth, canvassing the rummage. It sounds like Brett was doing exactly what Rocky Milano sent him here to do, bargaining for perishables with the farmers and hustlers and thieves, digging through the scrap piles for things the restaurant could use: toilet paper, dish soap, candles, firewood, plates and spoons. And no one, it seems, saw the man on Tuesday morning.

As I work, the rummage gets busier, the noise and bustle increasing as the morning wears on. There's a loud sharp burst of noise, two men throwing punches at each other's head among the blankets of third-tier material, violently arguing over a battered Falcons football helmet. The proprietors of the rummage rush over, a collection of thin and rugged men with very short haircuts, swarming like a rugby team, chanting "out, out, out, out" as they hustle the combatants to the exit.

At a booth that says simply MISCELLANEOUS is a heavy-set woman with ghastly red hair piled and curled on her head, smoking a long and thin cigarette.

"Excuse me," I ask her. "Do you have toys?"

"You mean . . ." She lowers her voice. The cigarette wobbles in the corner of her mouth. "Like, weapons?"

"No," I say. "I'm looking for a particular toy. For a friend."

She lowers her voice still further. "You mean, for sex?"

"No. Forget it. Thank you."

Backing away I collide with someone and turn around, murmuring "excuse me." It's one of the proprietors, and he doesn't say excuse me in return, just stands there with his arms crossed, sinewy and grave. He's a wiry thug with two teardrop tattoos, one beneath each beady eye. They examined me carefully when I came in here, these guys, asked me three times how I knew McGully, skeptically appraised the old Mr. Coffee I had brought in, reluctantly, for barter.

Now this one looks me up and down: my suit jacket, my policeman's shoes. He stinks of early-day beer and some kind of oily hair product.

"Good morning," I say.

"You finding everything okay?" His voice is gravelly, deadpan. I get the message. "Come on, boy," I say to Houdini. "Time to go."

*　*　*

Halfway from the Elks rummage to my next stop I get off the bike in the heart of downtown and just take a long slow turn around the deserted sprawl of Main Street: crushed glass, broken shop windows, a couple of drunk teenagers on top of each other on a bench. It's a ghost town. It's one of those Western cowboy outposts they used to keep preserved as a living museum: Here there used to be a bookstore. Once upon a time, this was a gift shop. Long, long ago, that was a Citgo station.

*　*　*

I stare at the front door of the Concord Police Department for a few minutes, but I can't go in. As a sworn officer I would push open that door, tip my head hello to the warm-eyed receptionist behind the bulletproof glass, and go get my assignment for the day. As a child, I would push through with both hands, and the warm-eyed receptionist was my mother.

Now, today, different world, I walk with my head down, anonymous and inconspicuous, counterclockwise around the building, past the sternly worded signs posted at ten-yard intervals on the cement berms ringing the perimeter. Sentries patrol the roof, among the bending thickets of antennae and the chugging generators, black-clad cops with semiautomatic rifles, slowly rotating their gaze, one way and then the other, like they're guarding a besieged consulate in a chaotic third world nation. I find a position about a half block up School Street, almost at the YMCA, and crouch behind a Dumpster.

"Come on," I say, waiting, watching the big garage doors that are now halfway rolled up, revealing a newly installed loading dock where the repair garage used to be. "Come on, buddy."

The personnel turnover in the last few months has been dramatic, the police force remaking itself, sinking deeper into its core missions—not stopping crime, not investigating it or containing it, just keeping as many people alive and unharmed as possible. Keeping everyone alive to die later, as McGully puts it. But there's at least one cop of my acquaintance who is still in there, and who I happen to know has recently taken up smoking, and who enjoys the day's first cigarette break every day at twelve o'clock.

I check my watch. "Come on."

Someone rolls up the big garage doors the rest of the way, and a pair of long flat metal ramps are clattered out off the lip of the loading dock. Cops scuttle down the cement steps to ground level, lining up pallets and carts and gesturing to one another and muttering into their walkie-talkies. I risk a closer look, ducking out from behind the Dumpster and walking slowly down the street, until I slump in the empty doorway of Granite State Ice Cream. The activity in the loading dock is increasing now, cops pouring in and out of the building, like robots, like ants, thick black uniforms heavy in the sun.

"Hello, Detective Palace. How's retirement?"

She's right on time and she's smiling, finding space for herself beside me in the narrow doorway, no more than five feet tall even in the military boots, her Plexiglas riot mask tipped back to make room for the noontime cigarette.

"Officer McConnell," I say. "I need your help."

"Really?"

A flash of excitement followed immediately by wariness. We always enjoyed working together, Trish and I, first as fellow patrol officers and then during my brief stint on the detectives. But everything is changed now. She drags on the cigarette. "Okay, well, first I should warn you that if my sergeant sees me out here talking to you, I'm going to have to pretend you're a perp, and probably tase you. I'm sorry."

"Sergeant who—Gonzales?"

"No, Belewski. Gonzales? Carlos is long gone. No, Belewski,

you don't know him, but he's looking for people to cut, and he doesn't like us holdovers."

She jerks her head, and we leave the doorway of the ice cream parlor, fall into step, walking uptown from headquarters.

"Is Belewski a fed?" I ask. "From out of town?"

"Can't tell you."

"Army guy?"

"I can't tell you that, Detective. Are you doing okay?"

"What do you mean?"

"You've got enough to eat?"

"I'm fine. I'm working on this case."

"Okay," she says, nods, and her voice goes all business. "What have you got? Arson?"

"Missing person."

"You kidding? Everyone's a missing person."

"I know," I say. "But this is different."

"Is it? Because a lot of people are missing. Like half the Eastern Hemisphere, just for starters."

We've stopped walking outside what used to be a Subway sandwich shop: shattered front glass, furniture overturned, extensive graffiti on the sneeze guard of the toppings line.

"Those are refugees," I tell her. "What I've got is a thirty-three-year-old Caucasian male, happy marriage, gainfully employed."

"Gainfully employed? Are you drunk? Do you know what day it is?"

"He disappears from his workplace at 8:45 in the morning,

never comes back."

"His workplace?"

"Pizza restaurant."

"Oh, dear. Maybe he fell into an alternate dimension. Have you checked the alternate dimensions?"

A small knot of policemen walk by, boots crunching on the broken glass on the sidewalk outside the Subway. One of them hesitates for half a second, looking from Trish to me; she stares back hard, gives him a curt nod. She wouldn't really tase me—I don't think so, anyway. McConnell looks different than she used to, more adult somehow; her small ponytail and short stature, which always struck me in the past as awkward and quasi-adolescent, seem this morning like the opposite: signs of maturity, readiness.

"Keep moving," says McConnell, when her fellow officers are gone. "Let's keep moving."

I brief her on my investigation as we circle the block, giving her the high points, from memory: Martha Cavatone, wild eyed, wringing her hands; Rocky Milano and his defiantly bustling pizza place; my late-night visit from Jeremy Canliss, his strong suggestion that Brett has a girl somewhere.

"So the guy is getting laid. Or he's getting drunk on a beach. What's the point?"

We've made the circuit and are now back at the Dumpster where I was hiding out before, trash spilling out on all sides. I've got a foot and a half on McConnell, easy, and now she stares up at me, CPD headquarters looming behind her like an alien planet.

"He used to be a cop," I say. "The husband."

"Oh, yeah?" McConnell's walkie-talkie crackles and mutters, and she looks at it, and then over at the loading dock, now swarming with bustling police.

"Yeah. A state trooper."

She looks back at me, uncertain for a moment, and then her face changes. "You want the file."

"Only if—"

"You asshole."

She's shaking her head but I press on, feeling bad, but I can't help it—she's the only person I've got left in there. "Concord is the HQ for the whole state now, right? So any paper related to state-force personnel will be here in the basement. Anything with the seal of the state of New Hampshire."

McConnell answers slowly. "It's not like it used to be, Hank. You don't just stroll down to the basement and fill out a form with—what was his name? Wilentz?"

"Wilentz."

She doesn't seem angry, just sad. Resigned. "You don't just go down and fill out a form and then Wilentz jokes around, makes you admire his stupid hat collection. I go down there now and request a file, I've got three supervisors who are total strangers to me asking what I want it for. Next thing you know that's it, I'm done. I'm out on the streets doing whatever you're doing all day."

"Reading," I say. "Teaching the dog some tricks."

"That drug dealer's dog? How's that going?"

"Poorly."

"They're paying, Palace. You know that, right? That's why I'm still in the uniform." She spits out the word *uniform*, like it's *cancer*. "A siren is going to blow, and then a truck rolls in." She glances at her watch. "In forty-five seconds. And the shit that's coming off there—food, water, supplies—as long as I'm in this gear, I get dibs. That's how they're doing this. That's how there is any law-enforcement activity of any kind: because the assholes in the uniform get first crack."

"I get it."

"Do you? I *cannot* lose my job."

McConnell's daughter Kelli is nine years old; Robbie, I think, is five. Their father took off four years ago, before the asteroid, before any of this. "Barry went Bucket List," Trish said to me once, "before Bucket List was cool."

"I'm sorry," I say. "I should have thought."

"Don't worry about it."

"Really, I'm sorry."

"Hank," she says, quieter. A different tone of voice.

"Yes?"

"One day, when the time is right, I'm going to escape to a mansion in the woods, somewhere in western Mass., and I'm taking you with me. How's that sound?"

"Sure," I say. "Sounds good."

And then McConnell, very quickly, reaches up and tugs on my mustache, hard.

"Hey."

"Sorry. Something I've always wanted to do. Carpe diem, right?"

"Right."

Then the siren goes off, loud and insistent, a tornado horn blowing somewhere on the roof of the CPD. McConnell mutters "shit" as her walkie-talkie blares to life, crackling out a string of code: "Team four-zero-nine, go alpha. Team six-zero-forty, go alpha." The CB code is unfamiliar, and I ask McConnell what it means.

"It means I've got thirty seconds to get across the street and get back in character." She grits her teeth and stares at me, shaking her head. "What's the guy's name?"

"Cavatone."

"He was a trooper?"

"Until a couple years ago. But Trish, seriously, forget it."

I feel bad now. She's right. I never should have put her in this position. I have a permanent mental picture of Trish's kids from a couple years ago, when she couldn't find a sitter and dragged them to someone's retirement party: Kelli, a thoughtful child with watchful eyes in a lime-green Hello Kitty shirt, Robbie sucking his thumb.

"Western Mass., Detective," says McConnell. "You and me."

She winks and flips down her mask, and she's smiling, I can see it in the lines of her brow above the Plexiglas. Then off she goes, dropping into a hustle as the eighteen-wheeler rumbles in, the driver clutching the big wheel, white-knuckled as he rattles the thing into place. The police swarm its flat metal flanks like bugs on the carcass of a forest animal.

"Trish," I call. I can't resist. "If there's coffee on the truck—"

Over her shoulder she flashes me her middle finger and disappears into the pack of cops.

* * *

Nico, my sister, is living in a used-clothing store on Wilson Avenue. That's where she is, holed up with a small rotating cast of poorly groomed, slack-jawed, paranoid-delusional chuckleheads. My sister.

I come here every couple days. I don't knock on the door, I don't go inside. I stand across the street or skulk through the mud-splattered alley behind the store, leaning in toward the open windows to hear her voice, catch a glimpse of her. Today I slouch down low on a bus bench across the street from Next Time Around with a six-month-old issue of *Popular Science* held up in front of my eyes like a spy.

The last time I spoke to Nico Palace it was April, and she was standing on my porch in a jean jacket, revealing with defiance and pride how she had taken advantage of her credulous policeman older brother, gulled me into using my law-enforcement connections to gain sensitive information about security at the New Hampshire National Guard facility on Pembroke Road. She had used me, not to mention her husband, Derek, who was likely executed or remanded to permanent custody as the result of her maneuvering. I was astonished and furious and I told her so, and Nico assured me—breathless with self-importance—that her machinations were all in the service of a profoundly important objective. She stood on my porch, smoking one of her American Spirits, eyes glittering with conspiracy, and insisted that she and her anonymous companions were working to save us all.

She wanted me to ask for the details, and I would not give her that satisfaction. Instead, I told her that this project, whatever it was, was the worst kind of dangerous nonsense, and we have not spoken since.

And yet here I am, turning the pages of *Popular Science*, reading for the millionth time about the soil composition under the Indonesian sea, and what that means for the ejecta that will be blasted into our atmosphere at impact—here I am, waiting to assure myself that Nico is safe. Once she was gone for two days, and I was anxious enough about her absence to spend three miserable hours crouched in that filthy back alley, listening through the windows until one of the scumbags within mentioned to another that Nico was down in Durham, mingling with the utopians and self-styled revolutionaries at the Free Republic of New Hampshire.

The details I ignored. I just needed to know, as I need to know now, today, that she's okay.

At last the front door opens and a fat twenty-something boy with greasy hair emerges to dump out a bucket full of some fluid—urine? cooking oil? bong water?—and I see Nico, slight and pale and smoking, just inside.

I wish I could abandon my sister to her cronies and her idiotic plans. I wish I could stop giving a flying fig, as my father used to say, about this selfish and petulant and ignorant child. But she's my sister. Our parents are dead and so is my father's father, who raised us, and it's my responsibility to ensure, for now, that she stays alive.

2.

"Sit anywhere, hon."

It's lunchtime but Culverson and McGully aren't here, and as I slide onto a stool at the counter I feel a roll of anxiety. Every time someone isn't there who is supposed to be, a part of my mind defaults to the certainty that they're dead or disappeared.

"It's early yet," says Ruth-Ann, reading my mind, as she comes over with the carafe of hot water and a tray of teabags. "They'll be here."

I watch her walk back to the counter. The asteroid will come and destroy the earth and leave behind only Ruth-Ann, floating in the vast blackness of space, one hand clutched around the handle of her carafe.

On the counter is the valedictory edition of the *Concord Monitor*, from a Sunday four weeks ago, and though I've surely read it cover to cover a hundred times by now, I pick it up to read it one more time. American and European bombing campaign against nuclear, general military, and civilian targets across Pakistan. The newly formed Mayfair Commission, subpoenaing the records of the Spaceguard Survey and the Arecibo Observatory in Puerto Rico. The massive twelve-deck cruise ship, flying the Norwegian flag, that plowed into Oakland Harbor and turned out to be carrying more than twenty thousand catastrophe immigrants from Central Asia, women and children "packed like animals" into its holds.

There's a long feature story on the back about a young woman, a former Boston University law student, who has decided to head eastward, to Indonesia, a CI in reverse, to await the world's destruction "in the epicenter of the event." The article has a gently amused, "well, what do you know?" sort of tone, except for the quotes from the kid's horrified parents.

And then, in the lower-left corner of the front page, the short, anguished mea culpa from the publisher: lacking in resources, lacking in staff, it is with great regret that we announce that effective immediately . . .

As Ruth-Ann centers my teacup on its saucer there's a rush of noise from outside, someone pushing open the front door. I swivel, knock the teacup with my elbow, and it shatters on the floor. Ruth-Ann pulls out a double-barreled shotgun like a gangster from under the counter and aims it at the door.

"Stop," she says to the trembling woman. "Who are you?"

"It's okay," I say, sliding off my stool, tripping over myself, rushing over. "I know her."

"He came *back*, Henry," says Martha, frantic, pleading, her face flushed and pink. "Brett came home."

* * *

I put Martha Milano on my handlebars somehow and bike her home like we're old-timey sweethearts. Once we're inside, once she's slammed the door and worked down the column of locks from top to bottom, she makes a beeline for the kitchen and pantry, the one with the cartons of smokes—then stops herself, slaps her thigh, retreats to the sofa, collapses in a heap.

"He was here?"

Martha nods vigorously, almost violently, eyes popped open like a frightened child's. "Right where you're standing. This morning. First thing this morning."

"You spoke to him?"

"No, no, I didn't, not actually." She shakes her head, starts chewing on a hangnail. "Didn't get a chance to. He disappeared."

"Disappeared?"

Martha makes a swift up-and-down motion, like a magician tossing pixie dust onto the stage, *whoosh*. "He was here and then, just—*disappeared*."

"Okay," I say.

The room looks exactly the same as it did. It's Martha who looks different. She is shakier on her feet than she was at our meeting yesterday morning, her pale skin even paler, marked by bright red splotches, like she's been picking at spots on her face. Her hair does not appear to have been washed or brushed, and it flies off in all directions, thick and messy. I get a nasty feeling, like her anxiety over her husband's disappearance has metastasized into something else, something closer to profound despair, even madness.

I take out my notebook, flip to a fresh page.

"What time was he here?"

"Very early. I don't know. Five? I don't know. I was dreaming of him, believe it or not. I have this dream where he pulls up to the house in his old cruiser, the lights spinning. And he climbs out, in his boots, and holds out his hands to me, and I run into his arms."

"That's nice," I say, seeing it in my mind like a mini-movie: the blue cop-car lights splashing on the sidewalk, Martha and Brett running into each other's arms.

"But then, so, I woke up because there was this loud noise. Downstairs. It freaked me out."

"What kind of noise, exactly?"

"I don't know," she says. "A crack? A thud? Some kind of noise."

I don't say anything, I'm remembering my own nighttime visitor, Jeremy Canliss, stumbling into Mr. Moran's solar still. But Martha reads judgment in my silence, and she changes gears, her voice becomes brittle and insistent. "It was him, Henry, I know that it was him."

I pour her a glass of water. I tell her to start at the beginning, tell me exactly what happened, and I write it all down. She heard the noise, she lit a candle, waited at the top of the stairs, breathless, until she heard it again. Not daring to call out, assuming it was a violent-minded intruder and preferring to be merely burglarized than raped or killed, she stared down the steps until she recognized him.

"You saw his face?"

"No. But his—you know, his shape. His body."

"Okay."

"He's short, but he's stocky. It was him." I nod, wait, and she keeps going. "I called out to him, I ran down the stairs, but like I said, he was . . ." Her face collapses into her hands. "He was *gone.*"

All of Martha's wild energy fades; she sinks back into the sofa while my mind runs through the possibilities, trying to give her what credit I can: It might have been a house thief, plenty of those, who chose at the last minute, for some reason, to leave empty-handed. Someone unhinged, bent on violence, suddenly frightened or confused by his prey.

Or, very possibly, it was nothing. The symptom of a desperately lonely and burdened mind, jumping at shadows.

I rove around the downstairs rooms, doing my policeman routine, crawling on hands and knees, looking for footprints in the shag carpet. I investigate the windows one by one, running my fingertips carefully over the frames. Undamaged. Unopened. No signs of forced entry, no scatter of glass on the carpet, no scratches on the locks. If someone came in, they came in with a key. I pause at the door, running my hand along the long column of dead bolts and chains.

"Martha, do you lock this door at night?"

"Yes," she says, "Yes, we always—I do all the . . ."

She stops, bites her lip as she realizes where I'm heading here. Brett could not have come in through this door without her letting him in.

"There are windows," she says.

"Sure. They are locked, though." I clear my throat. "And barred."

"Right. But . . ." She looks around the small house helplessly. "But it was his house. He installed all those locks, all the bars, and—I mean—he's *Brett*. He could—I mean, he could have gotten in if he wanted to. Right?"

"I don't know," I say. "Of course. Anything's possible."

I don't know what else to say. The expression on her face, of pure and fierce belief, untroubled by evidence or common sense—it's maddening, in its way, and all at once I'm infuriated and exhausted. I remember Detective McGully, questioning my motives, teasing but not really: *That's not a kind of money.* I hear Trish, too: *Have you checked the alternate dimensions?*

Behind Martha on the wall is a flat-screen TV, a flat cold rectangle, and I am struck by the object's profound uselessness, a receiver for an extinct species of signal, a reminder of all that is already dead, a tombstone hung on the wall.

Martha is muttering now, rubbing the sides of her face with the flats of her hands, working herself back up. "I know that it was him, Henry," she says. "I told you that he was going to come back, and he came back."

I wander the apartment, try to focus my mind, see things from my client's point of view. Brett comes back but doesn't approach her, doesn't stop to talk. Why? He's not back, but there's something he needs her to know. He wants to leave a message. I nod, turning this over, okay . . . so where's the message? On the sofa, Martha Cavatone is clutching her face with both hands, her fingers covering her cheeks and chin and eyes like vines crawling up the wall of a house.

"He was here," she's murmuring, talking to herself now, "I know that he was here."

"Yes."

"What?"

I'm calling from the kitchen. I'm in the pantry. She rushes in and I turn around to stare at her. "Martha, you were right. He was here."

Astonished, I detach the perforated cardboard top of the uppermost carton of Camels. "Here," I say. Martha's eyes are as wide as paper plates. "He left you a note. Hid it where he thought you'd be sure to see it."

And I'm almost laughing, because this is what happens when you decide that a case is pure smoke—no solution, no chance. You find a clue, clear and incontrovertible. It's got a date on it, for heaven's sake. July nineteenth. Today's date. I sit beside her on the couch to read what Brett Cavatone has written carefully in neat script.

17 GARVINS FALLS #2 // MR. PHILLIPS // SUNSHINE SUNSHINE MINE

ALL MINE

Martha's anxiety has drained out of her. She stands up straight, as steady as I've seen her, her brow untroubled, a gentle gleam in her eye. Her faith rewarded.

"Does this note make sense to you?" I ask.

"The last part does," she says, softly, almost whispering. "Sunshine, sunshine, mine all mine. He would always say that to me. When we first got married. Sunshine, sunshine, mine all mine." She takes the cardboard slip from me and reads it again, murmurs the words to herself. "He's telling me so I know it's him."

"And the rest of it? Garvins Falls?"

"No. I mean—it sounds like an address, but I don't know where it is."

It is an address. Garvins Falls Road is a winding industrial street, east of the river, south of Manchester Street. An industrial section, unmaintained and gritty even before the beginning of our current environment.

"What about Mr. Phillips?"

"No."

"You sure?"

"I don't know who that is."

Gently, I take the piece of cardboard from her hands and read it again. "Martha, I have to be sure of something. There was no one else who knew about this. 'Sunshine, sunshine, mine all mine,' I mean. This code phrase?"

"Code phrase?" she says.

Martha's eyes focus on me and she's giving me this pitying and perplexed expression, which I recognize from the old days, when I used to do things that surprised her—politely say "no, thank you" to

a second glass of chocolate milk, or rise to turn off the TV immediately after our permitted half hour had elapsed.

"It's not a code phrase, Henry," says Martha. "It was just a sweet
little thing that we said to each other. A loving phrase we used. Because we loved each other."

"Right," I say, slipping the piece of cardboard in my pocket.
"Of course. Let's go."

3.

Martha and I leave the bike chained to her cement birdbath and walk together from the Cavatones' home toward Garvins Falls Road, skirting downtown, sticking to the quiet backstreets, the neighborhoods with active residents-association patrols. Marginally safer; nothing is safe.

My mind is buzzing with questions. If Brett really came back, if it was really him, then why? Why leave and then return? Who abandons his wife and comes back to leave a forwarding address?

Martha is untroubled by the specifics. Martha is borne forward by gusts of joyful anticipation. "I can't believe it," she says—sings, almost, like a schoolgirl. "We're just going to walk in there, and Brett's going to be waiting for me. I can't believe it."

But she can believe it. She does. She's walking so fast down Main Street on the way to the bridge that I have to hurry to keep up, even with my long stride. I loop my arm through hers, try to temper her pace. Walking quickly isn't safe—too many loose stones and ruts in the sidewalk. She's in a simple black cotton dress and I'm in my suit, and when I see our reflection in one of the remaining plates of the plate-glass window at what used to be Howager's Discount Store on Loudon Road, we look like time travelers, like voyagers rocketed forward from another era; the roaring twenties, maybe, or postwar, a fella and his dame out for a noonday stroll, who accidentally took a wrong turn and came out on a rubbled path in a collapsing world.

There's no sign to identify the building on Garvins Falls Road, no indication of what businesses are here, or used to be, just the number "17" stenciled in rust-colored paint on the brick wall outside. Inside, the lobby is decrepit and bare, and there's no passenger elevator—just a heavy fire door with the single word STAIRS, and the rusting gated doors of a freight elevator.

"All right," I say, looking slowly around. "Okay."

But Martha is already in motion, rushing across the empty room and tugging open the door to the stairs. Then she steps back, confused, and I whistle lightly in surprise. Behind the door is nothing: the stairs are gone, literally gone, it's just an empty shaft with a railing running up the walls. Like the staircase has turned invisible, like it's a staircase for ghosts.

"Huh," I say. I don't like this. It's purposeful, defensive, a fortification. Martha hugs herself as she stares up into the darkness of the stairwell.

"We've got to get up there," she says. "What do we do?"

"Freight elevator. I'll go first. You wait here."

"No," says Martha. "I need to see him. I can't wait anymore."

"We don't know what's up there, Martha."

"He is," she says, jaw set, certain. "Brett is up there."

The doors of the elevator open immediately when I press the button, and Martha gets on, and I get on behind her, and my stomach tightens as the doors draw closed behind us. We lurch into motion. There's a skylight in the ceiling of the elevator car and another one way up somewhere at the top of the shaft, sending down twice-distilled sunlight like a message from a distant star. As the car works its slow way upward, Martha, for all her bravado, tenses and takes a step closer to me. I can hear her murmuring prayers in the darkness, and she gets as far as "who art in heaven" when the elevator shudders to a stop and the doors groan open and reveal a room full of supplies: crates, pallets laden with jugs and cans, water bottles, shelving. And then a man hoots and launches himself into the elevator car, directly into my midsection, knocking the breath from me and forcing me backward into one dark corner. He lands on top of me and clamps a hand down over my face. I am smashed into the dirty floor with this man crouched above me like a wolf, a lycanthrope, his knees pinned into my shoulders, holding my mouth shut and jamming something hard and cold into the side of my head.

I writhe. I try to speak and cannot. The stranger's eyes are bright and narrow in the dim refracted light.

"It's a staple gun," coos the man in my ear, low and lover-like.

"But I modified it. Juiced it up a little."

He digs the staple gun harder into my temple, and I try to twist my head away and cannot. In the corner of my eye is Martha Cavatone, her mouth agape, her eyes distorted with fear. A tall woman is behind her, one hand pulling Martha's head back by the hair and the other holding the keen end of a cleaver to her neck. Their pose is biblical, brutal, a lamb at the slaughter point.

We're in this tableau, the four of us, as the doors of the elevator creak closed and we start down again, listening to the rusted clang of the chains.

"It takes about thirty-five seconds for the elevator to get down to the ground floor," says the man on top of me, leaning his body forward to flatten me further. "The way we do it is, it touches down, the doors open, we roll out the bodies and hit the Up button."

Martha screams and thrashes in the grip of the tall woman. I breathe through my nose, deep breaths.

"I don't know what happens to the bodies. It seems too early for cannibalism, but who knows? They keep disappearing is all I know."

The man's chin is square and jutting. His hand is rough and it smells like Ivory soap. I started counting seconds as soon as he started talking; there are twenty seconds left.

"What I did was, I rigged the staple gun to the motor of a hedge trimmer, so it can really do some business. I got guns, but I'm saving up my bullets. You know how it is."

The man grins, shining white teeth, a gap between the two in front. The elevator descends, the chains rattling deafeningly like exploding ordnance. T-minus ten seconds—T-minus nine—who's counting?

"My friend Ellen, she just uses a butcher's knife. No imagination, you know?"

"Fuck you, you dick," says the woman holding on to Martha, glaring at the man. He puffs out his cheeks, looks at me like *can you believe this one?* T-minus two. One. The elevator touches down with a thud. My bones rattle. I brace myself.

"Who are you?" says the man, and takes his hand off my mouth, and I say, "My name is Henry Pal—" and he fires the staple gun with a whir and a click and my brain explodes. I scream, and there's another scream, in the corner, it's the woman, Ellen. I crane my neck and try to see through the pain-sparked flickers, red and gold stars flaring across my field of vision. Martha is biting the woman's arm, kicking free.

"Fuck!" screams Ellen, raises her knife like a butcher, and Martha screams, "Phillips! Mr. Phillips!"

"Oh," says the man, and eases off. "Well, shit."

Ellen lowers the knife, breathes heavily, and Martha sinks down against the back wall of the elevator car, her face in her hands, sobbing.

A password. Of course. *Mr. Phillips.* Palace, you idiot.

Blood is rushing from the side of my head, down my forehead and into my eyes. I raise one finger and touch the wound, a hole the size of a dime, the small sharp object of the staple buried in the thin flesh of my temple.

My assailant tosses his weapon on the floor of the elevator. "Ellen, hit the Up button, will you, honey?"

* * *

There are more goods than I saw in that first glimpse, many more: a room full of boxes, each box overflowing with things—useful things. Batteries, light bulbs, portable fans, humidifiers, snack foods, plastic utensils, first aid supplies, pens and pencils and big pads of paper. The man, the one who just shot me in the head with his staple gun, he pats me on the back and grins wolfishly, opens his arms and does a proud half-turn around the room.

"Pretty nice, right?" he says, and then answers his own question, settling back in a swiveling chair. "It's *very* nice. I obtained an Office Depot."

He pilots himself across the room on the wobbly wheels of the chair and docks behind a wide L-shaped glass-topped desk, where he puts up his feet and unscrews the lid of a plastic jug of pretzels. I'm holding my palm up to the side of my head, blood flowing freely down my wrist, pooling inside my shirt sleeves. Martha is holding herself, trembling, looking fearfully at the woman with the butcher knife. A couple years ago, at this time, Martha Cavatone would have been at Market Basket, picking up something for dinner, or maybe at the bank, the dry cleaners. A year from now, who knows?

"See, I had a friend," says our host from behind his glass-top desk. "An acquaintance, really, who owed me just a disgusting amount of money. This was last December. And you know, I had a feeling how this was going, this business with the asteroid. It was in the darkness still, hidden by the moon."

When he mentions the asteroid, he gets a sort of wistful contented glimmer in his eye, like it's the best thing that ever happened to him. Conjunction, is what he means. In December $2011GV_1$ was still in conjunction, aligned with the sun and impossible to observe. It was not "hidden by the moon." My eyes have landed on the water—boxes of jugs, ten jugs to the box, two stacks of ten boxes, side by side. Twelve jugs of water per box times ten times two.

"And this cat, this poor fellow, I went to him and said, look, forget the money. Because this guy, when he wasn't making bad bets on sports, he was the manager of the Office Depot in Pittsfield. And the thing about Office Depot is that they don't have just *office* things. They have a really extraordinary variety of merchandise."

He sounds like a commercial for Office Depot, and he knows he does. He laughs, tosses his shoulder-length hair.

"Anyway, so the shit goes down, they say the world's gonna end, and I'm in a position, you know? I had a copy of this guy's keys, I had some friends lined up, I had a truck set aside, I had some gasoline." He winks again. He shrugs. "So I obtained an Office Depot."

"*We* did, Cortez," says Ellen, curtly. "We obtained it." She's at the door of the empty stairwell, still holding her butcher knife.

Cortez grins at me, rolls his eyes slightly, like we're in cahoots, he and I, boys versus girls. I study him, long black hair, bulging forehead, jutting jaw—he reminds me of a houseguest we had once when I was a child, a noted poet my father invited to give a lecture at St. Anselm's. My mother said he was "ugly, in that handsome sort of way."

I take another look at Martha, make sure she's okay. She's sitting down at a desk; the room is full of desks, glass-topped desks, hutch desks, imposing oak-top desks; many of them with locked drawers. A room full of stashes, hidden places, things squirreled away.

"Do you know this man?" I say, bringing the photograph of Brett out of my pocket.

Cortez gasps theatrically, puts his hands in the air. "Oh my God, you're a fucking policeman."

"No, sir."

"Do it again," he says, grinning. "With the picture. Ask me again."

I place the photograph down in front of him. "Do you know this man?"

He slaps his desk, delighted. "A real-life policeman. It's like an acid flashback."

"Yes," says Ellen quietly, from her side of the room, still holding the butcher's knife. "We know him. He was here yesterday. You're his wife?"

Cortez gives Ellen an irritated look while Martha nods, her eyes filling with refreshed hope as she looks around the room. She's thinking, *here—in this room*. She's reveling in the fact of his proximity, in space if not in time: *He was here.*

"Yes. He was here." Cortez is looking me over, up and down, marveling still at the real-live policeman. "And he said that the woman would be coming alone, which is why I shot you with my staple gun."

"It's okay," I say.

"I did not apologize."

"Can I just . . ." Martha swallows. Her hands are trembling. She looks from Ellen to Cortez and then back to Ellen. "What did he want?"

"Stuff," said Cortez simply.

"What?" says Martha.

I'm looking around again: the desks, the filing cabinets, the boxes of impulse-purchase nonfoods, fruit snacks and goldfish crackers and granola bars.

"What do you mean, what?" says Cortez, grinning. "That's what he wanted. Stuff! Stuff for *you*, sweetheart."

"I'm sorry," says Martha. "I don't understand."

"Oh, honey," says Ellen, glaring at Cortez, laying her hatchet down at last and putting an arm around Martha. "He paid us to take care of you. Until afterward."

"Take care of?" says Martha, eyes wide. "What does that mean?"

"It means, *give a bunch of fucking shit to*." Cortez sidles over to their side of the room and scoops up the big knife. "It means, *not let to become dead*."

"Shut up, Cortez," says Ellen. "It means he paid up front for us to provide enough stuff for you to make it till the end. Food, water, batteries, flashlights, clothes, tampons. Whatever."

"And if you're afraid of things going bump in the night, we do protection." Cortez walks back to his desk, slides Ellen's butcher knife into a drawer. "Right up until the end."

"But not afterward?" I ask.

"Afterward?" Cortez cackles, kicks his legs up on the desk like a corporate raider. "Anyone making promises for afterward is a liar and a thief."

I'm holding my bloody forehead, thinking this through, realizing along with Martha exactly what it means. Brett wanted her to be taken care of, which is a nice thing, except it means he knew that he was leaving. There is no longer any question of accident or foul play. Brett Cavatone left his wife with foresight, efficiency, and decisiveness. Martha is staring straight ahead, lost behind the large desk like a schoolchild in her daddy's office.

"Excuse me," she says, suddenly sitting up straight, her voice carefully controlled. "Do you have any cigarettes?"

"Yes, honey," says Ellen, unlatching a trunk the size of a small bathtub. "Thousands of them."

The pain from my new injury has reignited an old one, like a pinball bouncing against a bumper and lighting it up: a raw spot where I was once stabbed, just below my left eye. It was the drug dealer who stabbed me, the one whose dog is at my house right now, waiting to be fed.

"This protection. This is a service you offer?" I ask Cortez. "Have been offering?"

"It is." He grins. "You interested?"

"No, thank you. How do people pay you for this service?"

"Stuff," he says, the strong chin, the lopsided grin. "More stuff. Things I can turn around and offer to other folks. Items I can hang on to for a rainy day. For the big rainy day."

"How did *he* pay you?" I say, holding up the photograph again.

"Ah!" Cortez rubs his hands together, eyes gleaming like coins. "You want to see?"

* * *

Pieces of metal, hunks of metal, scraps and stacks of it. Gleaming silver, contoured black plastic, glass and dials. I look at the pile, look at Cortez.

"It's a vehicle."

Cortez waggles his eyebrows mysteriously, having fun. We took the elevator down together in silence and then had to go outside, around the back, and down a rickety flight of basement stairs accessible now only by a sidewalk trapdoor. The basement of 17 Garvins Falls has a concrete floor, dim overhead bulbs hooked up to a noisy and foul-smelling biofuel generator. I lift one long flat plane of reinforced iron and find words painted on the other side in a childlike comic-book font: CALIFORNIA: GOLD RUSH COUNTRY!

"A U-Haul," I say, and Cortez's jagged grin widens. "Can you believe it?"

I can. I do. Rocky Milano was lying: he didn't have his beloved

son-in-law and right-hand man hauling furniture around the county
on a ten-speed bicycle. That's how a restaurant stays open: get ahold
of a working vehicle, scam or barter for a supply of gas or some boot-
leg biofuel, make a reliable map of DOJ checkpoints to be avoided.
No wonder Rocky is so aggrieved. He didn't just lose a son-in-law
and a top employee; he lost his most valuable capital asset. I wish I
could go back to that room and ask him again, press him on all the
half-truths and evasions. I'm not a cop, I'd say. I'm just a guy trying
to help your daughter.

"What I told him is, if you're gonna leave this, you gotta take
it apart," says Cortez. "I'll get more on it, piece by piece, don't you
think?"

I don't hazard a guess. I lift a gritty metal pole the length of my
arm.

"Steering column." Cortez titters, angles out his chin.

I wander among the pieces of the van, identifying the pedals,
the seat belt straps, the slanting beveled iron of the loading ramp. The
fractured shapes of something as ordinary as a U-Haul truck, it's like
a vision from distant memory, like I'm inspecting the butchered carcass of a mastodon. The two tire rims are stacked, one atop the other,
the fat black rubber wheels beside them.

I straighten up and I look at Cortez, the Jesus-style hair, the
mischievous smile. "Why would he trust you?" I ask. "To honor a
bargain?"

He splays a hand across his breastbone, offended. I wait.
"We've known each other, going back, that cop and I. He knows

what I am." He smiles like a magical cat. "I'm a thief, but I'm an honorable thief. He's seen me get arrested, seen me get out and build right back. Because I'm dependable. A man of business has to be relied upon, that's all."

I pull the wad of gauze away from the side of my head—it's soaked in blood—I put it back in place. Rocky Milano has not closed his restaurant, even though we're in countdown land: he's doubled down, intensified his commitment to his operation and his self-identity. So, too, with Cortez the thief.

"Plus, he said that if I went back on him, if I let anything befall his wife, he'd come back and murder me," adds Cortez, almost off-handedly. "I've known people who say that and don't mean it. It was my strong impression that this was a man who meant it."

"And he gave you no indication of where he was going?'

"Nope." Cortez pauses, smirks. "I'll tell you one thing, though. Wherever he was going, he was in a goddamn hurry to get there. I teased the man about it. I said, for someone who is here to cut up a working vehicle and leave it behind, you sure want to get going. He didn't laugh, though. Not one little bit."

No, I think. I bet he didn't. If Brett was as much of a straight shooter as I am sensing he was, if he was the decent and honorable character that emerges from everybody's recollections, then he *hated* coming here. I can picture him, on the way to Garvins Falls Road, in this stolen van—tasting the bitterness of the measure he was taking, of putting his trust in this weasely and self-regarding man. Brett Cavatone disassembling a U-Haul van, working swiftly under

Cortez's glittering gaze, not looking at his watch, just doing the job carefully and well until it was done.

My missing person was a man dying to leave, in a fever to leave, but who knew that leaving was wrong. He made a compromise with himself, struck a moral balance, did what he had to, to make arrangements for the woman he'd be leaving behind.

I say "thank you" to Cortez. He says "you're very welcome" and bows. I go up to collect Martha.

* * *

On Garvins Falls Road, outside, the late-day sunlight a perfect golden gleam along the rutted sidewalks, I look back up at the building and Martha looks down at the street. It's hotter than yesterday but still not uncomfortable. There's a pair of perfect clouds teasing each other across the bright blue sky. Martha seems calm and composed, surprisingly so, considering what she has learned.

"I told you," she says, very softly, and I say, "Excuse me?"

"I told you, he's like a rock, that man. That's how he is. He thinks of things. He's so thoughtful. Even—" She smiles, turns her face up to the sun. "Even leaving me, he was considerate about it."

"Yes," I say. "Sure."

In the distance, all the way back in downtown Concord, the deafening holler of the tornado siren. I can picture the truck rumbling into its dock, McConnell and the rest of the cops hurrying into place, forming their perimeter, preparing to unload.

"So, just to be absolutely clear, Martha," I say, as gently as I can. "You no longer want me to find your husband?"

"Oh, no," she says, startled. "Now I want you to find him more than ever."

4.

People talk about the asteroid that killed the dinosaurs, like it just happened one day. All the dinosaurs were hanging out, all together in an open field, and the asteroid slammed down and destroyed them, killed them all and all at once.

Not so, of course. Some died on the day, no doubt about it, and probably a lot—but the whole business took years. Generations, maybe. They can't say for sure. They know that a ten-kilometer asteroid exploded into the crust of the earth in the Yucatan Peninsula 65.6 million years ago, tearing a great gash from the planet and darkening the sky, and some of the dinosaurs drowned and some burned and some starved when the plants stopped growing, and some stumbled on through the new cold world. They ate what they could find and fought for scraps and forgot there had been an asteroid. Brains like walnuts, creatures of need, they knew only their hunger. A lot of species died. A lot of species didn't.

This time, too, it'll go both ways: Most people will die in October and in the brutal cataclysms that follow, and then many more will die later. The sudden death versus the lingering; the instant and certain versus the drawn-out and unpredictable. My parents both died suddenly, a finger-snap, a crack in time: One day my mother was here, and then she was buried, and then soon after that my father, bang, gone. With Grandfather, it was the long way: diagnosis, treatment, remission, relapse, new diagnosis, the wayward course of illness. There was one afternoon when we huddled at his bedside, Nico and I and a handful of his friends, said our goodbyes, and then he got better and lived for another six months, pale and thin and irritable.

Naomi Eddes, the woman I loved, she went the other way, the first way: bang and gone.

The best available scientific evidence suggests that on the day itself, the earth's atmosphere will be riven by flame, as if by a prodigious nuclear detonation: over most of the planet, a broiling heat, the sky on fire. Tsunamis as tall as skyscrapers slam into coasts and drown everyone within hundreds of miles from impact, while around the globe volcanic eruptions and earthquakes convulse the landscape, splintering the crust of the world at all its hidden junctions. And then photosynthesis, the magic trick undergirding the entire food chain, is snuffed out by a blanket of darkness drawn down across the sun.

But no one knows. No one really knows. They have computer models, based on the Yucatan event, based on Siberia. But it all depends on final velocity, on angle of approach, on the precise makeup of the object and the soil below the impact spot. Probably not everyone will die. But probably most people will. It will definitely be terrible, but it's impossible to say exactly how. Anyone making promises for afterward is a liar and a thief.

* * *

When I get home there's a thick manila envelope jammed between the screen door and the front door, so that when I pull open the door the package falls out and lands on the porch with a thump. I crouch down and tear open the envelope with one finger and slide out a single manila file folder, thickly packed, stamped NEW HAMPSHIRE STATE POLICE FILE: BRETT ALAN CAVATONE (RET.).

"Thanks, Trish," I murmur, and turn eastward toward School Street to toss her a salute, soft and sweet as blowing a kiss.

Stepping inside I close the front door carefully, not wanting a sharp slam to wake Houdini, who is snoring lightly on the sofa, curled with his face smushed into his own warm side. In the kitchen I light three candles and make tea. The police file is written in the clipped language of all such reports: a short story written in brief static bursts of institutional prose. The subject is referred to throughout as O. Cavatone. "O." for officer. O. Cavatone graduated the police academy on such-and-such a date. On such-and-such a date he was assigned to Troop D of the Division of State Police with the rank of Trooper I; transferred north, then, to Troop F; recognized with a commendation and a small ceremony for saving the life of a traffic accident victim; promoted to Trooper II. Taken together, the pages speak to an admirable, steadfast career: no citations, no warnings, no blemishes on the record.

"The Governor's Medal," I say to myself quietly, turning a page, nodding appreciatively. "Very nice, O. Cavatone. Congratulations."

Halfway down the fourth page, the quick log-line bursts of information give way to one long detailed paragraph, delving in some detail into one particular incident. It begins with the arrest report: four suspects accused of trespassing. The location is a slaughterhouse operated by a dairy farm called Blue Moon, near Rumney. The apparent mission of the alleged trespassers was to install hidden videotaping equipment, but they tripped alarms and were apprehended fleeing the scene. Subsequently, the suspects explained to the arresting officer—O. Cavatone—that their action was intended to gather evidence of inhumane and unhealthful treatment of the cattle: to "provoke horror and outrage," says the report, "toward Blue Moon in particular and U.S. agricultural practice in general."

The case rings a bell, the thing about the slaughterhouse. I get up and pace around the dark kitchen a little bit, try to remember it. According to the date on the file it was two and a half years ago, this arrest. I probably read about it in the *Monitor*, or maybe they went over it with us in the academy. An interesting sort of crime, an unusual category of motivation for this part of the world: political provocation, college kids in tie-dyed ski masks, planting video cameras.

Houdini murmurs in his sleep, growling a little. I sip my tea.

It's cold. I lift the file again, read the names of the perpetrators, all of whom had been charged with trespassing and two counts of criminal mischief. Marcus Norman, Julia Stone, Annabelle Demetrios, Frank Cignal.

I read these names again, study them, tapping my fingers. Why does O. Cavatone's file include a detailed report of this particular case, why the full paragraph on this one arrest, when there must have been hundreds over the course of a six-year career?

The answer, as it turns out, is not hard to find. It is, indeed, highlighted—literally highlighted, on the next page of the record.

"Charges against all suspects dismissed; O. Cavatone failing on several occasions to provide appropriate testimony."

The Blue Moon incident is the end of Brett Cavatone's file. There is no discharge information, no report given of his dismissal or early retirement. The rest of his story I already know, more or less: Brett leaves the state troopers a few months later, at age thirty, and takes a job at his father-in-law's new pizza restaurant. And then, three days ago, he disappears.

I rise and stretch, feeling my bones ache along the length of my body. My body is crying out for sleep—for sleep or for coffee. There's a dull throbbing at my temple, and it's only when I raise one finger to the small divot beside my eye do I recall that I was shot earlier today with a staple gun. I gently move Houdini over and lie down beside him in the darkness and then a few minutes later I'm up again, reopening the file—reading it again—and again—unable to stop—the impulse to discover speaking up in me like morning birds, like unruly children.

* * *

"I'll have the lobster Thermidor," says Detective Culverson.

"We don't have that," says Ruth-Ann, sighing elaborately.

"Coq au vin?"

"We don't have that either."

"You're kidding."

"Sorry."

It's midmorning the next day, Friday, and Culverson and Ruth-Ann are doing the kind of flirtatious give-and-take that I normally find amusing, but now I'm rat-a-tatting my fingers on the edge of the booth, shifting impatiently while they go through their bit. Detective McGully isn't here yet, but that doesn't matter, it's Culverson's opinion I want.

"Here," I say, as soon as Ruth-Ann turns and heads back to the kitchen. "Okay." I slide him the file. Not the whole thing, just the last two pages. "Tell me what you see."

"This is the Bucket List guy?" He slowly unfolds his reading glasses. "Your babysitter's boyfriend?"

"Husband."

"Oh, I thought boyfriend."

"Can you just have a look?"

Culverson lifts the pages and scans, glasses perched on the end of his nose, and quickly comes to the exact same conclusion that I did. "Looks like he got fired."

"Yes."

"But someone doesn't want to say that."

"Yes!" I beam at him. "Exactly."

"Where the hell is McGully?" says Culverson, straightening up and peering at the door.

"I don't know," I say quickly, and tap the file. "But the question is why, right? Why is this guy fired? I mean, so he fails to testify."

"Right. But he's not getting fired for a no-show."

"Right." Pause. Take a breath. "But, what if he *couldn't* show up."

"What do you mean? You saying he was a drunk?"

Ruth-Ann returns with two bowls of oatmeal. "Lobster Thermidor," she says, putting one down in front of me. "And coq au vin," giving Culverson his.

"No," I say, when she's gone. "No, not a drunk."

"Listen, Stretch, if you got some kind of stunning breakthrough to lay on me, then go ahead and do it," says Culverson. He tucks a napkin into the collar of his shirt, spreads it down across his chest like a bib. "Maybe you haven't heard, but life is short."

"Brett named the specials."

"What?"

"At the pizza place. Rocky told me—that's the boss, the father-in-law—he told me. Brett leaves the force after this thing at the dairy farm, he comes to work at his wife's father's pizza restaurant, and one of his first jobs is: name the specials. All of them get classic rock names. Layla: a very unusual and specific name. Hazel: unusual and specific. Sally Simpson: unusual and specific. And then—Julia."

He looks where I'm pointing, where I've laid my finger across the case file, at the list of suspects. Marcus Norman, Julia Stone, Annabelle Demetrios, Frank Cignal.

"Palace."

"Of all the girls' names in all the songs in the world?"

"*Palace.*"

"Even all the girls' names in all the Beatles songs? Who picks Julia?" I jab my finger at the page. "Who but a man with a woman on his mind?"

"I'm not really a Beatles man," says Culverson, stirring honey into his oatmeal. "You got any Earth, Wind, and Fire related clues?"

"Come on, Culverson."

"I'm teasing you."

"I know. But do you think it makes sense?"

"Honestly? No." He grins. "You have gone for a walk, my young friend. You have wandered so far from the available evidence that I cannot see you anymore, tall as a telephone pole though you may be."

"Maybe," I say. I cross my arms. "But I'm right."

"It's possible," he says. I've known Culverson for longer than anyone now living, except for my sister. Long ago, when I was still a child, it was Detective Culverson who solved the murder of my mother. "And hey, you know what? The world's about to blow up. So, you know, knock yourself out. You have a last-known address for young Julia?"

"Yeah," I say, tapping the file. "Durham."

"Durham?" he says.

"Yeah. At the time of the incident, she was a rising junior at UNH."

"So her last-known is on the grounds of the Free Republic. You're ready to go door to door down there?"

"No. Maybe." I grit my teeth. This is the hard part. "I actually know someone who might be able to help."

"Oh yeah?" Culverson raises an eyebrow. "Who's that?"

I'm saved by the bell. The door chimes, and McGully comes in with an old Samsonite suitcase like a traveling salesman. We look at him, Culverson and I, and Ruth-Ann looks over from her spot at the counter, at old McGully with his suitcase and his boots. No one says anything. That's it—it's like he's already gone, fading from full color to black and white before our eyes. He stands at the threshold of the restaurant, in the antechamber by the cash register where the pictures still hang of the owner, Bob Galicki, shaking hands with various politicians, where there's an old-fashioned gumball machine. The gumballs are gone now, the glass sphere shattered a long time ago.

Culverson leans back in his seat; McGully stares back at us in silence.

"Wow," says Culverson. "Where to?"

"New Orleans," says McGully. "I'm going to hoof it to 95, look for a southbound bus."

Culverson nods. I don't say anything. What is there to say? In the corner of my eye, Ruth-Ann is ramrod straight at the counter, carafe in hand, watching McGully in her doorway.

"You tell Beth?" Culverson asks.

"Nah." McGully flashes his monkey's grin, real quick, and then looks down at the floor. "I've been telling her, you know, we should get outta here, we should make a change, but she's . . . she's settled, you know? She's not leaving the house. Her mom died in that house." He looks up, then down again, mutters into his shirtfront. "I left her a note, though. Little note."

"Hey," I say. "McGully—" and he says, "No—no, you shut up," and I say, "What?" and then suddenly he's hollering, furious, stalking across the diner toward me. "You're like a little kid, you know that?"

He leans over me in the booth. I shrink back.

"In your tidy little universe, with your notebooks, and the good guys and the bad guys. That shit is moot, man. That shit is over."

"Easy," says Culverson, half rising, "take it easy now," but McGully keeps his finger in my face. "You just wait until the water runs out. You just fucking wait." He's snarling, showing his teeth. "You think this trooper you're looking for, you think he's a bad guy? You think I'm a bad guy?"

"I didn't say that," I murmur, but he's not listening. He's not talking to me, not really.

"Well, you wait until the taps stop working. *Then* you'll see some fucking bad guys." He's bright red. He's out of breath. "Okay?"

I don't say anything, but he seems to want an answer. "Okay," I say.

"Okay, smart guy?"

"Okay."

I meet McGully's eyes and he nods, eases off. No one else says anything. The boots squeak on the linoleum as he turns around, Ruth-Ann tsk-tsking at the scuff he's leaving on her floor. Then the door chimes, and he's gone: off and running. We look at each other for half a second, me and Culverson, and then I stand up, my oatmeal untouched on the table.

"So," says Culverson mildly. "UNH, huh?"

"Yeah. Just a day, I figure. There and back."

He nods. "Yup."

"The only thing is, there're these kids." And I tell him about Micah and Alyssa, the business with the sword, and he says sure, he says he'll look into it. We're talking quietly, carefully, not moving much, McGully's angry energy still buzzing around the room.

I tear the relevant piece of paper from my notebook, and Culverson tucks it into his shirt pocket.

"Go on ahead, Henry. Solve your case," he says. "Get it right."

* * *

I sit on my bus bench across the street from Next Time Around, the vintage clothing store, for thirty seconds, a minute maybe, gathering my nerve. Then I stand up, march over there, and knock on the front door.

No one answers. I stand there like a dummy. Somewhere farther down Wilson Avenue there's a loud, muffled clang, like someone banging two trash can lids together. I knock again, harder this time, loud enough to rattle the glass panes of the door. I know they're in there. I'm bending to peek in the curtained window when the door is jerked open and here's the fat young man with the greasy hair, wearing a wool cap despite the heat.

"Yeah?" he grunts. "What?"

"My name is Henry Palace," I begin, and Nico rushes over, rushes right around this guy's hunched frame to hug me like a maniac.

"Henry!" she says. "What the hell?" But she's happy, grinning, stepping back to look at me and then forward to hug me again. I take a look at her, too, take her in, my sister: a man's white undershirt and camouflage pants, an American Spirit hanging like a lollipop stick from the corner of her mouth. Her hair has been cut short and choppy and dyed black; the change is dramatic and entirely for the worse. But her eyes are the same, twinkling and wicked and brilliant.

"I knew it," she says, looks up at my face, still grinning. "I knew I hadn't seen the last of you."

I don't reply, I smile, I peer past her into the cluttered room, the rolling racks and overspilling bins of clothes, the mannequins arranged in a variety of obscene poses. There's a man in there on the floor asleep, shirtless, in a tangle of sheets, a woman sitting Indian-style, dealing herself a hand of cards. There's an ersatz table, just a piece of plywood laid across two sawhorses, strewn with drawing paper and old newspapers. The store smells like must and cigarettes and body odor. The squat man in the wool cap leans across the prone body of the sleeper to reach a Bunsen burner and light his cigarette on its blue flame.

"So, what's up?" says Nico. "What do you want?"

What I want, suddenly and fiercely, is to get my sister the hell out of this filthy squat, to extract her like one of those private detectives who pull kids from cults and reunite them with their parents. I want to tell her she has to leave this—this—this dorm, this hostel, this squalid storefront where she has decided to spend the last days of human history bedded down with this collection of lice-infested conspiracy theorists. I want her to give up whatever fantasies are driving her actions at this point and come stay where I can see her. I want to scream at her that for God's sake she is all I have left, she's the only person still living that I have a claim on, and her poor decision-making makes me depressed and furious in equal measure.

"Hen?" says Nico, dragging on her cigarette and blowing the smoke out her nose.

I don't say any of those things. I smile.

"Nico," I say. "I need your help."

PART THREE

Signs and Shibboleths

Saturday, July 21

Right Ascension 20 03 13.8
Declination -60 44 02
Elongation 139.9
Delta 0.844 AU

1.

If I can find the woman, I'll have the man.

Culverson's right. When you look at it objectively, my plan is a long shot at best. It's the plan of a rookie or a plum fool: going to look for a person in the one place in New England where it's probably the hardest to find anyone. A woman for whom I have no physical description, just an age and a stale address. And why? Because this woman may or may not have had a relationship two years ago with the man I'm looking for now.

And the thing is, McGully's right, too—I'm not unmindful of that. There is an aspect of my character that tends to latch on to one difficult but potentially solvable problem, rather than grapple with the vast and unsolvable problem that would be all I could see, if I were to look up, figuratively speaking, from my small blue notebooks. There are a million things I might be doing other than putting in overtime to make right one Bucket List abandonment, to heal Martha Milano's broken heart. But this is what I do. It's what makes sense to me, what has long made sense. And surely some large proportion of the world's current danger and decline is not inevitable but rather the result of people scrambling fearfully away from the things that have long made sense.

That's what I like to tell myself anyway, and it's what I'm telling myself now, as I take off for Durham, biking by night, east-southeast on Route 202 with my madman sister for a sidekick, buoyed forward on a cloud of instinct and guesswork. It's only about forty miles from Concord to Durham, an easy bike ride with no vehicular traffic going either way, just mild summer weather and the trill of night birds. Sometimes Nico rides ahead and sometimes I ride ahead, and we shout jokes to each other, small observations, checking in:

"You doing okay?"

"Yeah, dude. You?"

"Yeah."

One time the headlights of a bus appear in the darkness like lanternfish, get close, zoom past. A mercy bus, running on some sort of rotgut fuel, jammed with singing clapping passengers, luggage racks strapped precariously to the top: off to do some good works somewhere in Jesus's name. We watch the taillights disappear into the westbound distance, the once-familiar sight of bus headlights on a highway at night as unfamiliar and eerie as if a tank had just rolled by.

I've haven't been to UNH, not recently. I've been before, in the old days, but not since Maia, and not since the bloodless "revolution" in January, when a group of students exiled the faculty and staff, took over the campus and rechristened it the Free Republic of New Hampshire. Supposedly the plan was to quickly forge a utopian society in which willing participants can live out the rest of time in communal harmony with their brothers and sisters, everyone contributing, everyone respecting everyone else's freedom to spend life's remaining hours doing what they saw fit.

Nico, as I had suspected, has been down there numerous times. Apparently, her little clubhouse in Concord has something of a satellite office in the Free Republic. And, most important, she claims to know exactly how to get me in. "Oh, yeah," Nico said, grinning, when I explained my dilemma, delighted to be in possession of something I need. "I know the place. I know it well. All the signs and shibboleths." And when I explained who the client was, that the man I was looking for was married to Martha Milano, that only sweetened the deal—Nico was happy to pack a bag and come help me navigate the terrain.

There was just one condition—and she said that, of course, narrowed her eyes like a gangster-movie tough guy and said, "There's just one condition . . ." After the trip, when I had what I needed, I had to promise that I would sit down with her so she could explain what she and her friends are up to.

"You bet," I told her. We were sitting in Next Time Around on two filthy beanbag chairs, speaking in low whispers. "No problem."

"I'm serious, Hen."

"What?"

"You have a way of saying you're going to listen to something, but then when the other person is talking you're up in your head having some sort of complicated policeman dialog with yourself about something else."

"That's not true."

"Just promise that when we sit down, and I lay it all out for you, you will listen with an open mind."

"I promise, Nic," is what I told her, extracting myself with difficulty from the beanbag chair. Then I even looked her in the eye, to make sure she knew I was listening to her and not to any voices in my head. "I promise."

And so now we're biking along 202, through the forested counties, past Northwood Center and Northwood Ridge, talking sometimes, singing sometimes, sometimes just gliding in silence, listening to the distant thud and whack of trees being cut down for firewood. It was harder for Nico than it was for me, everything that happened, the series of catastrophic events that marked our childhood. I was twelve and she was six when our mother was murdered in a Market Basket parking lot, and our father hung himself with a window cord, and we were sent to live with our stern and disinterested grandfather.

It would be difficult for me to disentangle these three sequential and overlapping traumas, tease them apart and judge which affected me the most. I can say with confidence, however, that as painful as all of it was for me, it swept over my sister like an advancing wall of water—pulled her under and never let her up. At six she was a small flickering gem of a child: agile minded, anxious, curious, quick witted, chameleonic. And here comes this great thundering wave and it knocked her over and dragged her around, filled her with pain like water in the lungs of a drowning man.

Somewhere east of Epsom, Nico begins to sing, something I immediately recognize as a Dylan song, except I can't place it, which is odd to consider, that she might know one I don't. But then Nico gets to the chorus, and I realize it's "One Headlight," the number by Dylan's son.

"Love that song," I say. "Are you singing that because of Martha?"

"What?"

I veer in close, pedal up alongside Nico. "You don't remember? That spring, she listened to that song nonstop."

"She did? Was she even around?"

"Are you kidding? All the time. She made dinner every night."

Nico looks over, shrugs. Invariably we refer to that grim doom-heavy period of our mutual memory as *that spring*, rather than by the more cumbersome formulation that would be more accurate: "the five months after Mom's terrible death but before Dad's."

"Do you seriously not remember that?"

"Why do you care?"

"I don't."

She gives herself a burst of speed, takes the lead again, and goes back to singing. "Me and Cinderella, we put it all together . . ."

Houdini is in the wagon hitched to the bike, among the supplies, panting, joyful, his weird little pink tongue tasting the wind.

* * *

It's past midnight when we get to India Garden, the terrible restaurant just off campus that was, for some reason, Nathanael Palace's dining selection when I was a high school junior and we came to tour the campus. Dim multicolored lighting, indifferent employees; abundant portions of barely edible food, strangely textured and overly spiced. I had zero interest in attending the University of New Hampshire anyway. You only needed sixty credit hours for the Concord PD, so that's what I did: sixty hours exactly at the New Hampshire Technological Institute and then off to the Police Academy. I figured Grandfather would be proud eventually, once I was on the force, but by the time I graduated he was dead.

Nico and I kickstand our bikes and wander through the abandoned restaurant like visitors from a foreign planet. The sign's been torn down and the windows and door smashed with a blunt object, but the inside is untouched, preserved as if for a museum display. Long rows of chafing dishes under long-cold heating lamps, rectangular tables tottering unevenly. The smell, too, is the same: turmeric and cumin and the faint resonance of mop water from the linoleum floor. The cash register, miraculously, has money in it, four limp twenty-dollar bills. I feel them between my thumb and forefinger. Worthless bits of paper; ancient history.

Houdini has fallen asleep in the wagon, nestled amongst my jugs of water and peanut butter sandwiches and Clif Bars and first aid supplies, eyes fluttering, breathing softly, like a child. I lift him out and place him gently in a bed of empty rice sacks. Nico and I roll out sleeping bags and arrange ourselves on the floor.

"Hey, what's she paying you for this gig?" she asks.

"What?" I say, pulling the little Ruger from my pants pocket and placing it beside my bedroll.

"Martha Milano. What's she paying you to find her deadbeat husband?"

"Oh, I don't know. Nothing really. I just . . ." I shrug, feeling myself get flush. "He promised her he would stay till the end. She's upset."

"You're a moron," says Nico, and it's dark but I can hear in her voice that she's smiling.

"I know. Goodnight, Nic."

"Goodnight, Hen."

* * *

The flag of the state of New Hampshire has been removed from above Thompson Hall, and a new flag has been raised in its place. It depicts a stylized asteroid, steel gray and gleaming as it streaks through the sky, with a long sparkling contrail flashing out behind it like a superhero's cape. This asteroid is about to smash not into the earth, however, but into a clenched fist. The flag is enormous, painted on a bed sheet, rippling buoyantly on the summer wind.

"You shouldn't be wearing a suit," Nico tells me for the third time this morning.

"It's what I brought," I say. "I'm fine."

We're making our way up the long hill, overgrown with crab-grass and onion grass, toward the imposing castlelike facade of Thompson Hall. Houdini trots along behind us.

"We're going to a utopian society, run by hyperintellectual teenagers. It's July. You should have put on some shorts."

"I'm fine," I say again.

Nico gets a pace or two ahead of me and raises a hand in greeting to the two young women—girls, really—coming forward off the steps of Thompson to meet us. One is a light-skinned African American girl with short tightly braided hair, green capri pants, and a UNH T-shirt. The other is pale skinned, petite, in a sundress and a ponytail. As we get closer, past the flagpole, they both raise shotguns and point them at us.

I freeze.

"Hey," says Nico, nice and easy. "Not with a bang."

"But with a whimper," says the white girl in the sundress, and the guns come down. Nico hits me with the smallest, sliest of winks—all the signs and shibboleths—and I exhale. This entire moment of peril has escaped the notice of my vigilant protector: Houdini is sniffing at the ground, digging up tufts of wild grass with his teeth.

"Oh, hey, I know you," says the short white girl, and Nico grins.

"Yes, indeed. It's Beau, right?"

"Yeah," says Beau. "And you're Nico. Jordan's friend. You were here when we put up the greenhouse."

"I was. How's that going?"

"So-so. We got great dope, but the tomato vines will not take."

The black girl and I look at each other during this exchange and smile awkwardly, like strangers at a cocktail party. We're not alone, I've noticed: Hanging out on the stone wall that extends from the right side of the building are two kids, all in black, each with a bandana pulled up over the lower half of his face. They're stretched out on the wall, relaxed but watchful, like panthers.

"You're working perimeter now?" says Nico to Beau.

"I am," she says. "Hey, this is my girlfriend, Sport."

"Hi," says the African American girl, and Nico smiles warmly. "This is Hank."

We all shake hands, and then Beau says, "Listen, sorry," and steps forward, and Nico goes "Totally okay," and they frisk us, one at a time, quick perfunctory pat-downs. They open the heavy duffel bag that Nico took with her from India Garden, unzip it, peek inside, then zip it back up. I'm empty-handed, just a couple of blue notebooks in the inside pocket of my suit coat; the handgun, Nico strongly suggested I leave back at the restaurant.

"Why are you dressed like that?" Sport asks.

"Oh," I say, looking down and then up. "I don't know."

I can feel Nico's irritation rolling off her. "He's in mourning," says my sister. "For the world."

"All right, you guys are clean," says Beau brightly. "As you know."

"Oh my God," says Sport, bending to pet the dog. "So cute. What kind of dog is she?"

"He," I say. "He's a bichon frisé."

"So cute," she says again, and it's like we're in one of those alternate dimensions, just some folks hanging out on the front steps of campus: green lawn, blue sky, white dog, a group of friends. Detective McGully has remarked on the gorgeous run of summer weather this year. He calls it nut-kicker weather, as in, "that's just God, kicking us in the nuts."

Good old McGully, I think in passing. *Off and running*.

The boys on the wall are not introduced, but their aesthetic and affect are familiar; the kinds of young men one used to see on the evening news, rushing through city streets in clouds of tear gas, protesting the meetings of international financial organizations. These two seem confident and calm, long legs dangling over the stone walls of the university, passing a cigarette or joint back and forth, strips of ammunition pulled across their chests like seatbelts.

"So, hey," says Nico. "Hank is coming in with me, just for the day. He's looking for someone."

"Oh," says Sport. "Actually—" She stops, tenses up, and looks to Beau, who shakes her head.

"You've been here before, so you're good," says Beau to Nico. "But unfortunately your friend has to be quarantined."

"Quarantined?" says Nico.

Quarantined. Terrific.

"It's a new system," Beau explains. She's a small woman with a small voice, but she's clearly not timid. It's more like she's insisting that the listener pay attention. "The idea came from Comfort, but there was a whole Big Group vote on it. In quarantine, newcomers are instructed in the function of our community. Divested of their old ideas about living in the self, and at the same time divested of their personal possessions." She's fallen into a rhythm, here, she's reciting a set speech. "In quarantine a newcomer learns the way thing are handled at the Republic, and to prioritize the needs of the community over their needs as an individual."

"There've been a lot of people just, like, wandering in," Sport adds more casually, and Beau scowls. She liked her official explanation better.

"What people?" says Nico. "CIs?"

"Yeah," says Sport, "But also just—you know. Whoever."

"And so in quarantine," says Beau, reclaiming the conversation, "we learn that the Republic is a system of responsibility, not just of privilege. That there is no such thing as a utopia for one—it must be a utopia for all."

Sport nods solemnly, picks up the phrase and murmurs it in echo: "no such thing as a utopia for one . . ."

Okay, I'm thinking. *Got it. Let's cut to the chase here.* "How long is quarantine?"

"Five days," says Beau. Sport winces apologetically.

Damn it. Julia Stone is in there somewhere, I'm sure of it, seated between the Doric columns of one or another collegiate hall, with

Brett Cavatone laying his heavy head in her lap. In five days, who knows? I take a look at Nico, who still looks relaxed, all smiles, but I can see the unease flashing in her eyes—this quarantine business is as much a surprise to her as it is to me.

"But it's easy," says Sport. "Seriously. It's in Woodside Apartments, the big dorm on the other side of Wallace? And in terms of the divestment or whatever, you can keep super-personal items. Family pictures and stuff."

"Actually, not anymore," says Beau.

"Really?"

"Yeah. Comfort just decided."

"When?"

"Yesterday."

"I didn't even know they were conferencing on it."

"Yes," says Beau. "No more personal or sentimental items. It's rearview."

She says the word "rearview" with a definite and meaningful emphasis, like it's been lifted from the language and glossed with a shiny new meaning, one accessible only to those who've undergone five days of quarantine at the Woodside Apartments. I look up at the banner, the flapping bed sheet, the proud standard of asteroidland.

"Come on, guys," says Nico. "Henry's not trouble. Can we give him a pass?"

"Like a hand stamp?" says Sport, but her laugh is fleeting; Beau is quiet, stone-faced.

"No," she says, and her hand drops back to the butt of her gun.

"The quarantine is a pretty firm rule."

"Well, yesterday—" starts Sports, and Beau cuts her off. "Yeah, I know, and they got serious shit for it."

"Right, right."

Sport looks at Beau, and Beau looks over her shoulders at the Black Bloc guys, the crows watching us from the wall. Nice egalitarian utopian society, I'm thinking, everybody making sure everybody else is following the rules.

"Listen—" I start, and then Nico turns a quarter turn toward me and stares, just for an instant, all the time she needs to tell me very clearly with her eyes and eyebrows to shut up. I do so. This is why I brought her, and I might as well let her do her thing; this is Nico's element, if ever she had one.

"Look, totally honest with you? This girl that Henry is looking for? Her mother is sick. She's dying."

Beau doesn't say anything, but Sport whistles lightly. "Sucks."

I follow Nico's lead. "Yeah," I say softly. "It's cancer."

"Brain cancer," says Nico, and Sport's eyes grow wider. Beau's fingertips remain on the handle of her gun.

"Yeah, she's got a tumor," I say. "A chordoma it's called, actually, at the base of her skull. And because the hospitals are all screwed up, so many doctors are gone, there isn't much they can do."

I'm picturing McGully, of course, big vaudeville hands: *six months to live . . . wakka-wakka.* It was Grandfather who had the chordoma, though; they're mostly seen in geriatric patients, but no one here seems likely to know that.

Sport looks at me, then at Beau, who shakes her head.

"No," she says. "We can't."

"All he's got to do is find her," says Nico softly, "let this kid know her mom is sick, in case she wants to say goodbye. That's all. If it's not possible, we understand."

"It's not possible," says Beau, immediately.

Sport turns to her. "Don't be a jerk."

"I'm just following the rules.

"It's not your mom."

"Fine," says Beau abruptly. "You know what? Fuck it."

She stomps over to the steps and sits down sullenly while Sport walks over to the two on the wall and whispers something to the one with the cigarette, jokingly plucks it from his hands. Sport and the anarchists crack up—one lunges for his cigarette, the other shrugs and turns away—Beau sulks on the steps. They're just a bunch of kids, these people: goofing around, flirting, fighting, smoking, running their principality.

At last Sport trots back over to us, flashing a small thumbs-up, and I exhale, see Nico smiling from the corner of my eye. We get four hours, Sport tells us, and not a second more.

"And come out through this exit. Okay? Only this exit."

"Okay," I say, and Nico says, "Thanks."

"She uh—" she angles her head toward Beau. "She told her mom she was gay. Because of the asteroid. Radical-honesty time, right? Her mother told her she would burn in hell. So." She sighs. "I don't know."

Beau is still sitting on the steps, glaring at the sky. There are times I think the world is better off in some ways—I do—I think in some ways it's better off. One of the anarchists slides down from the wall and ambles over, skinny and sloe-eyed, black bandana draped loosely at his collarbone. "Hey, so, four hours, man," he says. He smells like hand-rolled cigarettes and sweat.

"I told them," says Sport.

"Cool. And in the meantime, we gotta hold on to your dog."

The skinny kid reaches out his arms. Nico looks at me—I look at Houdini. I scoop him up, rub his neck, hold him for a long second. He looks into my eyes, then shakes his body and pulls for the ground. I put him back down, and he resumes chewing grass under the watchful eyes of his captors.

"Four hours," I say, and Nico heaves her duffel bag onto her shoulder, and we're ready to go.

2.

Once, in high school, as part of a short-lived and ill-fated campaign to gain the attention of a "cool" girl named Alessandra Loomis, I accompanied some friends to a day-long popular-music festival hosted by the Manchester radio station Rock 101. This is like that, what I'm looking at now, standing at the rear exit of Thompson Hall gazing down the long slope toward the main quad. It's like the rockfest but to a factor of ten: brightly colored tents and sleeping bags stretch out in all directions, studded by what look like giant shipping cartons, overturned and transformed into baroquely decorated forts. Long snaking lines of drummers move through the crowds, dancing in rhythmic interlocking circles. At the center of the quad is a towering junk-shop sculpture painted in neons and pastels, built of car doors and computer monitors and children's toys and aquarium parts. Puffs of cigarette and marijuana smoke float up, drifting over the crowds like smoke signals. It's like a concert with no stage, no bands, no electricity; a concert that's all audience.

Nico was right. I should have worn shorts.

"So great," murmurs my sister. She leans back, throws her arms open and closes her eyes, breathing it in—the marijuana smoke, certainly, but all of it, the whole thing. And I am surprised to be feeling how I do, confronted with the massive and chaotic scene—not at all how I felt driving the long hour back to Concord after a day at the Rock 101 festival, my ears ringing alternately with Alessandra Loomis's kind but unequivocal demurrals and Soundgarden's egregious cover of "Buckets of Rain."

We make our way down the slope and into the crowd. I unknot my tie and take it off. Nico laughs. "There you go, Starsky," she says. "Deep cover."

"Shut up," I say. "Where are we going?"

"We gotta find my man Jordan," says Nico. "He's got this place wired."

"Okay," I say. "And where's Jordan?"

"In Dimond," she says. "The library. If his committee is sitting. Follow me."

I follow her down into the wonderland, trotting a few paces behind as she picks a route through the crowded tents and revelers. Nico pauses here and there to say hello to people she knows, ducking into one tent to hug a fine-boned girl in a miniskirt, jog bra, and elaborate Native American headdress.

At the far end of the main quad the crowd thins and we pick

up a narrow winding path and follow it into and out of a stand of thin sapling elms. After a few minutes of walking, the noises of the drums and the singing have faded, and we are wandering through the campus, passing nondescript low-slung brick academic buildings—Geology department, Kinesiology, Mathematics. After ten minutes or so we come out onto a plaza where there's just a single drummer, tapping away all on his own, wearing sweatpants and a Brooklyn Dodgers jersey. The chiseled brick cornerstone says PERFORMING ARTS, and a sandwich board is propped up at the base of the wide steps, between the columns, advertising a lecture: "The Asteroid as Metaphor: Collision, Chaos, and Perceptions of Doom."

Nico peers at the sign.

"Is this where we're going?" I ask.

"Nope."

"Do you *know* where we're going?"

"Yup," she says, and we keep walking. I'm picturing Brett Cavatone making his way through the campus in his heavy policeman boots, looking for Julia Stone just as I am now. How did he circumvent the perimeter guards, I wonder? If I had to guess, his stratagem was more tactile than mine, more direct. He would have cased the campus, selected the least-defended of the various checkpoints, and employed overwhelming but nonlethal force to get past one of these skinny twenty-somethings playing tough guy.

I keep following Nico, who is still lugging her heavy duffel bag, deeper and deeper into the bewildering campus. The paths roll back on themselves, the woods grow thick, then thin out again. On a volleyball court outside the athletic complex is a row of young people clutching Civil War–style bayonets, practicing their form: someone yells "Charge!" and they charge, sprinting full bore, lunging with bayonets extended, stopping on a line, laughing, retreating.

I'm growing more and more concerned about Nico's sense of direction every time she pauses at a forking path and chews on her lip for a moment before plunging forward.

"Here, wait," I say. "Here's a map."

"I don't need it," she says. "I know where I'm going."

"You sure?"

"Stop asking me that."

It doesn't matter; the map, when I look closer, has been imaginatively graffitied, the place names all crossed out and replaced: "Perdition." "Deathtown." "Dragons Here There Be."

"We're fine," says Nico, taking a seemingly arbitrary left turn onto a narrower path with a light handrail. "Come on."

We cross over a brown, bubbling creek and pass one more building, a dorm, with loud insistent music pouring out along with a series of modulated groans. There's a man on the roof, naked, waving to passers-by as if from a parade float.

"Holy moly," I say. "What are they doing in there?"

"Oh, you know," says Nico, looking down, blushing, uncharacteristically. "Fucking."

"Ah," I say, "right."

And then, thank God, we get to where we're going.

* * *

In Dimond Library, on the way to the basement stairs, I see a pale boy hunched over the desk in a carrel, sipping from a Styrofoam cup, surrounded by books, reading. His face is gaunt and his hair a greasy mass. On the ground beside him is a clotted leaking pile of discarded teabags, and beside that a bucket that I realize with horror is full of urine. There's a tall stack of books on one side of him and a taller stack on the other: out pile, in pile. I stand for a second watching this guy, frozen in place but alive with small action: muttering to himself as he reads, almost humming like an electric motor, his hands twitching at the edges of the pages until, with a sudden flash of motion, he turns the page, flings it over like he can't consume the words fast enough.

"Come on," says Nico, and we continue down the hall, passing four more of these carrels, each with its quiet intent occupant— earnestly, frantically reading.

* * *

In the basement, Nico slips in through a pair of green double doors marked BOOK REPAIR and I wait outside, until a moment later she emerges with a friend behind her. Jordan, presumably. In the few seconds before the door swings closed I glimpse a big workshop with the tables pushed to the sides, people sitting cross-legged on the floor in loose concentric rings. As the door opens, someone is saying

"Agreed, with reservations . . . ," and the rest are raising their hands in the air—two hands up, palms out—and then the door closes all the way.

"So this is the brother, huh?" says Jordan, sticking his hand out. "I seriously don't think I've ever met a real cop before."

"Well," I say, shaking his hand, and I'm going to say that I'm not a cop anymore, actually, but then he says, "What's it like to shove a nightstick up someone's ass?"

I let go of his hand.

"I'm totally serious," he says. And Nico says, "Jordan, don't be a moron."

He looks at her, all innocence. "What?"

I just want to find my missing person. That's all I want. Jordan and Nico lean against a wall in the hallway, and I stand across from them. He's short, baby faced, fatuous, with a pair of Ray-Bans pushed back high on his head. Nico pulls out a cigarette and Jordan gives her an expectant expression, and she lights one for him, too, on the same match.

"How's Ars Republica?" she asks.

"Boring. Stupid. Ridiculous. As usual." Jordan looks over his shoulder at the BOOK REPAIR door. "Today it's immigrant policy: take 'em or leave 'em, basically." He talks fast, taking quick little puffs of the cigarette between choppy sentences. "Crowd mood is definitely take 'em, especially now with this quarantine jazz. How'd you get him in, by the way?"

"We told a story."

"Nice." Then, to me, "Like that outfit, by the way. You look like a funeral director." He keeps chattering, hyper and self-important. "Not that many of 'em are making it up here. The CI's I mean. Coasties must be doing a bang-up job of rounding 'em up and taking 'em camping. Oh, wait, not *camping*. *Internment camp*. My bad."

He smirks, then leans his neck one way till it cracks, and then the other way. "Okay, what do we need?"

"I'm looking for someone."

"Aren't we all."

"Someone specific, jackass," says Nico, and sticks out her tongue at him.

If it turns out that my sister is romantically involved with this man, I might actually have to murder him.

"A former student here," I say. "Would have been a senior last year, when all of this started up. Whatever this is."

"'Whatever this is'?" Jordan's face becomes serious. "I'll tell you what this is, asshole, this is the apex of civilization. Okay? This is what democracy looks like, real democracy, you fucking Nazi cop asshole."

Jordan stares at me and I grope for some sort of placating language, wishing more than anything in the world that I didn't need help from this particular person—and then he drops the stone face and giggles like a hyena.

"I'm jerking your chain, man." He points back over his shoulder at the committee meeting. "These dingleberries are in there for forty-five minutes arguing about toilet paper rationing, even though the world is about to explode. It's fucking retarded."

"I see," I say, speaking slowly to control the anger in my voice. "If that's how you feel, why are you here?"

"Resources. Recruitment. And because I happen to know that the world is *not* about to explode. Right Nico?"

"Damn right," she says.

"The woman that I'm looking for is named Julia Stone." I give him the campus address that I have from the file: Hunter Hall 415.

"She won't be there," he says. "Nobody's stayed put."

"I figured. I need to know where she is."

"You got a picture?"

"I do not."

He whistles, jogs his head back and forth, blows out a plume of smoke.

"Well, Nico's brother the cop, it shan't be easy. Everything is scrambled like an egg around here. I'll do what I can."

"Okay," I say. I'm thinking of Brett slipping away, further and further into the future—thinking, too, of the four hours I've been given by my new friends at the entrance to Thompson Hall. That dog has suffered enough already. "How long?"

"How *long*?" Jordan turns to Nico. "Is that how policemen say thank you?"

"God," she says, laughing, shoving him lightly in the chest. "You're such a prick."

"Meet me in the grub tent in an hour and a half," Jordan tells me. "If I don't have something by then, I never will."

* * *

Around the corner from Dimond Library is a cluster of residence halls, each shaped like a parenthesis and arranged around a shared courtyard, where, at present, there's a dozen or so young people playing a game. A kid in some sort of Victorian derby hat shakes a Styrofoam cup to spill dice out onto the sidewalk with a loud clatter, and the other players cheer and then start racing around the courtyard. A chalk sign says ANTIPODAL VOLCANISM WORKING GROUP.

"Do you know what that means?" I ask Nico, and she shrugs, lights a cigarette, disinterested.

The players aren't just running, they're drawing, stopping to make marks on a massive game board that's been drawn out on the pavement. The kid with the hat gathers up the dice, puts them back in the cup, and hands it to the next player, a homely girl in a flowing skirt and *Dr. Who* T-shirt. These kids remind me of certain people in high school I was never friends with but always liked, the ones who played D&D and worked backstage: scruffy, unstylish, ill-fitting clothes and glasses, deeply uncomfortable outside their small group. The girl tosses the dice, and this time everyone yells "ka-boom!" I take a step closer, and now I can see that it's a map of the world they've drawn, laid out on the hot unshaded pavement of the courtyard, a big blown-up Mercator projection of the earth. Now they're unspooling long loops of ribbon along the map, tracing trajectories somehow keyed to the numbers that came up on the roll of the dice. The ribbons go off in various directions, out from the impact site:

one wave of destruction rolling over southern Europe; another through Tokyo and on across the Pacific. A dark-haired young man is squatting over cities, one after another, joyfully marking them with big red X's.

"No! Not San Francisco!" says another, a girl with an awkward pixie haircut, snorting laughter. "That's my old apartment!"

At last I let Nico lead me away, follow her back through the paths of what used to be UNH. Again I find myself imagining O. Cavatone, if he really was here, picturing him navigating these tortuous paths. What did he make of it, the tents, the kids, the antipodal volcanism working group? The tough and righteous state trooper in the land of the permanent asteroid party? Then I stop myself, shake my head. *What do you think, Henry? You think that if you imagine him hard enough, you can make him appear?*

* * *

All the food in the grub tent is free and hot and delicious. There is a no-nonsense woman in a stained yellow apron, serving tea and miso soup and gooey chocolate desserts from a long table. Dinner rolls and cups of tea are help-yourself. I look down the buffet line, daring to hope—it's a different world, a different infrastructure, you never know—but there is no coffee. People drift in and out of the tent, pushing back the flap and saying "hey" to the cook and grabbing food and trays; most of the citizens of the Free Republic are of college age or even younger, although there are a handful of grown-ups.

In fact, there's a middle-aged man with a long gray beard and a potbelly seated next to Nico and me at our picnic table, wearing a loud-print bowling shirt and shooting what I presume to be heroin into the veins of his forearm, having tied off above the elbow with an extension cord.

I try to ignore him. I break my roll and open a small foil packet of margarine.

"So," I say to Nico. "Jordan. Is he your boyfriend?"

She grins. "Yes, Dad. He's my boyfriend. And I'm thinking about going all the way. Don't tell Jesus, okay?"

"That's hilarious."

"I know."

"Well, just for the record . . ." I dab on the margarine with a plastic knife. "I don't like him."

"For the record, I do not care." Nico laughs again. "But, to tell you the truth, I don't like him much, either. Okay? He's part of my thing, that's all. He's a teammate."

I lean back and bite into the roll. This whole time Nico has been lugging around her mysterious duffel bag, large and ungainly, and now it is slung on the bench beside her. The potbellied heroin addict at the end of the table makes a low grunt and depresses his plunger, grits his teeth, and throws back his head. There is something horrifying and mesmerizing about him doing this in front of us, almost as if he were performing a sexual act or a murder. I look away, back to Nico.

We chat. We catch up. We tell each other stories from the old days: stories about Grandfather, about our mom and dad, about Nico and her screw-up friends from high school, stealing cars, drinking beer in homeroom, shoplifting. I remind her of our mother's zealous and misplaced encouragement of Nico's early-life interest in gymnastics. My comically uncoordinated little sister would do some poorly executed somersault, land painfully on her tiny butt, and my mother would clap wildly, cup her hands into a megaphone: "Nico Palace, ladies and gentlemen! Nico Palace!"

We finish our soup. I check my watch. Jordan said an hour and a half. It's been fifty-five minutes. The heroin addict babbles to himself, murmuring his way through his private ecstasies.

"So, Henry," says Nico, in that same tone of voice that Culverson always used, fake casual, innocent, to ask if I'd been in touch with her. "How are you?"

"In what sense?"

"The girl," she says. I look up. The roof of the grub tent is not properly joined; there's a diagonal slash of open air, blue sky. "The one who died."

"Naomi," I say. "I'm fine."

"Yeah?"

"Yeah."

Nico sighs and pats me on the back of the hand, a sweet simple gesture glowing faintly with the ghost light of our dead mother. I can imagine my sister and me in some future that never will exist, some alternate dimension, Nico appearing on my doorstep on Thanksgiving Day or Christmas Eve, whatever dipshit husband she ended up with still parking the car, my beautiful sarcastic nieces and nephews tearing through the house, demanding their presents.

"Random question," I say. "Do you know the name Canliss?"

"No. I don't think so."

"It's not someone we went to school with?"

"I don't think so. Why?"

"No reason," I say. "Forget it."

She shrugs. The chef in her apron is singing, opera, something from *Marriage of Figaro*, I think. A new group wanders in, three boys and two girls, all of them in matching bright orange shirts and sneakers, like they're some sort of athletic team, and they're arguing, loudly but not angrily, about the future of humanity: "Okay, let's say that everybody's dead but ten people," says one of the men. "And let's say one of them opens a store . . ."

"Capitalist pig!" interrupts one of the women, and they all crack up. The heroin addict's forehead hits the table with an audible *thunk*.

"Hey. You should come back to Concord with me," I say suddenly to my sister. "After I settle this case. We'll hole up in Grandfather's house. On Little Pond Road. We'll share resources. Wait it out together."

"Wish I could, big brother," says Nico, amused, eyes dancing. "But I gotta save the world."

* * *

Jordan slips through the flap of the grub tent right on time, as good as his word, Ray-Bans and shit-eating grin firmly in place. He's written Julia Stone's information on a tiny slip of cigarette paper, which he slides into my palm like a bellhop's tip.

"She's on R&R," he says cheerfully to Nico, who says, "No kidding?"

"What's R&R?" I say.

"One of the—whatever they call them. One of the grand committees," Nico says.

"Okay," I say, looking at the paper. All it says is what he just told me: *Julia Stone. R&R.* "So where is she?"

Jordan looks me over. "Do you have some kind of philosophical or moral objection to thanking people for things?"

"Thank you," I say. "Where is she?"

"Well, it's tricky. R&R meets in a series of rotating locations." He lifts his sunglasses and winks. "Kinda top secret."

"Oh, come on," says Nico, lighting a fresh cigarette.

"Why are you looking for her?" asks Jordan.

"I can't tell you that."

"Really?" he says. "You can't? You came this far for this tiny piece of information, and you're not prepared to barter for it? How are you gonna do when it's cannibal time, and you've gotta negotiate with Caveman Stan for a bite of the baby?"

"You're such a dick, Jordan," says Nico, exhaling.

"No, no," he says, "I'm not," and he turns on her, suddenly serious. "You come to me for information, because you know I can get it. Well, how do you think that happens? Information is a *resource*, the same as food, same as oxygen. Geez Louise!" He throws his hands in the air, turns back to me. "Everybody just wants, wants, wants. Nobody wants to *give*." He drops his cigarette in the dirt, jabs me in the chest. "So. You. *Give*. You're looking for Julia Stone. Why is that?"

I stay silent. I keep my arms crossed. I'm thinking, *no way*. I've got most of what I want, and I can figure out the rest on my own. I stare back at him. *Sorry, clown*.

"There's a man looking for her." Nico, mumbling, looking at the dirt. "A former state trooper."

"Nico," I say, astonished. She doesn't look at me.

"The trooper is in love with the girl. My brother is trying to find him. For the guy's wife."

"No kidding?" says Jordan thoughtfully. "See? That's interesting. And . . . and . . ." He looks me up and down, his mouth slightly open, eyes squinting, like I'm a manticore or a griffin, some exotic species. "And why are you doing this?"

"I don't know," I say. I've had enough of this. I'm ready to go. "Because I told her that I would."

"Well, well."

He gives me the rest of the information I need: R&R stands for Respect and Restraint, and they are meeting in Kingfisher room 110, a big lecture hall. They're meeting "right this exact second," as a matter of fact, so I better hurry up. I stand and Jordan takes Nico by the elbow and murmurs in her ear. "You're staying with me, right? Because we have big fun things to discuss."

"Henry?" Nico's eyes are bright again. She reaches up and pats me on the cheek. "See you in a few?"

"Sure," I say, swat her hand away.

I'm close—I'm this close. I start to go, and then I stop. "Nico? What's in that duffel bag?"

"Candy," she says, and laughs.

"Nico."

"Dope."

"Really?"

"Handguns. Human skulls. Maple syrup."

She cracks up, they both do, and then they're walking away arm in arm, the two of them slipping through the front flap of the grub tent and off into the crowded campus. Nico Palace, ladies and gentlemen. My sister.

3.

Lining the approach to Kingfisher Hall are stately oaks, flanking the pathway, upright and orderly as a praetorian guard. They're strung with banners, primary colors and simple bold fonts, each announcing an extinction or near extinction: the Justinian Plague, 541 A.D. Toba supereruption, 75,000 years ago. The Permian Extinction. The K-T Boundary Extinction . . . on and on, a parade of pandemics and catastrophes and species genocides festooning the approach.

In I go, into the building itself, into a spacious and sunlit atrium with a vaulted ceiling, then down a long hallway lined with bulletin boards, somehow untouched, still offering grants, scholarship money, internship opportunities for engineering students.

When I push open one of the big double doors to room 110, my immediate impression is that here we have another party, an auxiliary of the ongoing festivities on the main quad. It's a big lecture hall, packed and noisy, citizens of the Free Republic relaxed and at ease in their varied costumes, from track suits to tie-dye to what appears to be an adult-sized set of My Little Pony feetie pajamas. People hollering or engaged in intense conversation or, in one case, stretched out over three seats, asleep. As I pick my way as inconspicuously as possible up the raked tiers of seating in search of an empty spot, I count at least three ice-packed coolers, full of small unlabeled glass bottles of beer.

It is only when I have found a seat, in one of the very last rows, that I can focus my attention on the front of the room—and the young man standing with his back to the crowd, naked to the waist with his hands tied behind him with a length of bungee cord. Across from him, seated at a folding table on the shallow stage, are two men and a woman, all of approximately student age, all wearing serious, intent expressions, huddled together and whispering.

I settle into my seat, cross my long legs with difficulty, and watch the stage. One of the three at the table, a man with glasses and a head of wild curly hair, looks up and clears his throat.

"Okay," he says. "Can we get quiet?"

The man with hands tied shifts nervously on his feet.

I look around the room. I've seen plenty of trials—this is a trial. The curly-haired man asks for quiet again, and the crowd settles down, just a little bit.

She's in here. Somewhere, in this crowd, is Julia Stone.

"So we're down with the decision to proceed?" says the woman at the center of the little triumvirate on the stage. "Can we go ahead and just by voice vote reaffirm the provisional authority of R&R over maintaining safety and peace in our community. Everyone?"

She looks around the room. So do the other two judges, the one with the hair, and the third, the one farthest to the right, who has a small pudgy face and a turned-up nose and who looks to me no more than eighteen years old, if that. Most of the audience seems to have little interest in the proceedings. People keep talking, leaning forward in their seats to poke a friend or back to stretch. From where I'm sitting I watch a man rolling what will be, if completed, the largest marijuana cigarette I have ever seen. Two rows up from me a couple is vigorously making out, the female partner shifting as I watch into a full straddle atop her companion. The guy on my right, a sallow figure with hairy forearms, is absorbed in something he's got in his lap.

"Hello?" says the young woman on the stage. She has sharp small features, black horn-rim glasses, and pigtails. Taped in front of her is an eight-by-eleven piece of paper reading CHAIR, a slap-dash designation of authority. "Are we okay to proceed?" The crowd, those paying attention, half maybe, make the under-arrest gesture I spotted earlier in the library, hands in the air with palms up. I take this to be some understood signal of assent, because the young woman nods, goes, "Great."

The defendant cranes his neck around nervously, scanning the crowd. I whisper to my seatmate, "Who is he?"

"What?" he says, looking up blankly. It's an iPhone he's got in his lap, and even as we talk he runs his thumb over the blank dead screen, absently, over and over.

"The defendant?"

The guy scrunches his nose, and I realize too late the word *defendant* might be considered significantly rearview. "What did he do?"

"I don't know, actually," he says, peering down at the shirtless shivering man at the front of the room as if for the first time. "Something, I guess. The next agenda item after this is the nudity policy. Pretty sure that's why it's so packed today."

"Oh," I say, and the guy turns back to his iPhone.

"So, okay," says the chair, addressing the defendant directly. "We should start by apologizing to you, as a member of our community. We understand there was some unnecessary violence involved in your, uh, your detention."

The prisoner mutters something I can't hear, and the chair nods. The other judges have notebook-paper signs, too. The curly-haired one's sign says VICE, and the pudgy-faced boy's says VICE TO THE VICE.

"If you couldn't hear, everyone," says the vice, "he said it's cool."

Scattered laughter from the crowd.

"Oh, great," someone yells sarcastically, and everyone turns to see who it is: a great big fat dude in overalls and a painter's cap. "It's cool, everyone. He's cool. Don't worry."

More laughter. More people seem to be paying attention now. Someone from a distant corner, by the door, shouts "Thank God!" The couple making out a few seats up pause in their exertions for a moment, glance in the general direction of the stage, and then get back to business. During all this back and forth, I'm trying to work out a plan, trying first of all to figure out how many people are in this room: maybe a hundred rows of seats, maybe fifty to seventy-five seats per row, maybe eighty percent occupied, maybe fifty-five percent female. I have no photograph of Julia Stone, no physical description of any kind: no race or ethnicity, no distinguishing characteristics, no distinctive mode of dress. All I know is that she is a female between twenty and twenty-four years of age, and I am seated in a room with between one hundred seventy-five and two hundred people matching that description.

"Okay, so," the chair is saying. "Theft from the community of the Free Republic is among our most serious infractions. It's a big fucking deal. There are a lot of things we might do to handle this sort of situation. But it's obviously important that everyone gets a chance to give their input and have their feelings on the subject heard."

I look around the room, trying to narrow down somehow who Julia might be. If I were Brett, who here would I fall in love with? Who would I follow to doomsday? But I'm not Brett. I've never met him. Forty-five minutes until I'm supposed to be back at the Thompson Hall exit, collecting my dog and getting out of here.

"And—sorry, were you done?" says the vice, glancing respectfully at the chair, who nods, shrugs. "And so anyone who wants to say something is invited to do so at this time." A handful of people are already making their way down the aisles, raising their hands to speak. The third judge, the vice to the vice, turns up his chin and watches them come. He's quiet, watchful, little beady eyes scanning the room over and over. He has yet to speak.

There is a woman with red hair, dark red, so dark as to be almost brown. She's three rows up from mine, across the aisle, and she seems to be taking notes or minutes on a pad of paper balanced on her bare knee. She's wearing a very short black skirt, black boots. Brett, I think, would have found her attractive.

The first speaker to offer his input is a small man in cargo pants and a plain red T-shirt. He stands in one of the aisles and reads rapidly, almost agitatedly, from a stack of index cards. "The whole idea of theft from a communal store is itself a reflection of capitalist thinking. In other words, the crime of theft cannot and should not exist in a postcapitalist society, because property"—he leans into the word, his voice charged with disdain—"cannot and should not exist." He flips to a new card; the vice to the vice looks irritated. "Our vigilance is required against attitudes that reflect not only explicit capitalist dogma, but vestigial reflections of same."

"Okay, thanks," says the chair. The little man looks up from his cards; clearly, he wasn't finished.

"Thanks," she says again, and someone says "Point of order" from the back—it's the fat man in the overalls, and the chair acknowledges him with a nod. "I just want to say, in regard to what that guy just said: That's stupid."

The vigilant anticapitalist looks around the room, doe eyed, wounded. The chair smiles softly and nods for the next speaker. Small lines are forming in two different aisles of the auditorium. I keep my eye on the dark-haired woman three rows up. What is my move here? How long do these meetings last?

The next speaker is a woman with long matted dreadlocks, who wants to propose a complicated redemption-based system, wherein those accused of rule breaking would engage in a dialog with the community about the nature of their transgression. This idea the vice chair gets excited about, nodding vigorously as the woman speaks, his curls bouncing. It goes on like this, speaker after speaker: someone wonders if today's proceedings might in fact inspire further infractions; a man asks politely if the public-nudity policy is still on the agenda, and the affirmative answer from the vice draws cheers; a young woman with earnest eyes and a single thick braid running down her back rises and says that she's been carefully noting the speakers at this meeting, as well as the six previous R&R meetings, and can report that people of color are participating at a ratio of just one in twelve.

"Huh," says the vice chair. "Maybe because radical movements have always been the province of the privileged?"

"Maybe because we're in fucking New Hampshire," says the class clown in the overalls.

In the laughter that follows, the woman with dark red hair looks around and sees me watching her. She does not look down: Instead she meets and holds my gaze. It occurs to me that I could pass her a note, and the idea is so absurd that I very nearly laugh out loud. *Are you Julia Stone? Check this box if yes.*

"Okay," says the chair. "I think that's enough. Just in terms of time?"

The vice looks surprised, but the vice to the vice nods. The defendant shivers, hunching forward, glancing from side to side. Male shirtlessness can in the right circumstances be powerful, leonine, but it can also make a person seem exposed and helpless, the knobs of the spine quivering and fragile like surfacing fish.

"I'm sorry," I say "Excuse me." I stand up. This is stupid. This is the stupidest thing I could possibly be doing right now. "What is it he is accused of stealing?"

A room full of people turn their heads toward me, the man who fits in least with this crowd now drawing the maximum amount of attention to himself.

"It's not really relevant," says the vice, after glancing respectively at the chair for permission to handle this one. "Our protocol says, given limited time and resources, to focus on outcomes when the cause of action is relatively straightforward."

"Yup," says the chair. "Bingo."

The vice vice's beady eyes are fixed on me, birdlike and unpleasant.

"But he has the right to know the charges against him," I say, nodding my head toward the defendant. The crowd has settled into near silence now, drawn out of their chatty genial atmosphere by this novelty. The guy next to me, with his iPhone, scootches over a little in his seat, putting some distance between us. My presumptive Julia Stone, the attractive woman with dark red hair, is staring at me with the same frank interest as everyone else. A wash of nervousness passes over me. This really was idiotic, but I'm still standing, so I go ahead and press my case.

"He also has the right to face his accusers," I say. "If someone is saying he stole something, he gets to confront them in open court."

The defendant cranes around, then glances anxiously back at his judges, trying to figure out if this mysterious interjection is aiding or hindering his case. I'm not sure, my friend, I tell him telepathically. I honestly don't know. Somewhere in the room, someone opens a beer bottle with a pop and hiss. On the seatback in front of me is graffiti, RON LOVES CELIA, etched by some bored undergrad in days gone by.

"It's not that we are unaware of the rules of evidence," says the vice, shifting back in his chair and squinting at me. "I went to law school at Duke, okay? But those rules are moot in this context."

"But how can you pass sentence—"

"We don't call it 'passing sentence'—"

"—without a fair trial?"

"Excuse me?" says the third judge, the vice to the vice, speaking at last and loudly, his voice high and reedy and charged with anger. "Who are you?"

I open my mouth but say nothing, cycling rapidly through a series of possible answers, sharply aware of the insufficiency of them all. They could kill me, these people—I could truly die here. The Free Republic of New Hampshire, for all its easy egalitarian spirit and New Age trappings, is a world unto itself, beyond the reach even of what little law remains; as the man said, certain rules are moot in this context. I could be murdered here, easily, if the mood of this crowd should change; I could be beaten to death or shot, my corpse abandoned in the dirt of the quad, my sister and my dog left to wonder why I never emerged.

"Well?" says the vice vice, rising from his chair. And then the chair says, "I knew it."

"What?" says the vice.

"I knew someone would be coming to find him."

She stares at me from the table on the stage—arms crossed, glasses, pigtails—and I stare back at her.

"Excuse me?" The vice vice says, glaring and confused. "What the fuck are you talking about?"

But Julia Stone is unconcerned with his bafflement, with the confused attention of the crowd. She gazes cooly at me.

"I told him they would come for him. That's what your kind do, right? You come for people."

The low murmur of the room is beginning to bubble up again, people leaning across one another to whisper and nudge, people exchanging questioning expressions. I ignore them, keep my eyes locked on Julia Stone.

"Um, yes, point of order," says the vice, while the vice vice stands stonily, arms crossed. "What are you talking about?"

"This man has entered our space on a false pretense," says Julia, and points at me with one steady finger. "He's not here to take part in our community; he's here to infiltrate it. He is on a mission to hunt down another human being like a pig or a dog."

Silence, then, the room suddenly alive with tension, everybody staring at me or at Julia or back and forth, me to her. I feel it again, the dread gut-level certainty that these people could kill me: that I might die here, in this room, and no one the wiser. And at the same time, nevertheless, I am feeling these wild waves of excitement, looking at the woman for whom Brett named a pizza, the woman who drew him from Concord and from his wife, the woman I went looking for and found. I want to take a picture of her and send it to Detective Culverson and say, "See? See?"

"You don't understand where you are," Julia tells me. "This is a new world. We have no room for police-style tactics here."

"I'm not a policeman," I say.

"Oh, yeah?" she says, "But you are police-style, aren't you?"

"What is going on, Julia?" says the vice vice, and he takes an aggressive step toward her around the back of the table, and the vice rises to stop him with one hand pushed against his chest. "Whoa."

Julia keeps her eyes on mine. "You'll never kill him," she says.

"Kill him?" I say. "No, I—his wife sent me."

"His wife?"

She stands breathing for a second, taking this in, deciding what to do with it, while I'm thinking: *Kill him? Who would be coming to kill him?*

"Sorry about this," says Julia to her colleagues on the tribunal, and then turns to address the room. "I call for an extraordinary postponement. I need to speak to this man alone."

"Oh, come on," says the vice vice petulantly. "You just asked for an extraordinary postponement yesterday."

"Yes, well," she says drily. "These are extraordinary times."

Julia Stone steps down over the lip of the stage and motions for me to meet her at the door. As I pick my way over legs down the tiers, the kid with his hands tied sits down, confused, and the vice chair moves that the meeting advance to the question of public nudity. Everybody cheers and raises their hands, palms up.

4.

The woman Brett loves, like the woman he married, is not beautiful, not in any conventional way. But where Martha Milano's plainness is redeemed by a sweet radiant quality and warmth of spirit, Julia Stone's small thin body and dark features are attractive in a whole other way. She doesn't speak, she *pronounces*, talking fast with her black eyes flashing, each word charged with energy.

"There," she says. "Those kids. On the roof. See?"

I look where she's pointing, to a cluster of busy shapes atop one of the dorm buildings off in the distance. "Exercise machines. Maybe twelve people up there now. Sometimes we get thirty or thirty-five. Bikes, treadmills. This is an example. You join us here, you do what you want, as long as, A, your action does not interfere with the ability of others to do what *they* want, and B, whenever possible, your action offers some concrete benefit to the community."

Julia pauses and stares at the air in front of her, as if scouring the words she has just said, satisfying herself of their soundness before plunging forward. We're on the roof of Kingfisher Hall: steam pipes, a wilted rooftop garden, a weather-beaten sofa someone lugged up the concrete stairwell and out the trap door.

"We have a team of engineering postdocs who rigged those machines to capture the electricity generated in a central battery. So that, for example . . . " She swings her arm until she's pointing at another building, much closer, where on the first floor the curtains are pulled shut tightly. ". . . *those* people can watch movies. A French New Wave festival at present. Then they do Tarantino. And so on. They vote on it. There's a committee."

"That's interesting," I murmur, still trying to get a read on her, on this conversation. *Where is he?* is all I want to ask. *Where's Brett?*

"Interesting?" Julia says. "Sure, it's *interesting*, but that's not the *point*. I'm answering your question from downstairs. How can we pass sentence on someone who might be innocent?" She glares at me through the thickness of her glasses. "Wasn't that your question?"

"Sort of."

"No, it was, that's what you asked. Don't backtrack. He didn't do it, by the way."

She thrusts out her chin, waiting for astonishment, anger, argument. And in fact I am a little astonished; I can see him clearly, the shivering nervous defendant, barely out of his teens, hands bound, waiting for the punishment of the mob.

But I hold my peace, I just raise my eyebrows, go, "Oh, really?"

"Yeah. Really. I set him up."

She's pushing, she's feeling me out, and I know exactly why. She thinks that she hates me and she wants to make sure. I come to her tainted by my association with Martha, with "the wife," and Julia Stone would therefore prefer to tell me to fuck off back to copland or wherever I came from. I therefore need to play it slow, hang back, save my questions until I think there's a chance she'll answer them.

"All I meant is that the kid deserved to be treated fairly," I say. "I didn't say he was innocent."

"Oh, he's not *innocent*," says Julia, "he's just not a thief. He's a rapist. Okay? Don't ask how I know, because I know what goes on here. I *know*. And I want him out of my community. But if I had him brought up for rape, then Jonathan—the vice to the vice? Remember him?"

I nod. Piggy eyes, flushed face, the sneer of a spoiled child.

"Jonathan would demand a hanging. Not because he gives two shits about violence against women. Because he wants to hang someone. I know he does. And once the hangings start—" She shakes her head, seeing the future. "Forget it."

I rub my forehead, finding the queer little divot in my temple, remembering when Cortez assaulted me in the elevator. Seems like a million years ago, a different lifetime. Julia is looking out over the campus again, brow furrowed, hands moving while she talks.

"Radical social theories when put into practice have a notoriously short half-life. They dissolve into anarchy. Or the people's power, even when carefully delegated to provisional authorities, is seized by totalitarians and autocrats. Can you think of a single counterexample?"

Julia flicks her gaze at me.

"No," I say. "I guess not."

"No," she says. "There isn't one."

Her passion, her confidence—I can see clearly how these qualities must have sung out to Brett Cavatone, whom I have come to see as quiet, quick-minded and intense, a philosopher in the thick tough body of a policeman. How, I wonder fleetingly, did he and Martha Milano end up together in the first place? How long did it take before he knew he had married the wrong sort of woman?

"We have this opportunity," Julia says. "We've struck this elusive balance between safety and personal liberty. This balance *always* gets fucked up, but now there's no *time* for it to get fucked up. We just have to keep the Jacobin shit at bay, keep from tipping over into *Lord of the Flies* for seventy-four more days." She's talking faster and faster, the words rattling along like train cars. "This is literally a unique opportunity in the history of civilization, and the preservation of public order trumps the specific form of justice doled out to one individual. Right?"

"Right," I say.

"Yes. Right. Is she paying you?" She turns to me, crosses her arms. "The wife?"

"No."

"So why are you doing it?"

"I don't know," I say, and give her a quick little half smile.

"Although people do keep asking me that."

"I'll bet." And then she smiles back, just the tiniest secret hint of a smile. There's a small gap between her front teeth, like a rascally ten-year-old.

"You thought before that I had been sent to kill him. Why would someone be trying to kill him?"

The smile disappears. "Why the fuck should I tell you?"

"Are you in love with him?"

"Love is a bourgeois construct," Julia says immediately, but nevertheless she turns away from me, gazes out over the rooftops and treetops of the transformed campus. I wait, allow her a moment alone with whatever memories she's replaying. And then I gently push forward, talking softly, telling her the story she already knows.

"Brett arrested you a couple years ago, in Rumney, but you gave him an earful from the bars of the holding cell. You made him see the justice of your cause, and he came to respect you. You talked him out of testifying. You developed feelings for each other."

Julia gives me a quick sour look at the word *feelings*, and I nod in acknowledgment of the fact that feelings are a bourgeois construct, but I keep going.

"But he wouldn't leave his wife. That wasn't in his character. So at the end of the summer you went back to school, and he left the state troopers and moved to Concord, and that was that."

She's not saying anything, she's not even looking at me now. Her eyes are fixed on her campus, her people: the exercisers, the movie watchers, the undulating swarms on the central quad. But neither is she interrupting, neither is she saying no. I keep talking, just a guy in a suit on a rooftop telling a story on a summer's day.

"But then the asteroid comes along. The countdown begins, and it changes everything. You think, well, maybe *now*. Maybe now Brett and I get our shot. You wrote him letters, told him all about the Free Republic and what you had accomplished here. You told him he should come and play chess and hang out with you until the end."

Now Julia raises a single finger, still staring straight ahead. "One letter. A couple months ago."

"Okay," I say. "One letter. And then yesterday, suddenly, he shows up."

I can picture the scene, Brett Cavatone slipping into the back of that crowded noisy auditorium as I had, and suddenly Julia spots him from her chair on the stage. Her jaw drops, her commanding pose of leadership wavers momentarily like a blurry TV signal as Brett smiles up at her, self-contained and formidable and affectionate. "He tells you he's here now, there aren't many days left and he wants to spend them with you."

"No," says Julia abruptly.

"No?"

At last she turns away from the rail and looks at me straight on, lips pursed with emotion, and I don't care if love is a bourgeois construct or not, I've seen love once or twice before and this is the face of a woman in love. She loves him and bitterly regrets what she says next.

"No, he did not come because there aren't many days left and he wants to spend them with me. He came for guns."

"He came for—" I blink. "What?"

Julia laughs then, once, a harsh bark, as I stare at her, open-mouthed with bafflement.

"Come on," she says, and flings open the trapdoor to the stairwell. "Let's take a walk."

* * *

Jeremy Canliss was right. Brett had a woman on his mind. But it was neither lust nor love that brought him to the University of New Hampshire to find Julia Stone; it was the lure of the weapons she had proudly described to him in that one letter, a couple months back.

Julia Stone leads and I follow, a pace or two behind, down the path leading away from Kingfisher, under the gauntlet of extinction—Permian, K-T Boundary, Justinian Plague—and off across campus. We don't speak, we just go, my nervous excitement making itself known in the loud rattling of my heart in my chest, my understanding of this case revolving slowly like a wall of books in a haunted mansion, revealing the hidden staircase behind. I have questions—more questions, new questions—but I just walk, allow myself to be led, Julia offering muted greeting to nearly everyone we pass on the twisting trails.

Our destination, as it turns out, is a compact concrete shed with a flat tar roof, built along a chain-link perimeter fence separating the

UNH facilities buildings from College Road behind them. The shed sits in the shadow of the hulking power station, now defunct, its coils and towers silent and cold.

Julia opens the padlocked shed and leads me inside. It's a single room, a perfect box: flat floor, flat ceiling, four flat walls. The sunlight filters in dimly through the low dirty windows. The walls are lined with hooks that are hung with guns: pistols, rifles, automatics and semi-automatics. On a shelf near the floor are a dozen boxes of ammunition, neatly arranged. The revolutionary Free Republic, Julia Stone explains, appropriated all this gear from the UNH ROTC program at the time of the "revolution." What Brett told her was that he needed "serious weapons"; he asked for a pair of high-powered rifles, M140s with bolted scopes. Julia gave him the guns and pinned their disappearance on the rapist.

"Not that the guns were mine to give," says Julia, shaking her head bitterly. "They belong to the community. I don't know why I let him talk me into it. He's just . . ."

She opens her hands, trailing off. But I know what she wants to say. I've heard it before: *He's just Brett.*

We step outside and Julia locks the door and we lean against one of the concrete sides, facing the power station, and I fight back a wave of anxiety, an intense consciousness of what's in the shed. The destructive capability of just this one tiny building, this single small room in a world full of them. Because I've seen rooms like this before, since the asteroid's slow approach became known. By now there must be millions of them, basements and attics, sheds and garages, lined with weapons silently waiting to be used, a world of tinderboxes ready to bloom into flame. I look at my watch and I am late—the deadline given to me by the guards at Thompson Hall has passed. I offer up a silent apology to Houdini, wondering whether those two girls or the guys in the black shirts would actually do anything to harm the dog.

I circle back around to my initial question.

"Julia, what is going on? Who is trying to kill Brett?"

"I don't know," she says. "Maybe no one."

"Is he in danger?"

"Danger? I mean, danger doesn't even . . ."

She shakes her head with bitter amusement. She's going to tell me, I realize—she's already started to tell me. For the first time I feel it with a wrenching ecstatic certainty: I'm going to find him. *I'm coming, Brett—I'm coming.*

"Julia?"

But her affect changes; her face gets tight with anger. "Why the fuck should I tell you?" she says, spitting the words. She wheels away from the wall of the shed, glaring. "Why should I tell you *shit?*"

I respond not to the anger but to the question. She wouldn't be asking if she didn't want an answer. She wouldn't have taken me to the guns. "You care about him. Whatever passed between the two of you, it meant something to you. Perhaps you don't love him, but you wish to keep him from harm. If I find him, maybe I can make that happen."

She doesn't answer. She pulls nervously on one of her pigtails, a small human gesture.

I'm coming, Brett. Here I come.

There's a motion by the chain fence, some animal or stumbling citizen of the Free Republic, moving in shadow. We both turn our heads, see nothing, and then look back at each other. I watch Julia intensely considering, weighing factors, deciding whether to reject the truth of what I've said, simply because I'm the one to have said it. I watch her weighing her loyalty to Brett, her anger at him, her desire to see him safe from harm.

"I won't tell you what he's doing," she says at last. "He made me promise to tell no one. I can't betray him."

"I understand," I say. "I respect that." And I mean it. I do.

"But I will tell you where he is."

5.

I'm sorry, Martha.

I can hear myself saying the words, imagine them hanging in the bright empty air of her kitchen, when I make it back to Concord, knock on her door like a cop with hat in hand to give her the news.

I'm sorry, ma'am, but your husband will not be coming home.

Had I been right, and had I found Brett Cavatone as I briefly imagined him, reclining on the thick grass of the quad, head in the lap of his long-lost love—or had I found him in a whorehouse or at a fuck-it-all beach party, staring up at the stars with something wicked sluicing through his veins—and had I then delivered Martha's message, reminded him that "his salvation depends" on his return . . . had it all played out that way, there might still have been some small chance of success, some sliver of hope, that he would remember himself, hang his head, and come home.

But now what I know is that he's out in the woods with two rifles. And whether he's plunged himself into some terrible danger, as Julia seems to fear, or he's performing some great act of end-days nobility, as Martha wants to believe, it is in all scenarios harder to see him having much interest in home.

I couldn't find him, I could say to Martha. *Neither hide nor hair of the man.*

But I've always been a terrible liar. Maybe the best thing to do is never report back to my client at all. I could stay here in Durham, or return to Concord but never to her house on Albin Road, let the final months roll by for Martha in hopeful silence. Let her die on October 3 with that small diamond of possibility still pressed in her palm, that Brett might return, turn up suddenly to hold her tightly as the world explodes.

*   *   *

"Sorry I'm late," I say, panting and out of breath. One of the anarchists in the black T-shirts looks up and goes, "Oh, what time is it?" and there's Houdini, perfectly fine, bounding around on the sloping lawn under the flapping flag of the Free Republic while Beau and Sport toss a Frisbee for his amusement.

"For God's sake," I say, and exhale. The girls' shotguns lie carelessly on the steps like pocketbooks; the Black Bloc guys are sitting languorously on the dirt by the wall, bandanas off, faces warmed by the sunshine.

Houdini barks in recognition as I come into view but does not, I note sourly, come racing for the lap of his master. He's having a great time, leaping delightedly between his captors, delivering the battered yellow Frisbee to each in turn. Beau crouches as if to protect him from returning to my ownership, and Sport waves merrily.

"Oh, hey," she says. "Check it out." She points to my dog. "Sit."

He sits.

"Roll over."

He rolls over.

"That's great," I say. "Wow."

This a clear case of canine Stockholm syndrome, and I explain this to Houdini as he reluctantly falls into step beside me and we trot away back toward Main Street and India Garden.

I eat a Clif Bar and a peanut butter sandwich, pour out a cup of kibble for the dog, reviewing my obligation in my head, my contract with my client: *I will do what I can to find your husband.* . . . The problem now is that I know where he is. The problem now is that I could be there on the ten-speed in an hour. The problem is that I want to go. I've come this far and I want to deliver my message. I've come this far, and I need to see the man with my own eyes.

The door rings brightly. "Hey, can I get a palak paneer, please?" says Nico pulling up a chair. "And a thing of naan bread?"

She's smiling her crooked clever smile, a cigarette hanging in the tough-girl style from the corner of her mouth, but somehow I'm not in the mood. I stand up and hug her for a long time, pressing her face against my chest and resting my chin on her head.

"What the hell, Henry?" she says when I let her go. "Did something happen?"

"No. I mean, yes. Not really." I sit down again. "You smell like beer."

"Yup," she says. "I drank a bunch of beer." She runs a hand through her spiky black hair, then flicks her cigarette butt into the corner. Houdini glances up disapprovingly from his food, sniffing at the smoke.

"So?" says Nico. "Did you find her?"

"My witness?" I say. "I did."

"What about Martha's husband?"

"Not yet. But I know where he is."

"Oh, yeah? Where?"

"Maine, south of Kittery. At a place called Fort Riley. It's an old state park."

Nico nods blankly, helping herself to a bite of my Clif Bar. This is as far as her interest goes in my ongoing investigation.

"All right," says, when she's done chewing. "You ready?"

I rub my forehead with one hand. I know what she means, of course. I promised that if she guided me to and through the Free Republic of New Hampshire, then I would listen to all the sordid details of Nico's Magic Plan to Save the World. I just wanted a couple more minutes. Just a moment or two of small normal happiness, a brother and a sister and a dog. *I'm not ready*, I want to say. *Not yet.*

But I promised. I did promise. "Okay," I say. "Fire away."

I cross one leg over the other and lean slightly forward and focus my energy on Nico, admonishing myself as she begins talking to listen with patience and good grace to whatever Hail Mary last-ditch song and dance I'm about to hear.

"The United States government," Nico begins, and I clap one hand over my mouth, "if it wanted to, could detonate one or more near-surface nuclear explosions in the space surrounding the approaching asteroid."

I tighten my grip over my mouth, clamp it closed, forcing myself not to speak.

"The effect would be to superheat the surface of the object, initiating what's called a back reaction and altering its velocity sufficiently to keep it from impacting the planet."

I shut my eyes now, too, and tilt my head forward in a position that hopefully looks like deep concentration, but is in fact a desperate attempt to keep myself from leaping to my feet and away from this monologue. Nico goes on.

"But certain officials, high in the government, have decided to suppress this information. Make it sound like it's too late, or impossible."

I can't take it any longer, I remove my hand from my mouth. "Nico." Just that, quietly. She doesn't hear, or chooses not too. Houdini smacks his lips in the corner.

"Those with the knowledge to perform the operation have been jailed or made to disappear."

This is talking points. I can smell it. I try again. "Nic?"

"Or, in one case, murdered."

"Murdered?" I'm done. I stand up, lean forward across the table. "Nico, this is crazy."

She leans back from me and says, "What?"

"This is the big secret? A nuclear explosion? Blast it from the sky? You can't do that. It turns the one big asteroid into a million smaller ones. You haven't heard that? There was a National Geographic special about it, for God's sake. It was on the cover of the last issue of *Time* magazine."

I'm speaking loudly. Houdini looks up for a moment, startled, then returns to his kibble.

"That's not what I said." Nico speaks softly, crossing her arms patiently like a kindergarden teacher, like I'm the child, I'm the fool. "You're not listening.

"We went to war to *prevent* Pakistan from shooting a nuke at the thing. Thousands of people died." I can still see the pictures; it was all in the *Monitor* before the paper went out of business: drones, air strikes, firebombs, the rapid annihilation of nuclear capability and concomitant destruction of civilian areas. There was quite a spread on Pakistan, too, in that same issue of *Time*, their farewell double issue. Cover headline: "And Now We Wait."

"I didn't say blast it from the sky." Nico rises from the table and leans against the buffet line, digs another cigarette from her pocket. "What I said was a nuclear explosion or explosions, near but not on the asteroid. This is called a standoff burst, as distinct from a kinetic impactor, which would be a ship or other object smashing into the surface. A standoff burst has the advantage of creating the desired velocity change while minimizing surface disruption and the resulting ejecta."

More talking points. I feel like she's going to hand me a pamphlet. I get up. I pace.

"A standoff burst. And you guys think no one has thought of that?"

"I knew you wouldn't listen," she says with sadness, shaking her head, tapping ash onto the floor. "I knew I couldn't count on you."

I stop pacing. Of course she knows exactly what to say; she has had a lifetime of making me feel bad for castigating her in the face of her outrages. I take a breath. I lower my voice. "I'm sorry," I say. "Please. Tell me more."

"As I said, it's not that the government—I should say the military, it's really the military, not the civilian government. They *have* thought of it. They even commissioned people to figure out how to do it, years ago, when this kind of danger was purely hypothetical. There has to be a nuclear package in a new shape, with a new kind of fuse, to deliver the payload in space."

"Right. But they never built those."

"Well." She smiles, winks. "That's what they want us to think."

"Jesus, Nico. This is crazy."

"You said that already." Her expression suddenly transforms from wry and knowing into kind of serene intensity—this is the part she's been waiting for. This is the kernel of the lunacy. "Certain conservative elements in the international military-industrial complex welcome the asteroid, Henry. They're *psyched*. The opportunity to rule over a decimated, miserable population? To consolidate the remains of the world's resources? They can't fucking wait."

I start laughing. I lean my head back and bark laughter at the ceiling, and now Houdini really jumps, skitters away from his dish. The absurdity of this, the whole thing, sitting here talking as if we two tiny people in this bombed-out Indian restaurant in New Hampshire happen to have privileged information about the fate of the universe.

Nico talks for a while, and I listen as best I can, but a lot of it just washes over me, a lot of it is just words. There's a rogue scientist, of course: Hans-Michael Parry, an astrophysicist formerly associated with the United States Space Command, who knows exactly how to do it, knows where these specially constructed fuses are housed and how they are operated. Nico's organization has found Parry in a military prison, and they're going to get him over to England, where sympathetic elements are ready to try this deflection maneuver with British bombs.

"Oh," I say, during this exegesis, over and over, just: "Okay." I pat my lap and Houdini clambers up. I scratch him behind the ears, mutter "that's a boy" before he escapes to chase a stray bit of kibble across the room.

There was a part of me, I realize as she's speaking, that wanted to be surprised. I wanted her to say something that would make me say *Holy moly! She's right!* But of course that was never really possible, was it? That, of all the people in the world, my sister is going to happen to be the one with a solution. No one has a solution. No one sitting in India Garden, no maverick astrophysicist rotting in the bowels of the U.S. Army prison system. It's all nonsense, so plainly so that it would be hilarious if I didn't know of at least one person who had already been sacrificed to my sister's belief that it's real.

"So what?" I finally ask. "You and your friends are going to spring this scientist from the pokey?"

"We did that already," Nico says, ignoring the sarcasm in my question. "Not me, not the New England group. Another team, in the Midwest, they already found him and secured his release. And now Jordan and I and the other New Englanders, we're just waiting to recon with the team."

I mouth the words disbelievingly. *Recon with the team.* All this B-movie dialogue. How many times, over the course of our lives, have I seen Nico's beautiful quicksilver brilliance dimmed: by grief, by alcohol and marijuana, by association with foolish minds.

"How can you believe any of this, Nico?"

"Because it's true," she says. She reaches into the warm refrigerator and pops the top on a mango soda. Summer rain taps against the glass and on the pavement outside.

"But how do you *know* that it's true?

"Because it is."

"That doesn't work," I say. "That formulation. You sound like Jesus Man."

"No, I don't."

"You do."

Jesus Man was the bright-eyed codger in the next bed over

from Grandfather, in his last month or two, the final round of radiation before they gave up on Nathanael Palace and we took him home to die. Jesus Man had the light of the Lord, and there was no pain or discomfort that he couldn't bear smilingly through God's grace. He was practically celebrating it all, welcoming every new misery as a step on the road to paradise. Grandfather hated him—almost, he told me once, whispering loud enough for the other man to hear, as much as he hated the cancer itself. Once Jesus Man told Nico and me, while Grandfather slept, that he hoped we had accepted the Lord in our hearts. I didn't say anything when he said that, just nodded politely and looked at the TV. Nico, age seventeen, smiled and said, "Thanks, mister. I'll think it over."

Now she shrugs, stands up. "That's the whole story, big brother. I can't make you believe if you don't."

"Nope," I say. "You can't. When are you leaving? To recon with the team?"

"Soon. Jordan says they're on the way now. Tomorrow or the next day, a helicopter is going to land in Butler Field to scoop us up."

"Nico, I love you," is what I say next, and I'm surprised to hear the words coming out of my mouth; she looks pretty surprised, too. She crosses her arms, and I press on. "I do. And I made you a promise."

"I release you from that promise," she says immediately.

"You can't."

"We were kids."

"You were a kid," I say quietly. "I was fifteen. I knew what I was saying."

"I release you."

"No," I say, suddenly regretting my tone, my skepticism, regretting everything about the conversation. *Don't go*, I want to say, *don't do it, just stay, come with me to Maine, come with me to Concord, Nico, don't go.* Houdini is done eating and has found a place to lie down. In the silence, his snoring fills the room.

"Good luck with your case," says my sister.

"Good luck," I say, the start of a sentence, but I can't think of anything to finish it. That's all I've got. "Good luck."

* * *

Another scene from childhood. A few years after that spring, a few years before Jesus Man. Nico was nine years old and already she was sliding in and out of situations: insulting teachers, shoplifting small items. Stickers, cans of soda. A girl gave her beer, an older girl, probably as a joke, but Nico drank it all and was drunk—ten years old and drunk, and in her still-forming brain the alcohol was acting not as a goad to more bad behavior but as a truth serum, and she was muttering and sputtering, processing all kinds of anger toward me, toward Grandfather, toward everyone. "You will, though," she said, when I tried to hug her, lift her, carry her home. "You will go away like they did. You'll die. You'll disappear."

"I won't," I said to her. I said, "Nico, I will not do that."

* * *

The rain has exhausted itself, for now, and the sky is clear and untroubled, the stars twinkling in their familiar places. I try to sleep but can't; I can barely keep my eyes closed, lying restless on the floor of the India Garden, sprawled out uncomfortably with my backpack for a pillow. At dawn I will get back on the bike, get Houdini situated among my emergency supplies and water bottles, and leave for southern Maine.

Willfully I focus my thinking, put Nico and her friends and their tactics on a shelf in the back somewhere, pull a blanket down over Grandfather, who for some reason has been traveling with me all day today, emaciated and furious in his hospital bed with death crouching at his shoulders. I turn my head from everything and zero in on my case, my trip, my tomorrow.

So why are you doing it? Julia asked, as Nico had asked, as McGully had demanded of me. There are undoubtedly other ways I could be spending my time, performing actions of more tangible value to myself or others. But an investigation like this has its own force—it pulls you forward, and at a certain point it's no longer profitable to question your reasons for being pulled. I stay up for a long time, blinking into the darkness of India Garden, thinking about Brett Cavatone.

He'll ask me, too, if I find him, out there in the woods with his rifles. *What are you doing here? Why have you come?* And I don't know what I'll say, I really don't.

PART FOUR

He's Dead, He's Dead, He's Really Dead

Sunday, July 22

Right Ascension 20 01 26.5
Declination -61 09 16
Elongation 139.2
Delta 0.835 AU

1.

Route 4 meanders eastward from Durham and then north-northeast along the line of the Piscataqua River, offering me a wide rolling view of Portsmouth Harbor: rusting lobster traps bobbing unattended; boats listing in their abandonment, paint peeling, hulls jutting out of the shallows.

It's just me this time, bright and early and out on my mission. Detective Palace, retired, on his ten-speed with the dog hitched to the back in the little red wagon.

Cutts Neck—Raynes Neck—the long span of Memorial Bridge reaching high over the harbor. Then the series of roundabouts that spit you out onto 103 East. I know this route by pure sense memory from our handful of summers at York Beach, before the bottom fell out of my childhood. I roll past the big blue donut that had marked Louie's Roadside Diner, now torn from its mooring by weather or vandals and lolling across the parking lot like a giant's abandoned toy.

The sun is almost all the way up now, it's close to nine, and I'm leaning into the curve of the third roundabout, navigating around the pits and gashes in the asphalt, speeding past the gates of Portsmouth Naval Station on the seaward side. *I'm coming.* The woods huddle in close against the road as 103 crosses the border and cuts into southeastern Maine, gives up its last pretense of being a highway and settles down into a crooked little two-lane road with a faded yellow line down the middle.

Here I come.

* * *

Fort Riley, when I find it, sits on the northern lip of Portsmouth Harbor, a castle keep built on a cliff wall, staring out at the sea. For a couple hundred years it was an active United States Army fort, minding the coast during the Revolution, the War of 1812, all the way up to World War II, when civil reserves in green helmets would sit in seaside redoubts like this one, up and down the coast, peering out at the northern Atlantic for U-boats. For half a century Riley was a state park and historical site; now it's where Brett Cavatone, my missing man, has come to make camp. I turn off the highway into the parking lot, a long narrow spit of gravel with dense woods to the left and, to the right, the high tumbling stone wall of the old fort itself.

I get off the bike and lift Houdini from the wagon and set him down in the gravel. My chest is thick with anticipation. The air smells like the sea. He's here, I'm thinking. This is it. *Hello, sir. My name is Henry Palace.*

I walk slowly down the length of the parking lot, hands out of my pockets and slightly raised, a picture of harmlessness, in case anyone is watching—anyone with a pair of sniper rifles and reason to be wary of visitors. There's one car in the lot, a gray Buick LeSabre with Quebec plates and all four tires shot out. In the backseat, a teddy bear and an Uno deck. The entrance to the fort is all the way at the end of the parking lot, an arched doorway just where the stone wall bends away to the south and the gravel ends in grass and weeds. Farther on is the ocean.

Put down your weapons, sir. Your wife would like you to come home.

"Okay," I say, to no one, or to the dog I guess, but then I see that he's decided to stay back by the bicycle. I turn around and he's way back up there where the parking lot begins, skittering back and forth between the chained-up ten-speed and our supply wagon. I gesture to my right, around the corner of the wall, into the fort proper.

"You coming?"

Houdini doesn't answer. He growls uneasily, sniffs at the ground. "All right," I tell him. "You stay there."

The buildings of the fort, half a dozen tottering stone piles and decomposing wooden ruins, are scattered over one big uneven hill—an acre or acre and a half of muddy grassland, sloping down toward a cliff over the water. The layout is as haphazard as might be expected of a centuries-old military campus, built piecemeal by different commanders at different times for different purposes. It's all centered around one structure, though: the blockhouse, a wooden tower on a sturdy granite base, rising high above the center of the fortland like a birthday cake. The blockhouse could be somebody's tidy colonial house, a charming white-sided vacation home overlooking scenic Portsmouth Harbor, except that it's perfectly octagonal and slitted all around its eastern faces with narrow rifle ports, for spotting incoming ships and shooting at them.

I shade my eyes and look up at the narrow windows. He might be up there. He might be in any of these buildings. Cautiously I pick my way through the mud and seagrass, over the foundation stones like flat gravestones, alert for the presence of Brett.

The rifleman's house is a square red-brick building, as small as a one-room schoolhouse. A cornerstone announces the structure's provenance of 1834, but there is no roof; maybe it was never completed, or maybe the tiles were repurposed by the army when this fort was decommissioned, or maybe they were stripped last month by looters and carted away like Sergeant Thunder's brick shed.

I linger there in the roofless shelter. This then will be the shape and the feel of the world: an abandoned shell, signs of old life, curious animals wandering in and out of ruins, the wilderness crowding in, overtaking all human structures and human things. In fifty years, everything will look this way, desolate and quiet and overgrown. Not even fifty years—next year—by the end of this one.

I make my way carefully down the gentle slope to the granite wall that rings the fort's easternmost edge. There's a narrow trench dug into the mud just in front of the wall, except it's not a trench at all, it's an entrance, a stairhead carved out of the wet ground. A gash in the base of the wall, and then a short steep staircase into a dark chamber with a wet clay floor. The room is dank and close, as long and narrow as the barrel of a gun. A brass plate screwed into the granite wall identifies the room with an unfamiliar word: caponier. It smells like brine and fish and ancient mud. Light seeps in through nine high slit windows along the eastern face.

I am too tall, in a room like this. It bears down on me, coffinlike, and I can hear my heart beating, experience an unexpected sharp awareness of my body's functioning as a machine.

I walk slowly across the room and lean into one of those slitted windows and squint. To the south there's a lighthouse, to the north, uninterrupted miles of Maine coast. Way out on the horizon is the tiny black dot of an incoming ship and, twenty degrees to its left along the blue-green horizon, the tiny black dot of another. I stare for a minute, watching them come.

They must come all day. Big ships, their holds packed with desperate cargo, famished and exhausted, people from all over the world, the Eastern Hemisphere emptying itself out.

As I watch I see a third one, another speck on the far edge of the horizon, almost to the lighthouse on the harbor's southern lip. I have a sudden vivid picture of the earth as flat, a tray, covered in marbles, and someone is tilting it, and the marbles are rolling, cascading, from east to west.

"It is hard to imagine the conditions onboard those ships."

A voice deep and calm, and then there's the scrape of a boot heel behind me, and I take a breath and turn around and there he is at last.

"The countries of origin, many of them, were impoverished to begin with," says Brett Cavatone, his voice soft, even, scholarly. "More so since Maia. The ships are packed with travelers. They live in darkness, below decks in miserable dank holds, crawling with rats and bugs." His beard has grown in more, thickened into a dense black jungle. His eyes are deep set and black as a well. "It is hard to conceive of what they eat, on those ships, or how they drink. Still they come."

"Officer Cavatone, my name is Henry Palace. I'm from Concord." He doesn't respond. I keep talking. "Martha asked me to find you. She wants you to come home."

Brett's face betrays no surprise or confusion at this announcement. He doesn't ask, as I have anticipated, how I found him or why. He just nods his head, once—message received.

"And has Martha found Mr. Cortez?"

"Yes."

He nods again. "And is Mr. Cortez honoring our bargain?"

"Yes," I say. "I think so."

"Good. Then Martha is safe? And healthy?"

"She's devastated. Heartbroken."

"She is safe and healthy?"

"Yes."

Brett nods a third time, nods deeply and closes his eyes, almost bows. "Thank you for coming."

I hold up my hands. "Wait. Wait."

It doesn't seem fair. It doesn't seem *real*, somehow, that at the end of this journey I should find a thirty-second conversation, a quick fair hearing and then goodbye, thank you for coming.

"Do you have a message for me to bring back to her?"

Brett closes his eyes and steeples his fingers. He's in camouflage pants but a plain white T-shirt, sandals on his feet. "You may tell her that the asteroid has forced some hard decisions in me, as it has in many of us. Martha will understand what I mean."

"No." I shake my head.

"No?"

"Respectfully, sir, the asteroid did not make you leave her. The asteroid is not making anyone do anything. It's just a big piece of rock floating through space. Anything anyone does remains their own decision."

A smile flits across his lips, down in the thickness of facial hair. "You asked me to provide a message, and now you disapprove of it?" His voice is deep, hushed, rhythmic, like an Old Testament prophet. "You have discharged your obligation, friend. Your work is done, and now I must return to my own."

"You are a married man," I say. I'm pressing my luck. He stares back at me in silence, impassive as a mountainside. "Your wife is confused. You've left her terrified and alone. You can't just abandon your promises because the world is over."

I'm aware, even as I am talking, that these arguments are doomed to be unavailing. It is clear that Brett Cavatone is as rooted in his purpose as the fort's stone walls, planted for centuries in this craggy soil, and my suggestion that he return to Martha and Rocky's Rock 'n' Bowl is not only impossible but ridiculous, juvenile somehow. Oh, why should he do what I say? Why, again? Because he *promised*?

"I am not coming home." He looks steadily at me, black eyes under furrowed brows. "Tell her that. Tell her our contract has been abrogated. She will understand."

I can see her, Martha Milano at her kitchen table, aghast with grief, hand trembling on her teacup, stalking back and forth to the cigarettes she will not allow herself. "No," I say to Brett. "I don't think she will understand."

"You said your name was Henry?"

"Henry Palace. I used to be a policeman. Like you."

"There are things you don't understand, Officer Palace. Things you cannot understand."

He takes a step toward me, compact and powerful as a tank, and my mind flies to the little gun tucked in the inside pocket of my blazer. But I have no doubt that Brett, if he wanted to, could be on top of me before I drew, hammering me with his fists. Condensation drips from the ceiling of the room, sweats down the walls. I have to say one more thing, though. I have to try.

"Martha says your salvation depends on it."

He repeats the single word, "salvation," lets it hang in the gloomy air between us for a moment and then says, "I'll need you to leave the grounds of this fort within ten minutes."

He turns on the steps, presenting me with his broad back, and takes the first step out of the darkness of the caponier.

"Brett? Officer Cavatone?"

He stops, speaks quietly over his shoulder, without turning around. "Yes, Henry?"

I pause, gut rolling. Seconds pass. *Yes, Henry?*

My investigation is over. Case closed. But I hear Julia's voice in my head, tense and taut with anxiety: *Danger? I mean, danger doesn't even . . .*

I find that I cannot leave. I don't know anything, but I know too much to leave. Brett is still waiting. *Yes, Henry?*

"I know what you're doing," I say. "I met Julia Stone, and she told me. She explained your intentions."

"Oh," he says calmly. "Well." He is incapable of being surprised.

"And I—I'd like to help."

Brett comes back down off the stairs and toward me, holding up his big hands like he's warming them over a fire. I get the feeling he's getting a sense off me, interpreting me like a crystal ball.

"Are you armed?" he says.

"Yes." I take out the Ruger and hold it up. He takes it, weighs it in his hands, drops it in the mud.

"We can do better than that."

* * *

Together we walk up the slippery and mossed steps of the caponier, and then together, silently, we cross the patched mud and seagrass of the fort to the blockhouse. Using a long stick with a curved hook on the end, Brett releases a rope ladder coiled at the elevated doorway, tumbles it down to where we can reach it to climb up. Brett goes first, swift and sure-footed, and I follow, heaving my ungainly body up the rungs, one at a time, all knees and elbows, like some kind of invading mantis.

I'm not sure what happens now.

* * *

"There's the Portsmouth naval base, there's a base at Cape Cod, and there's what used to be the coast guard station at Portland, Maine. That is all. Three stations and by my count eight or nine cutter ships. There was a nuclear submarine called the *Virginia* assisting them, but no one seems to have seen it in months. AWOL, maybe, or else they've run it south to help in Florida."

I nod mutely, my stomach a tight ball of astonishment and unease, as Brett tells me his plan. Our plan.

"I have renderings from all of these facilities. We can't know precisely what the state of readiness is, but we can presume it is lower than we might have found pre-Maia, due to desertions and technical limitations related to resource depletion."

While he talks Brett runs his fingers delicately over the maps and blueprints he has taped all around the walls of the blockhouse.

He's papered over the historical displays and the park-service time-lines, but they peek through, the glowering faces of old soldiers from old wars, staring sternly at the portraitist or daguerrotype man. I think that Brett is wrong about our likelihood of success. I think we may find these naval and coast guard bases, like the Concord police department, better defended than in the past, not worse. I would predict multiple checkpoints, added layers of fence-line security, skittish base patrolmen operating under strict shoot-first orders.

It is clear though that Brett's calculation of these dangers is purely abstract. One does not contemplate failure, or even death, when one believes oneself to be on a crusade. Brett's intention is to commit murder in the name of a greater good.

Danger? I mean, danger doesn't even . . .

"This strikes me," I say quietly, "as more than a two-person job."

"Well, it was a one-person job until ten minutes ago," says Brett. "Our obligation is to do what we can with what we have. That is all we can do, and the results are up to God."

I nod again.

We are going to break into the naval and coast guard stations—shoot guards if necessary—shoot seamen—set fire to the ships. Whatever means necessary to prevent further missions by those vessels. A one-man crusade to stop the interdiction and internment of catastrophe immigrants along the northern Atlantic coast. A two-man crusade, I correct myself. We are going to the Portsmouth naval base first, and if our efforts are successful there, then we will come back here, to Fort Riley, resupply, and make the longer trip to Portland later in the week.

"I believe, Officer Palace, that you were sent for a reason," says Brett, turning away from his wall of Scotch-taped plans and barracks blueprints. "To ensure the success of this work."

There's a rusting piece of artillery in the center of this room, a cannon with its nose thrust out the centermost window toward the sea. Beside it Brett has a heavy trunk, and now he kneels and pops it open and starts to sift through the supplies inside, jugs of water and rolls of gauze and iodine capsules and plastic grocery bags full of jerky and cheese; as he's sifting through, something catches my eye, a flash of bright color, out of place. Then he shuts the trunk and hands me my gun, exactly the gun I was expecting: the second of the M140s that Julia Stone boosted for him from her stash at UNH. He presses the gun into my hands. I feel my simple missing-person case crumbling under my feet, melting beneath me.

"When do we go?" I ask.

"Now," says Brett. "Right now."

We throw the weapons down from the top of the blockhouse, and they land with two overlapping *thuds* in the dirt and then we begin to climb down, hand over hand, Brett first again and me behind. And when he's just touched down and I am two rungs from the bottom I lose my grip on the ladder and tumble down, landing squarely on Brett's back and knocking him over, and he goes, "Hey," while I roll off and land on one of the rifles and come up pointing it at his back.

"Don't move," I say. "Stop."

"Oh, no, Henry," says Brett. "Don't do this."

"I am sorry to have been duplicitous, I really am." I am speaking quickly. "But I can't allow you to proceed with a plan calculated to result in the death of servicemen and -women."

He is kneeling in the mud, head slightly down and turned away from me, like a praying monk. "There is a higher law, Henry. A higher law."

I knew he was going to say that—something like that.

"Murder is murder."

"No," he says, "it isn't."

"I am sorry, Officer Cavatone," I say, my eyes watering, read-justing to the summer brightness. "I really am."

"Don't be," he says. "Each man in his own heart takes the meas-ure of his actions."

The M140 is a bigger weapon than I'm used to handling, and I was unprepared for the weight of it. There are no iron sights on it, just the scope, long and thin like a flashlight bolted to the top of the gun. I'm trembling a little as I hold the thing steady, and I focus on controlling my hands. I will them to be still.

Brett is still on his knees, his back to me, his head slightly tilted upward, toward the sun.

"I understand," I say, "that you disagree with the interdiction and internment policy being carried out by the Coast Guard."

"No, Henry. You don't understand," he says softly. Mournfully, almost. "There is no such policy."

"What?"

"I thought you understood, Henry. I thought that's why God sent you."

The idea of that, that God or some other force of the universe sent me here, renews my sense of unease and distress. I adjust my hold on the big weapon.

"It's not interdiction. It's slaughter. Those cutters open fire on the cargo ships, they sink them when they can. They shoot the survivors, too. They don't want anyone to land."

I blink in the sunlight, my rifle trembling in my hands.

"I don't believe you."

After a moment Brett speaks again, calm and ardent. "What do you think is easier for the Coast Guard—what remains of the Coast Guard? A massive and resource-intensive interdiction effort, or the simple and efficient operation that I've described? They could stand down, of course, stop their sorties entirely, but then the immigrants get through. Then they arrive in our towns, then they are so bold as to want to share resources, share space. Then they want to be given their own chance at survival in the aftermath. And we are determined, God forgive us, we are determined that not be allowed."

He is crying. His head is bent toward the green of the fort, and his voice comes out choked with lamentation.

"I thought you understood that, Henry, I thought that's why you came."

My rifle is trembling now, and I force myself to steady it, trying to figure out what happens next, while Brett gathers his voice, keeps talking. "But perhaps God has given you eyes that cannot see that deeper kind of darkness. And that is a blessing in you. But I beg of you, Henry, to let me be to carry out my mission. I beg that of you today, Henry, because if I can save even one boatload of those people, even one child or one woman or one man, then I will have done God's work today. *We* will have done God's work."

I think of those dots on the horizon, the tiny ships I saw from the slitted window of the caponier, steaming closer, even now.

"Brett—" I begin, and suddenly he ducks and rolls into the mud and comes up with the other rifle, all in one swift motion, ends up on his knee facing me, the gun angled up toward me, as mine is angled down toward him.

I didn't fire. I couldn't. How could I?

I shake my head, trying to shake the sunlight out of my eyes, shake the sweat off my forehead. *Figure this out, Palace. Handle this.* Then I just start, I start talking:

"Does anyone know where you are and what you're doing?"

"Julia."

"Julia thought that someone else knew. She thought someone would try to come and stop you."

"That was an assumption on her part. She's wrong. No one knows."

"Where did you get all the—the blueprints and so on? Of the various bases?"

"From Officer Nils Ryan."

"Who—"

"A former colleague of mine from Troop F. Also a former

chief petty officer in the Coast Guard."

"But he doesn't know what you wanted them for?"

"No."

I don't need to ask why this man, this Officer Ryan, would turn over such documents: because he asked. Because he's Brett.

"Okay," I say. "So no one knows about this. No one knows where you are. Just me and you and Julia."

"Yes."

"So let's—" I look away from his gun barrel, into his eyes. "Brett, let's end this right now. I do not want to harm you."

"Then don't. Go."

"I won't. I can't."

And then we stand there, my gun pointed at him, his at me.

"Please, Officer."

"These are human beings with no chance left but one." Brett, with his soft rumble of a voice, slow train rolling. "Who have risked everything, traveled thousands of miles crammed and sweating in shipping containers and overstuffed holds, and maybe it's a fool's chance they're taking, but that is their right, and they do not deserve to be murdered thirty yards from shore."

"Yes, but . . ." *But what, Officer Palace? But what?* "We were sworn in once, you and I. Right? As officers of the law. We still have an obligation to do what's lawful and what's right."

He shakes his head sadly. "Those two things you said there, friend. Those are two different things."

I'm standing on a slight rise, looking down at him in his crouch, feeling very tall indeed. A bird flickers past overhead, and then another, and then there's a wind, stronger than usual, a summer wind carrying up the scent of fish and a pinch of gunpowder from the churning breakers. We can just hear the rushing of the tide, barely reaching us way up here above the cliff face.

"On the count of three," I say, "we will lower our weapons, both together."

"Fine," he says.

"And then we will figure out what to do next."

"Good."

"On the count of three."

"One," says Brett, and lowers his gun a little bit off his shoulder, and I lower mine an inch or two, my muscles crying out with relief.

"Two," we say, together now, and now both rifles are at forty-five-degree angles, pointed at the ground.

"Three," I say, and drop my rifle, and he drops his.

We remain frozen for about a quarter of a second, and both of us start to smile, just a little, two honorable men on a green field, and then Brett is starting to get up and he's extending his hand and saying "My friend—" and then as I raise my arm there is a sharp bang, a crack in the sky, and my arm explodes in pain, hot and savage, a roaring pain, and I whirl behind me to find the shooter, and by the time I turn back around Brett is on the ground, flattened in the dirt with arms and legs windmilled out in the grass. I leap to him, screaming his name and clutching my arm. I land beside him and lie there panting for five seconds, ten seconds, waiting for more shots. I'm trying to summon up the protocol for victims of gunshot trauma in the field, trying to recall my training regarding rescue breaths and compressions and so on, but it doesn't matter. The bullet caught Brett dead between the eyes and half the front of his face has been swallowed by a hole. It's useless—there's nothing to be done—he's dead.

* * *

The first thing to do is tourniquet my arm. I know that—that much I remember, and besides it's obvious, the wound is bleeding like a rushing faucet, great gouts of bright red blood exploding out of my arm, darkening my shirt and coat and puddling between my shoes in the mud and the dirt. Brett's dead body beside me on the ground.

It's funny because I'm watching it, this fountain of blood, and it's happening to someone else, like this is some other man's arm exploded arm, another man's torn suit coat and pulsing wound. That one sharp instant of terrible pain I felt at impact has completely receded, and the wound, high on my right arm, at the biceps, is something I can see, and register as severe, but not *feel*.

This is shock. This absence of feeling is the result of the adrenaline flooding my system, rushing through my veins like seawater crashing the breached holds of a ship. I examine my arm like it's a joint at the butcher's counter: a gunshot trauma to the brachial artery, and I'm losing blood quickly, too quickly, precious milliliters gushing out onto the dirt field of Fort Riley. I've had general first aid and CPR training and annual continuing education courses per Concord Police Department regulations, and I know what to expect here: blood loss, dizziness, coldness, clamminess, and finally a high risk of fever, high risks all the way around, gunshot wounds in general requiring immediate medical assistance—arterial gunshot wounds in particular. "High risk of loss of limb and/or death."

I need to stabilize the wound and get to a hospital.

Brett is lying three feet away from me, sprawled out in the dirt. The horrible front-face wound, the stillness of his body. *"That contract has been abrogated."* Why did he say that? What does that mean?

Focus, Palace. Tourniquet the wound.

"Okay," I tell myself. "Geez."

I scrabble in the dirt and come up with a short thick piece of wood. This is not going to work, not long-term, but I need to staunch the bleeding immediately—I needed to have done it thirty seconds ago—to remain on my feet, get to the bicycle and my first aid kit. I can use my necktie to cinch the wound, for now, but I reach up and my necktie is gone. I slipped it off, just yesterday—was it yesterday?—on the quad at UNH and now it's lying somewhere along those winding paths like a shed snakeskin in the desert. I extend my left hand, trying as hard as I can to move only that side of my body, don't jostle the wound; I lean forward and slowly pry off one shoe and then one sock. Wincing, I take the tip of the sock between my teeth and tie it off around my arm like a heroin addict, recalling the shabby gentleman I encountered in the grub tent, the old bearded addict. *Here's to you, sir,* I think crazily as I jam the stick between the thin fabric and the flesh of my arm above the wound. I twist the sock tight around the stick and feel a radiating tingle as the blood starts to slow. I look down at the ragged hole in my arm and I can see the spurting of the blood begin to slow, to calm, turning into a bare trickle.

"There we go," I say to my arm. "There we go."

It still doesn't hurt. The shock will wear off somewhere around a half hour from now, and then the pain will set in and intensify steadily over the following six to eight hours. I can see the words on the sea-green stapled booklet we got at EMT-First Responder training in the break room, black Helvetica lettering against the green background of the leaflet: TIME IS OF THE ESSENCE. Stabilize the wound rapidly and keep it stable until the victim can be moved to a hospital.

Hospital, Henry? What hospital?

The sock begins to loosen as soon as I release the grip of my teeth. It'll last me maybe ten minutes. I stumble to my feet and limp toward the parking lot, toward my Red Rider Wagon full of supplies.

* * *

He's Brett, is what everybody told me, *he's just Brett*. Now I have some understanding of what they meant. A fascinating man, a force of nature. Charismatic, thoughtful, righteous and strange.

I've paused for a moment to rest at about the halfway point between the field where we were shot and the spot at the entrance to the parking lot where I've chained up my bike.

That contract has been abrogated, he said. What an odd word to import into the language of love: *abrogated.*

Among my regrets about what has just unfolded is that Brett never did ask me why I had come to find him, why I cared. I had my answer all figured out. *Because a promise is a promise, Officer Cavatone, and civilization is just a bunch of promises, that's all it is. A mortgage, a wedding vow, a promise to obey the law, a pledge to enforce it. And now the world is falling apart, the whole rickety world, and every broken promise is a small rock tossed at the wooden side of its tumbling form.*

I explain all of these things to Brett as I trudge along, tugging my sock-tourniquet tighter and gasping at the first tingling promise of pain. I give him my answer even though he's dead, and with each passing moment the odds are climbing that I'm going to die out here, too.

* * *

By the time I get to my bike, my improvised tourniquet is a dark bloody rag, and as soon as I peel it off the blood bursts forth. I fumble on the black pneumatic tourniquet from my first aid kit, cinch the cuff high on my arm, upstream of the wound, and inflate it as fast as I can, closing my eyes tightly as I squeeze and squeeze the bulb.

I pause, then. I am not dizzy yet, not yet experiencing severe pain. I can think now, for a moment I can think. From here I can see the road, the elbow bend in Route 3, and I can look up at the towering trees crowding in on the parking lot from all sides.

What hospital, Hank? I ask myself, dragging the question out of my consciousness and into the light—not meaning, which hospital will you choose? but rather, what operational hospital might be within biking distance of a fatigued man who has already suffered significant loss of blood? As much as a liter, maybe, half a liter easily. Portsmouth is the closest city, and I don't even know if they have a functioning hospital anymore or if it's all private duty. What about Durham? There must be a medical tent somewhere on the grounds of the Free Republic of New Hampshire, as there is a grub tent; somewhere in one of those basements some premed is boiling clamps and hypodermic needles in a lobster pot.

Will it be easier, I wonder, without the wagon? And I'm looking down at it, debating how risky or wise it might be to jettison the water and food and gauze and antiseptic to gain maybe three or four m.p.h. of travel speed. I'm crouching to look through how much water I have left anyway, and wishing it were more.

There. Now. Pain. There it is.

"Jesus." I say the word, and then I scream it: "Jesus!" and throw my head back and scream again, louder. It hurts—it does—it hurts so much, a hot iron pressed against my biceps. I clutch the wounded arm with the other one and immediately let go and scream more.

I sink down, into a crouch, and close my eyes, and rock on my heels, and take a series of short and shallow breaths. "My God, my God."

The pain is circling out from the impact site and burning into my shoulder, my chest, my neck, all the circuits of my upper body. More deep breaths, still down in my crouch, in the parking lot by the roadway. After several long moments the pain recedes, and I open my eyes and see on the ground with hallucinogenic clarity a single bright-orange leaf.

But it's not—it's not a leaf. I stare at it. It's a fake leaf. I pick it up with my left hand. It's made of fabric—a synthetic fabric—a synthetic leaf.

The thought appears in my mind not word by word, but wholly formed, like someone else had the thought and placed it there: *This does not make sense.*

Because I know what this is, this artificial leaf. It's a piece from a ghillie suit, the full-body camouflage worn by professional snipers and police shooters, a costume of shrubbery worn so that they can wait unseen for long periods, buried in the scenery. I know what a ghillie suit is, not from my police training but from my grandfather, who took me hunting exactly three times, trying to cure me of my total disinterest in that pursuit. I remember he pointed out a fellow sportsman, crouched in a blind in a suit of leaves, and scorned the man: "Those are for hunting men, not rabbits." I remember his caustic expression, and I remember the term, *ghillie suit*; it seemed such a comical name for something designed for the purpose of killing human beings.

The pain returns like an inrushing tide and I gasp, sink down farther into the gravel of the parking lot, still clutching the strange alien leaf. *This does not make sense.*

When the pain is gone—not gone, but dampened—I look past the stone wall, up onto the rise, try to pick out the spot where the shooter waited on the woody ridge between the road and the fort. I trace the bullet's line in my mind, a bright red ribbon leaping from the gun muzzle and across the field. I eyeball it. I estimate. Three hundred yards. It was a sniper shot, no question about it, three hundred yards easy, through the barrier of my outstretched arm and right between Brett's eyes. What I just witnessed was Brett's assassination by a military sniper from the Coast Guard or the Navy. A professional killer who tracked him here and waited in his ghillie suit and fired from the woods between the road and the fort. A preemptive strike against his madman's crusade.

So what is it? Why doesn't it make sense?

I know the answer while I'm still formulating the question: because Brett said no. No one knew about it. He had told no one where he was. Just Julia, and Julia had told me.

How could the military have sent a sniper to take him out, before he carried out his raids, when no one knew that they were coming?

New pain. Worse. The worst. I throw my head back and howl. Nausea is rolling up in churning waves from my stomach and into my throat. The pain leaps out from the wound site in bursts. Spots buzz to life in front of my eyes and I hunch back over, count slowly to ten, dizziness seeping in around the back corners of my brain. Brett told me that nobody else knew. Brett had no reason to lie.

But what about the friend, from the troopers, the Coast Guard man who provided the blueprints? Did he suspect the full scope of what Brett was up to? Did he sound the alarm? Track him down?

There's something else, something—I take a breath, try to remember—something in the blockhouse that didn't belong there. The pain makes it hard to think. It makes it hard to move—to *be*, even. I sit down in the gravel of the parking lot, lean against the wall, try not to look at my arm.

A color.

A flash of pink from inside that trunk.

I get up and stumble back down to the gravel, where the killer disappeared onto the highway, on his own ten-speed.

Or hers, I remind myself, thinking of Julia Stone, thinking of Martha Cavatone—my mind suddenly racing, evaluating motives, performing a quick roll call of everyone I've met on my circuitous route to Fort Riley, thinking about all the guns I've seen: Julia's M140s, Rocky's paintball guns and target range, my little Ruger. Jeremy Canliss had a snub-nose pistol tucked up in his jacket when I met him outside the pizza place. No, no, he didn't. I imagined that. Didn't I?

It doesn't matter. This is America in countdown time. Everybody has a gun.

"A hospital." I find the words in my throat and pronounce them gravely, lecturing myself, stern. "Forget the guns. Forget about Brett. Get to a hospital."

I look out at Route 103, where the asphalt is melting in the sun, letting off a blackish gummy steam. I'm swaying on my feet. The green pages of the stapled EMT booklet flutter in the wind before me, the all-caps text informing me that my dizziness will escalate from mild to extreme. In four hours the pain will begin to ease, as my soft tissue runs out of blood and the arm begins to die.

I'm staring vacantly at the bike and I realize that my decision has been made. It's already too late. The idea of hopping on a bicycle right now and getting myself to a hospital, to any hospital, is ridiculous. It's insane. It was already too late half an hour ago. I can't ride a *bike*. I can barely walk. I laugh, say the words aloud:

"Henry, you can't ride a *bike*."

I look back over my shoulder. Brett's corpse is still lying out there, facing up toward the sun. The missing-person case must be declared unsuccessful. I know why he left, yes, and even where he went, but he's dead and I couldn't protect him from dying.

I do, however, have some thoughts about who might have shot him, a few stray and feverish ideas on the subject.

* * *

It takes forty-five miserable and crawling minutes to retrace my steps—all the way down the length of the parking lot—through the stone archway back into the fort proper—across the spongy terrain to the foot of the blockhouse. The pain only gets worse now, never better, intensifying as it gains in territory, colonizing the farthest reaches of my body. By the time I reach the wavering shadow of the blockhouse I'm breathing unevenly, bent over, deteriorating in speeded-up motion like a man dying of old age in a cartoon. I collapse and land on my wounded right arm and shriek like a child from the electric pain and roll onto my back under the dangling rope ladder and the sheer wooden side of the building.

I stare up at that ladder. The thick hempen rungs I recently clambered down, just behind Brett, seemed like child's play an hour ago, like one of the playground structures we used to tear around on in White Park. Now it's a rock wall, a mountain's face that I am somehow supposed to drag myself up, exhausted and one-handed.

I stand, slowly, look upward and squint. The sun is burning the top of my head.

"One," I say, and take a deep breath and grunt and haul my entire weight with my one good arm, lift myself just enough to get my footing on the second rung of the ladder.

Then I wait there, gasping, barely three feet off ground level, with my head tilted up and my eyes closed, sweat pouring off of my scalp and pooling in my collar line. I wait for strength—for—I don't know—a few minutes? Five minutes?

And then I say: "Two."

Breathe—steady—grunt—heave. And then three—and then four—again and again, finding my footing on each new rung, humping myself laboriously upward and then exhaling—and waiting—panting—the sun baking me against the wall—sweat running down my spinal column and my arms, gathering in my waistband and swamping my armpits.

Halfway up the ladder, at rung number ten, I conclude that this is, in fact, impossible. I won't get any farther. This is as good a place as any to die.

I am too tired and too hot and too thirsty—increasingly it is my thirst that is the main problem, superseding the exhaustion and the dizziness and even the nascent feverishness—superseding even the pain, heretofore the great champion among my tormentors. I have forgotten, at this point, just what I am hoping to find up there in the blockhouse, what if anything.

Doesn't matter. I am too tired and too impaired and too thirsty to keep going. I will die here, plastered with sweat and crusted blood against this two-centuries-old wooden building, burned into the side by the afternoon sun. Here Maia will find the empty shell of my body and carry it away to sea.

The dog barks at the foot of the building. I can't see him, of course. But I hear him. He barks a second time, loud and sharp.

"Hey," I say, the word drifting feebly off in the air like a dead leaf. I clear my throat, lick my lips, and try it again. "Hey, boy."

Houdini keeps barking, probably because he's hungry or scared or maybe just happy to see me, even my long spindly bottom half. He's probably been lost in the woods, chasing squirrels or being chased for the last two hours. But in my dizziness and fatigue I imagine his frantic yips as encouragement: He is insisting that I continue up, that I assault the next rung and the next.

My little dog has reappeared at the crucial moment to insist in his rough canine language that salvation waits at the top of the ladder. I keep going. Up I go.

* * *

When at last I'm on the floor of the blockhouse I just lie there for a while, coughing. My throat is shutting down, collapsing in on itself like a dusty mineshaft. I roll over when I can and crawl to the trunk under the cannon and manage to open it and find a two-gallon jug and heave the heavy thing to my lips and drink like the lost man in the desert, letting water spill out and soak my face and my chest. I come up for breath like a surfacing dolphin and then drink more.

I let the empty plastic jug drop from my hands, and it bounces with a hollow sound on the wooden beams of the blockhouse floor.

Then I go back to the trunk, and a minute later I've found it. The pink paper, buried—not even buried—half hidden at best, beneath a change of clothes and a flashlight, a single sheet of pink notebook paper, worried and blackened at the edges where Brett's fingers, stained with dirt and gunpowder, have picked at its corners. Folded and grimy but still bearing the faint smell of cinnamon.

I laugh out loud, a nasty dry rasp. I take the page from Martha's diary and wave it in the air, pump it crumpled in the fist of my working hand. The page is torn and jagged at one edge, ripped out as if with force. I look up at the roof of Brett's cloister and press the paper to my chest and grin, feeling the grime on my face crack and fall away. I read it and reread it, and its meaning starts to well up around me, and then I'm getting dizzy and cold, so I press the torn-out scrap of notebook paper to my chest and lean back against the old wooden wall and shut my eyes.

* * *

He's barking, down there. Houdini is shouting, beautiful and faithful creature, hollering to keep me awake, or maybe at some interesting clouds, or maybe he's just giving his little voice box a workout, as dogs are famous for doing.

I should—I open my eyes, stare at the opposite wall, struggle to form the thought—*I should check on him.* I roll from sitting down onto my belly and crawl back to the doorway. The arm is starting not to hurt, which though a relief is nevertheless a very bad sign. I peer over the edge, and there he is, barking, purposeful, sending his voice up along the side of the building to where I can hear him, way up here.

"Good boy," I whisper, smiling down at him.

The sun is lower now and not as bright and I can see clearly where, down at the base of the blockhouse, my dog has built a little pyramid of dead birds. And I am not sure whether this is supposed to be a kind of sacrifice in my honor, or a tribute, or some sort of bizarre enticement: *Here, master, here! If you survive this situation, you can eat these birds.*

"Good boy," I say again. "Good dog."

* * *

It is some time later. If I check my watch I will know what time it is, see how many hours have elapsed with most of my arm cut off from my circulating bloodstream like it's downriver from a dam, and discover thereby how close I am either to dying or to losing my right arm forever.

There is an ache up and down the length of my body. In olden days they would strap you, hands and feet, to a machine, turn a wheel to make you talk. Or even not to, just to watch you experience it. Or because there was someone visiting the court who had never gotten a chance to see the machine in action. Another one of those things that makes you think, well, okay, the end of the human race, what are you gonna do?

I read it again, the pink page, Martha's slightly slanted all-block-letter handwriting, just like the quote from St. Catherine above her sink. But different in tone, so different:

HE'S DEAD N. IS DEAD HE'S REALLY DEAD

I'LL NEVER SEE HIS FACE AGAIN OR KISS HIM AGAIN

WHEN I CLOSE MY EYES THERE HE IS THE GOLD-CAPPED SMILE THE HAND-ROLLED SMOKES THE SILLY TATTOOS

BUT THEN I OPEN THEM AND HE'S GONE AGAIN

OK SO LET THE WORLD DIE NOW IT'S DEAD ALREADY WITHOUT HIM BUT

It ends like that, in the middle of a thought, to be continued on the next page. There's a date at the top, July fifth, just a couple weeks ago.

He's dead, she wrote, *N.'s dead he's really dead.*

Who, Martha? Who is N.?

I still don't check my watch, but I can feel it getting later. The day is wearing itself down, the sunbeams appearing and disappearing in the slitted windows. I wish I could send out my thoughts like medieval telegraph crows to gather clues and bring them back to me, up here in my doomed chamber.

Who was N., Martha? With gold teeth and hand-rolled cigarettes and funny tattoos?

How many guns are left in that storehouse by the power station, Julia Stone? Would you run and check for me? Do you even
need to look, or is it you who's spirited one away?

Officer Nils Ryan—Brett's buddy from the trooper days—Nils
starts with N. But there's another one, another N., and I can't remember it. The world spins. This case was like a straight line, simple
and clean: A man is missing. Find the man. And now it's like the
wilderness is crowding in along the road, turning the world into a
thicket, a maze, a tangle.

I squeeze up and down along the edges of my arm and feel
nothing and meanwhile my breath is ragged and uneven. At a certain
point I will cross a threshold where it won't matter either way; "loss
of limb and/or death," the double-conjunction pivot point resolving
decisively on "and."

The kids are going to be okay. Alyssa and Micah Rose at
Quincy Elementary. I gave that over to Culverson, and Detective
Culverson will stay on top of it. I smile at the thought of Culverson—at the Somerset right now, dining alone, asking Ruth-Ann politely what he owes her.

The sun is losing its luster. It's late afternoon. Next will be
nighttime.

The only thing is that it's too bad about Nico. Because I did, I
promised her I would protect her until one or both of us were dead.

She was drunk and I was fifteen, but I promised her and I meant what I said. I tell her I'm sorry, in my mind somewhere. If there is anyone that I *can* send a telepathic message to, it's my sister, and I let my mind go blank and launch it into the air, Nico, my dear, I am sorry.

* * *

I open my eyes and see my watch without meaning to. It's 5:13. Approximately six and a half hours since impact, since the bullet tore the hole into my biceps.

I haven't heard from Houdini in a long time. Perhaps he decided to abrogate our contract, escaped into the woods, evolved into a sea dog or a wolf. Good for him. I reach up to my face as if to make sure it's still there. It's dirty. Cragged. Lined in a way I don't remember. The edges of my mustache are growing in weird, all fuzzy and uneven like a disintegrating coastline. I hate that.

I read Martha's journal page again. He's DEAD N. IS DEAD HE'S REALLY DEAD.

* * *

When the shooting begins it begins all at once, not one or two but a hundred guns firing all at the same time, and of course I can't move, can't go down there to the water's edge; all I can do is look from the narrow windows of the blockhouse and watch the horror unfold.

At some point during this long hot strenuous expanse of a day, one of those tiny dots I saw out on the horizon this morning has made its way into the harbor and dropped anchor out by the lighthouse; a cargo ship with long iron sides, anchored and massive, maybe half a mile offshore, with dozens of tiny crafts bobbling at its sides like suckling children. Six or seven of these little boats have been let down and are on their way in, maneuvering for shore, crowded with passengers, their small motors puttering. And now—as I'm watching—those boats are coming under withering fire.

"No," I whisper.

But it's just as Brett said, it's a Coast Guard cutter, the sleek lines and the iron prow, the bristling masts and antennae, the noble shape of it parked in the water perpendicular to shore, offering not a lifeline to the incoming boats but a cannonade.

The small boats perform useless evasive maneuvers, rowboats and rafts wheeling unevenly this way and that while the cutter strafes the water, kicking up mountains of churning foam.

Seabirds dart overhead, flying fast, away from the pop of the guns.

"No," I say, way the hell up here from my tower window, uselessly, ridiculously. "No."

The rafts begin to capsize, tipping their inhabitants into the water, where they paddle and scream and grab for one another—children, old women, young men—and me just watching, helpless, trapped inside the blockhouse, inside my injury, coughing and lightheaded, watching them drown, watching them swim, watching the cutter send out speedboats to gather up those who remain.

"Stop," I whisper, my eyes rolling up into my head. "Police."

Children clutching at one another, little bodies boiling up in the breakers, lashed by the wake of the ships, opening their mouths to scream even as they are pulled under by the waves.

* * *

In the silence when it's over I slip into sleep, and in my fever dream Brett is alive and squats beside me with his M140 pointed out the slit window of the blockhouse. He does not say "I told you so." That is not his style. What he does say though is, "It was abrogated. Our contract was *abrogated*." I want to warn him that the barrel of his rifle is poking back into the blockhouse at the next window over, a cartoon image, like it loops around out there and comes back in, pointing right at his own face.

Don't do it, I say, *don't shoot*. But my mouth moves and the words don't come and he fires and an instant later topples over backward, somersaults and rolls till he's still.

In the next dream, the next scene, he's got a skeet gun and we're up on the roof, me and him, and this time he smiles and when he smiles his mouth glows and he leans back and shoots up, up, up and the asteroid tumbles out of the sky, and Houdini goes and retrieves it, a burning planet of rock and metal clutched in his teeth like a fetched duck.

* * *

I wake up, because of a distant unfamiliar noise, and the first thing I think is that *he wanted to leave.*

He was not unfaithful to her; she was to him.

Oh, Martha—

She had taken a lover, the man she identified as N., and then that lover was killed in the riots on Independence Day.

And Brett had not left Martha, but he had been yearning in his heart to leave. He had information, he had a plan, he knew the good he wanted to do in the world. He even knew where he could go to get the guns that he needed to do it. But he could not and would not go, because he had made promises before his wife and before God and he would not release himself from those promises.

There's a thrumming out there. What is the noise? The ship must be back, or a new one is coming, a fresh engagement threatening on the horizon line. The image of the dead and dying from the boats returns, as clear and detailed as a photograph. I try to lift my head but cannot. I stay inside the hole I'm in, close my eyes to what I've seen and instead return to considering my case, piecing it together.

When Brett found his wife's diary page he reacted not with anger but with fierce and secret joy. He tore out that page and took it like a ticket, because this was permission to go and do what he wanted to. He made arrangements with the thief Cortez and off he went; by the grace of God his wife had been unfaithful, their contract had been abrogated, and he felt himself released and he left. He ripped out that page and held it to his heart and ran off to his seaside tower and his righteous crusade.

The thrumming is getting louder. I raise my arm and it lifts slow, dense, like it's made of bundled sticks. *Please don't be another ship. Please.* I don't want to witness any more.

It's a beating of wings, out there. Close by, much closer than the water. A motor.

I have to move then, I have to drag myself, and I do. I use my legs but not to walk, to launch myself forward like a worm across the small room and into the doorway and stick out my head and there it is—there she is—the great green-sided helicopter hovering in the sky above the blockhouse, rotors beating, the noise a great thundering rush.

I raise my working hand in the threshold of the blockhouse and wave it, feebly, and I'm trying to scream but there is no noise escaping my throat. It's not necessary, though, because she's already seen me. Nico leaning from the doorway of the helicopter, clutching the frame, laughing, shouting: "Hank! Hank!"

I can't really hear her, I can just see her lips moving, just make out the words—"I told you so!"

PART FIVE

Savage Land

Tuesday, July 24

Right Ascension 19 57 36.4
Declination -61 59 14
Elongation 137.9
Delta 0.817 AU

1.

Martha, oh Martha, you hid your heart from me.
Martha, oh Martha, oh why?

So here I am, I'm crouched with Martha Milano and the door of the Easy-Bake oven is slightly ajar, and together we're feeling the warmth of the one little bulb on our faces. I'm lying in the shadow of the blockhouse staring at Brett's blasted skull. I'm slouched slack-jawed in a helicopter and my sister is slapping me, trying to keep me awake. I'm awake. Strange smells are drifting out of the Easy-Bake oven. There are low murmurs somewhere in the back of my brain, people talking in another part of the house.

I open my eyes. The strange white room is dim and candlelit, but my corneas burn with the brightness. I shut my eyes.

Martha, oh Martha, oh why?

She lied. A sin of omission, at the very least.

Where am I? What happened to Nico? The helicopter—the fort—the dog, where's the dog?

She had a lover—Martha did. His name was N. Who was N.? *She* was untrue. *She* was the one who broke her marriage vow, who abrogated the contract, who risked her own salvation. There was a man who came into Rock 'n' Bowl just as I was leaving. Norman. Wasn't it? *"Mr. Norman is here." "No kidding? Already?"*

I'm floating through textured air, bobbing and dipping. The smell is bad now, strong and acrid, like disinfectant, like maybe Martha and I are baking a mop head. Where am I? My God, and how?

Is there anything else you need to tell me, Martha—didn't I say that? Didn't I ask her? Anything else about your husband, your marriage? I try to peer from this distance into Martha's secret heart: She must have felt that it didn't matter, whatever she had done and with whom. She must have thought it irrelevant to the task at hand: her husband had gone, it didn't matter why, and she just wanted him back.

But Martha, oh Martha, he's not coming back.

I see Brett's face again, the empty cratered space and the sharp sickly clean odor is all around me now. I sniff gingerly, my eyes still closed, like a newborn bunny rabbit, tasting air with the dew of the womb still drying on my nose. Bleach? Cleaning fluid?

More murmuring, more quiet voices.

And then suddenly a giant has got hold of my right side and is squeezing, huge brutal fingers digging into my flesh, trying to yank my arm off my torso like a flower petal. I writhe, remembering my injury. I feel like a broken toy, like I've been hurled from a height down onto cobblestones.

"Hank." One of the voices, clear and loud. "Hank."

I've never noticed before how sharp and clinical that name sounds, *HANK*, how curt and cold, *HANK*, onomatopoetic for the clink of a metal chain on a metal desk. My mind is moving, fast and strange. "Hank," says the voice again, and it's real; there's a voice in the room. I'm in a room and there's a voice in it, a person in it, standing close by me, saying my name.

I decide to go one eye at a time. I crack the right eye, and the light floods in. Silhouetted in the glare is a face I recognize. Two eyes, each encased in a glass circle, peering down at me like an amoeba on a slide. Above the pair of glasses a slash of bangs, a skeptical irritated face.

"Dr. Fenton?" I whisper. I open the other eye.

"What happened to you?" asks Alice Fenton.

"I was shot."

"Thanks," she says. "That's literally the only part of the story I already know."

"You're upstairs," I tell her.

"Yes. I quit the morgue," she says. "Not enough doctors. Too many people who need help. Plenty of idiots getting themselves shot."

I try to banter back at her but our conversation thus far has already exhausted me. I let my eyes drift closed again. Alice Fenton is a legend. She is or was the chief medical examiner of the state of

New Hampshire, and for a long time I idolized her from afar, her technical mastery and perspicacity. A few months ago I had the opportunity to work with her for the first time, and her forensic skill helped me figure out who it was that killed some people. Naomi Eddes, for example, whom I loved. She is—Fenton is a legend.

"Dr. Fenton," I say. "You're a legend."

"That's great," she says. "Go to sleep. We'll talk later."

"Wait. Hold. Wait."

"What?"

"Just one second."

I inhale. I get my eyes to open. I prop myself on my elbows and look around. The bedsheets and blankets are yellow-green in the pale light of the room. I'm in a flimsy powder-blue gown. I'm home. There's an iron arm that once held an in-room television, now angling uselessly out of the wall like a metal tree branch. I need to go to Albin Street. I have to check in with my client. *Hey, Martha? I've got a couple questions for you.*

Dr. Fenton stands at the side of the bed, a stack of clipboards under one arm, her short compact form quivering with impatience.

"What?" she says again.

"I have to get going."

"Sure," she says. "Nice to see you."

"Oh," I say. "Great."

She waits as I shift my legs toward the edge of the bed and my stomach heaves and thickens inside my body. Visions roll across my brainpan, double time: Martha crying; Brett staring; Nico smoking;

Rocky in his office with his feet up. Naomi Eddes unmoving in the darkness where they found her. I stop moving my legs and tuck my chin down into my neck and manage not to vomit.

"Ether," says Dr. Fenton with the barest trace of merriment. "You're coming down out of a cloud of ether. My colleagues and I are down to the dregs of our pain meds. The DOJ promised a shipment of morphine and MS Contin by Friday, along with new fuel for the generators. I'll believe it when I see it. In the meantime, ether. Everything that's old is new again."

I nod. I focus on not being sick. My arm feels like one big tender bruise. I try to move it, to see if that would hurt it more or less, and I discover that it won't move at all.

"I should say, Hank," says Dr. Fenton, and I note that there is no remaining amusement in her voice, "it is very much within the realm of possibility that you are going to lose that limb."

I listen, numb. *Lose the limb*. Sure. Of course. My pillow smells like dust, like other men's blood.

Fenton is still talking. "I repaired the blood vessels in the ruptured brachial artery by excising the injured segment and performing a graft. But I—" She stops, gives a quick shake of her head. "I don't know what I'm doing. I was cutting up corpses for the past twenty-five years, and now I've been doing general surgeries for approximately two weeks. Plus, you probably haven't noticed, but it's fucking *dark* in here."

"Dr. Fenton," I say. "I'm sure you did your best." I reach laboriously across the bed with my good hand and pat her on the arm.

"I'm sure I did, too," she says. "But you still might lose the limb."

I try again to move my legs, and this time I get them a little closer to the edge of the bed. I'm visualizing my swiftest route from here, Concord Hospital at Pleasant Street and Langley Parkway, all the way to Albin Street in North Concord. *I'm not cross with you, Martha. I just want to know the truth.* The machines around us beep dully, their blinking lights dim and pale, feeble back-up-generator lights. My legs refuse to go any farther for the time being. My arm throbs and my body aches. The world swells up and gently spins around me. I feel myself slipping down, not unpleasantly, back into my cloud of ether. Naomi is standing where Fenton just was, gazing sweetly down at me, and my heart shivers in my chest. Naomi was bald, in life; apparently in the world to come she's growing out her hair and it looks beautiful, like soft moss on a sea-washed stone.

I let my head fall back onto the pillow and the helicopter roars into view, Nico hollering from the hatchway, and then I'm in it, on it, feverish and confused, the wind rushing in and around us, Nico's choppy hair fluttering like a field of black grass. The pilot is nervous and unsure—and young, so terribly young, a girl in her late teens or early twenties, wearing aviator glasses and jerking the levers uncertainly.

Nico and I fought for the whole trip: forty-five minutes of arguing, voices raised, screaming to be heard over the clatter of the copter blades and the deafening wind, telling each other not to be stupid. I told her she had to get out with me in Concord and stay with me at the farmhouse on Little Pond Road until the end, like we'd discussed. Nico refused, urged me instead to stay with *her*, went on and on about the asteroid, the bombs, hydrodynamic simulations and necessary changes in velocity. And through all of this we're jerking back and forth in the skies over New Hampshire and my fever is climbing and then suddenly were descending haphazardly toward the landing pad atop Concord Hospital.

And as I was clambering out Nico said—what did she say? Something insane. As I stepped uncertainly onto the landing pad and turned around and pleaded with my sister through my haze of fever and pain to remain under my protection until the end—she told me not to worry.

"I'll be fine," she hollered, her hands cupped together. "Just e-mail me."

I wake myself up laughing in the hospital bed. *Just e-mail me.* The words, the *concept*, like something from an unfamiliar language: Urdu or Farsi or the Latin of the Romans.

I ease my head back onto the pillow and breathe and try to steady myself a little. I can't believe I let her go.

* * *

The insistent noise and fuss we have learned to expect from hospital rooms is absent now. No one charges down the hallway outside, no nurses in scrubs slip in and out of the door to check my fluid levels or bring dinner or adjust the bed. Every once in a while I hear a scream, or the squeaking wheel of a rolling cart, from some other room or from around some corner.

Eventually I get my legs off the bed and my feet on the floor, and I make my way over to where my clothes are heaped in a pile.

My arm is in a sling, wrapped elaborately in bandages and cinched tightly against my side. I find my watch. I find my shoes. I survey my clothing. The pants are wearable, but my blood-soaked shirt and jacket must be left behind, and I will stay in the hospital gown until I can stop at home and change.

After Martha's house. First I'm going to stop at Albin Street and ask Martha a few questions.

Dr. Fenton is at the nurses' station in the hallway, writing rapidly on the top clipboard on her pile. She looks up at me, shambling along the hall toward her, and looks down again.

"So—" I say.

"I get it," she says. "You're going."

From an examination room behind Dr. Fenton there's a steady anguished groaning. From another, someone is saying, "Just take it easy—just take it easy—just take it *easy.*"

"You should stay for twenty-four hours at least," says Fenton. "You need to be observed. You need a course of antibiotics."

"Oh," I say, and look back over my shoulder at the desolate room. "Well, can I get that now?"

"I said you *need* a course of antibiotics," she says, grabbing her clipboard and striding off. "We don't have any."

* * *

Houdini is waiting just outside the main lobby door of Concord Hospital, like a mafia bodyguard stationed at the sickbed of the capo. As soon as I emerge blinking into the parking lot in my pale blue gown he nods at me, I swear to God he does, and off we go.

2.

My watch says it's 11:15, and I know that means 11:15 a.m. because the sun is high and bright as Houdini and I make our way north across Concord. But I don't know what day it is—I literally have no idea. I was dead in the dirt at Fort Riley for who knows how long, and then I was on a helicopter and then I was in a bed on the fourth floor of Concord Hospital floating in and out of ether for years and years.

I walk as fast as I can manage across the city toward Martha's house, my dead arm tight in its harness, sweat dripping down my back and plastering my hospital gown against my spine. Looking around, examining the city after being gone, it's like one of those puzzle pages in a children's magazine: Look at these two pictures and spot what's changed. Down Pleasant Street and then up along Rumford. Walls with new graffiti; cars that had one wheel gone and the hood popped open are now down to the rims all the way around, or the glass of the windshield's been pried out with a crowbar. Or they're actually burning, thick black smoke pouring out of the engine. More houses that have been left behind, front doors yawning wide. Telephone poles made into stumps.

Last week Pirelli's Deli on Wilde Street was bustling, a cheerful violence-free dry goods rummage, with a couple of guys giving haircuts, of all things, in the back. Now the chain grate is pulled down over the doors and windows, and Pirelli stands on the sidewalk scowling, a strip of ammunition across his chest like a bandito.

Houdini is growling as we walk, bounding out ahead of me, his eyes fierce yellow slits. The sun beats on the sidewalks.

* * *

"Martha?" I bang on the door with my left hand, pause for a moment, then bang again. "Martha, are you in there?"

The Cavatones' lawn had been the only one mowed, but now it's starting to catch up with the others, wildness creeping in, the trim green fuzz growing out like uncut hair. My arm pulses suddenly, painfully, and I wince.

I knock again, waiting to hear those locks being thrown open, one by one. Nothing. I shout. "Hey, Martha?"

Across the street a window blind snaps open, a wary face peers out. "Excuse me?" I call. "Hey—" The blinds shoot closed again. A dog barks somewhere, down the street, and Houdini twitches his small head around in search of the challenger.

My fist is raised to knock again when the door jerks open and a strong hand grabs my wrist, and somebody in one quick motion drags me inside and kicks the door closed behind me. I'm pushed against a wall, my right arm sending out spasms of pain, and there's hot breath in my face. A tumble of hair, a crooked chin.

"Cortez," I say. "Hello."

"Oh, shit," he says, the good-humored voice, the laughing eyes. "I know *you.*"

Cortez lets go of my wrist, steps back, embraces me like I'm an old friend he's picking up at the airport. "Policeman!"

His staple gun is dangling from his right hand, but he leaves it angled down, pointed at the ground. Houdini is out on the porch, barking like a madman, so I step over and open the door, let him in.

"Where did you come from?" Cortez asks. "Why are you dressed for the mental asylum?"

"Where's Martha?"

"Oh, hell," he says, and flings himself into the Cavatones' fat leather Barcalounger. "I thought *you* were going to tell *me.*"

"She's not here?"

"I don't lie, Policeman."

Cortez watches with amusement while I search the small house, working my way through the closets of the living room, opening all the ones in the bedroom and peering under the bed, looking for Martha or evidence of Martha. Nothing. She's gone, and her clothes are gone: her dressers empty, wooden hangers dangling on her side of the closet. Brett's sidearm is also gone, the SIG Sauer he left behind for his wife's protection when he went off to play crusader in the woods. In the kitchen, sunbeams still play across the warm wood table, and the brass kettle sits happily in its place on the stove. But there's no sign of Martha, and my case has come full circle: It's a missing person, just a different person than before.

I return to the living room and point an angry finger at Cortez.

"I thought you were supposed to be watching her?"

"I was," he says, the staple gun lying across his lap like a kitten. "I am."

"So?"

"So, I failed," he says, and looks up at the ceiling with theatrical misery, as if to ask what kind of God could allow this to happen. "I absolutely failed."

"Okay," I say, "okay," patting my pockets for a notebook, but of course I have no notebook—I have no pockets—and my right hand is my writing hand. "Just tell me the story."

Cortez needs no prompting. He stands, gestures animatedly while he talks.

"On Saturday I came by three times. Three times I came." He holds up forefinger, middle finger, pointer, and his rhythm is like a Bible story: Three times I called your name and three times you refused me. Three times Cortez the thief came from Garvins Falls Road on a bike-and-wagon, laden with supplies for Martha, three times he did a "comprehensive walkaround" to ensure the safety of the small home, checking the doors and windows, checking the perimeters.

Morning, midday, sunset. Three times he made sure all was well; three times he paraded himself around with large and visible firearms, so any thugs or rapists would be aware of the presence of an armed defender. Sunday, Cortez says, same thing: morning visit, noon visit, nighttime.

"And I told her, anything else you need, I provide it." Cortez looks around the living room. "You want a muscular gentleman with a baseball bat sitting on this sofa all night long, you can have that. You want someone on the porch with a rocket launcher, we can make that happen."

I raise an eyebrow—they do not sell rocket launchers at Office Depot—and Cortez grins, happy to explain, but I wave my hand for him to go on. I'm not in the mood.

"The woman is not interested in protection inside the house, but otherwise she is happy," Cortez says. "Happy to have us around. As her husband had arranged."

"Okay. And?"

"Okay, so same yesterday. But then today, I am here in the morning, just the same, and the woman is standing out on the porch, shaking her head and waving her hands."

"She's on the porch?"

"Yes, Policeman. With a suitcase."

"A suitcase?"

"Yes. Suitcase. And she says, no thank you. Like I'm selling Girl Scout cookies. Like I'm a goddamn Jehovah's Witness." He puts on a mocking, feminine voice, says it again: "No thank you."

Martha, oh Martha, what secrets had you hidden in your heart?

"It was like she was waiting for someone," Cortez says, rubbing his chin. "Someone other than me."

"Wait—" I say. I'm trying to capture all these details, arrange them in my head. "Wait one second."

"What is it?" Cortez looks at me curiously. "You need me to repeat something?"

"Nothing," I say, "No. Just—what day is it?"

"It's Tuesday." He grins. "Are you okay?"

"I'm fine. I just didn't know what day it is. Please continue the story."

What happened next is Cortez told her it wasn't up to her, with all due respect he had been contracted to take care of her, and this wasn't her arrangement to undo. If she didn't want to see him, she could stay inside the house and he or his friend would drop off supplies and protect her from the outside. She insisted, no thank you, told him to leave her be, and then someone hit him on the side of the head.

"Someone hit you or her?"

"Me. I said me."

"With what?"

"I do not know. Something hard and flat." Cortez ducks his head, embarrassed. "I was hit very hard. I was knocked unconscious." He steps back, raises his hands, looks at me wide eyed, like, *Sounds impossible, I know, but that's what happened.* "I was out cold for I don't know how long, not long I think, and when I woke up, she was gone.

I went inside and ran up and down, three times I searched for her. But the house was as you see it. She is gone."

"Holy moly," I say.

"Yes," says Cortez drily, and now it's my voice he puts on, flat and solemn. "Holy moly."

"So what are you doing here now, Mr. Cortez?"

"Waiting for her. A friend I have, Mr. Wells, is out looking while I wait—often the missing simply return. Ellen, meanwhile, minds the home front. Listen, I don't care if that girl wants to be found or not. We're going to find her. That cop comes back and finds her gone, I'm finished."

"That contract, I think, has been abrogated."

"Why? Oh—dead?" Cortez does not look saddened by this news. "Who killed him?"

"I'm working on it."

He pauses, tilts his head. "Why?"

"I don't know yet. I'll know when I find the killer."

"I don't mean why was he killed. I mean, why are you working on it?"

I take one more turn around the small house, Houdini close at my heels. I check the locks on the window, look for fingerprints, footprints, anything. Did someone do this to her, or did she do it herself, slip out from under the protection that Brett had arranged? Was she kidnapped? The suitcase says she was waiting for someone, presumably the mysterious Mr. N. But the mysterious Mr. N. is dead, right?

For a long time I stare into Martha Milano's empty closet, and then I go back downstairs, find Cortez lounging in the recliner, his cigarette raised like a scepter.

"I tell you, this whole thing, it's a bad sign," he says. "Me losing track of someone I'm supposed to look after? That is a bad fucking sign."

"For what?"

"Oh, shit, you know. For all of mankind. The whole human race."

* * *

Back on Albin Street I look up at the sun. The city is hotter than it was last week, and you can smell it on the air—the reek of untreated sewage water drifting up off the river, of garbage that's been dumped in the streets and out of windows. Sweat and body odor and fear. I should go home and change clothes, see if any damage has been done while I was away. Make sure that nothing has been taken from my store of food and supplies, all that we left behind.

"We really should, buddy," I say to Houdini. "We should go home."

But we don't. We go back the way we came, down Albin, down Rumford, up Pleasant Street.

What few people there are on the streets are moving quickly, no eye contact. As we get closer to Langley Boulevard a man rushes past in a windbreaker, head down, carrying two whole hams, one under each arm. Then a woman, running, pushing a stroller with a giant Deer Park bottle strapped into it instead of a child.

I realize suddenly I have not seen a police car or a police officer or evidence of police presence of any kind since I returned to Concord, and for some reason the observation floods my stomach with a churning dread.

My legs are getting tired; my busted arm joggles against my side, tight and uncomfortable and useless, like I'm lugging a ten-pound weight around, to prove a point or win a contest.

* * *

I find Dr. Fenton right where I left her, working her way down her towering pile of charts, leaning against the counter of the nurses' station, her eyes blinking and red behind the round glasses.

"Hey," I start, but then another doctor, short and bald and bleary eyed, stops and scowls. "Is that a fucking dog? You can't have a fucking dog in here."

"Sorry," I say, but Fenton says, "Shut up, Gordon. That dog's more hygienic than you are."

"Clever," he says, "you fucking hack." He disappears into an adjacent exam room and slams the door. Fenton turns to me. "What happened, Detective Palace? You get shot again?"

* * *

We take the unlit stairwell down to the crowded first-floor

cafeteria: dirty linoleum tables and a handful of stools, a big plastic bin filled with mismatched cutlery, boxes of supermarket teabags and a row of kettles lined up on camp stoves. Dr. Fenton and I take our tea out to the lobby and sit in the overstuffed chairs.

"When did you stop working in the morgue?"

"Two weeks ago," she says. "Three, maybe. The last month or so, though, we weren't doing autopsies. No call for it. Just intake, preparing bodies for burial."

"But you were still down there when Independence Day happened?"

"I was."

The front door of the hospital crashes open and a middle-aged man stumbles in carrying a woman in his arms like a newlywed, her bleeding profusely from the wrists, him just yelling, "God you idiot, you idiot, you're such an idiot!" He kicks open the door of the stairwell and lugs his wife inside, and the door slams closed behind them. Fenton lifts her glasses to rub her eyes, looks at me expectantly.

"I'm trying to I.D. a corpse that came in that night."

"On the Fourth?" says Fenton. "Forget it."

"Why?"

"Why? We had three dozen corpses at least. As many as forty, I think. They were stacked like firewood down there."

"Oh."

Stacked like firewood. My neighbor, sweet Mr. Maron of the solar still, he died that night.

"We weren't able to process them properly, is the other thing.

No photographs, no intake records. Just bagging and tagging, really."

"The thing is, Dr. Fenton, this particular corpse would have been rather distinctive."

"You, my friend," she says, tasting her tea with a moue of displeasure, "are rather distinctive."

"A man, thirties probably. Gold-capped teeth. Humorous tattoos."

"How so, humorous?"

"I don't know. Zany, somehow." Dr. Fenton is looking at me bemusedly, and I don't know what I had imagined: a tattoo of a rubber chicken? Marvin the Martian?

"Where on the body?" Fenton asks.

"I don't know."

"Do you know the means of death?"

"Weren't they all—gunshots?"

"No, Hank." The words are dry with sarcasm, but then she stops, shakes her head, continues quietly. "No. They weren't."

Dr. Fenton takes off the glasses, looks at her hands, and in case I am correct in my impression that she is silently weeping I avert my gaze, try to find something interesting to look at in the dimness of the hospital lobby.

"And so," she says abruptly, shifting back into her characteristic tone, "the answer is no."

"No, there wasn't anybody matching that description or, no, you don't recall?"

"The former. I am relatively certain we did not see a body

matching that description."

"How certain is relatively certain?"

Dr. Fenton thinks this over. I wonder how it's going upstairs for the desperate man and his wife, bleeding from her wrists, how they're faring under the charge of Dr. Gordon.

"Eighty percent," says Dr. Fenton.

"Is it possible a victim might have been taken to New Hampshire Hospital?"

"No." she says. "It's closed. Unless someone took a body there and didn't know they were closed and dumped it in the horseshoe driveway. I understand—" She pauses, clears her throat. "I understand some bodies have been deposited in such a way."

"Right," I say absently.

She stands up. Time to get back to work. "How's the arm?"

"So-so." I squeeze my right biceps gingerly with my left hand. "I don't feel much yet."

"That's appropriate," she says.

We're walking back to the stairway. I set my half-empty teacup down carefully on the floor next to a full garbage can.

"As circulation improves over the next couple weeks, you'll start to get a persistent tingling, and then you'll need physical therapy to work toward regular functioning. Then, around early October, a massive object will strike Earth and you will die."

3.

"So I go over there on Friday night, maybe two hours after you take off, and the playground is a no-man's-land. The swings are cut down, just chains dangling, you know? The fence is kicked over, and the—what do you call it?—the jungle gym, it's over on its side. I'm thinking maybe I've got the wrong place."

"You're at Quincy Elementary?"

"Yeah," says Detective Culverson. "Quincy. The play field behind the school."

"That's right."

The diner; the booth; my old friend with an unlit cigar, stirring honey into his tea, telling me a story. A fat double-bread-loaf indentation in the vinyl where McGully used to sit.

"So there I am like a dummy, holding this samurai sword. And don't even ask how I got it, by the way. I'm standing there and I'm thinking, Okay, so, Hank's little buddies have moved along, they've found some other squat. But then I see that there's a flier: *If you are the parent of . . .* You know? One of those. It looks like they got scooped up."

I exhale. This is good news. This is the best possible outcome for Alyssa and Micah Rose. A mercy bus came and took them somewhere indoors, with food and organized play and prayer circles three times a day. Ruth-Ann is sitting at a stool by the counter. She's got her hot-water carafe, her pens arranged behind her ear, her little order notebook jutting out of the front pocket of her apron. Culverson is in his undershirt, off-white and yellowed and stained at the pits, because he's lent me his dress shirt, which puffs out at my stomach and gaps at the collar.

"Was it the Catholics?" I ask him.

He shakes his head. "Christian Science."

"Sure," I say. I've started in drumming the fingers of my working hand on the tabletop. Now that I know that my kids are okay, that they didn't suffer from my absence these last few days, I'm ready to move on, lay out my case. I hustled down here to make sure I caught Culverson within the loose bounds of the lunch hour, so I could run down my missing-person-turned-murder, see what he thinks.

"So I went to the address on the flier. Warren and Green. I didn't have descriptions so I asked for the names."

"How are they doing?" I ask. "Are they happy?"

"That's the thing," says Culverson. "They're not down there."

"What?" My fingers freeze. "They're not?"

"Nope. A lot of other kids are, though. I found one named Blackwell."

"Stone," I say. "Andy Blackstone."

"Yup. Funny kid. But Andy says that your guys . . ." Culverson flips through his notes; he's got a steno pad like we used to use for case notes; I bet he helped himself to a box from the CPD supply closet before we were cleared out of the building. "He says they were there but then they left before the head count."

"Oh."

"And that's as far as I could get."

"Oh," I say again, and stare down at the grimy linoleum. I can't believe I let them go. They were my responsibility, those kids, a self-imposed responsibility but a responsibility nevertheless, and I treated them casually, like objects—a file that could be turned over to a colleague. I chose instead to follow the case of Martha Milano's missing husband, and every choice forecloses on other choices; each step forward leaves a thousand dead possible universes behind you.

I think of the small broken boats I saw from the window of the blockhouse: the drowning, the dead.

"Detective Palace?" Culverson says. "Your turn. Tell me about your case."

I nod. I look up, take a breath. This is why we're here. I've come this far. I talk fast, giving him the highlight reel: Julia Stone at UNH, Brett Cavatone at Fort Riley. The gunshot, the orange leaf from the ghillie suit, the diary page. Detective Culverson stops me after the mysterious Mr. N.

"Wait," he says. "Slow down." He clears his throat, looks thoughtful. "So, you got a girl who comes to you for help. Husband is Bucket List, she wants him back."

"Yeah."

"You find the husband, and right away he's shot."

"Yeah. By someone who knows how to shoot."

"Military?"

"Maybe. I don't know. Someone who knows how to shoot."

"Okay."

"And then you get back home," says Culverson. "How do you get home?"

"In a helicopter—that's a whole other . . ." I shake my head. "Don't worry about that. Skip ahead. I get home, I go over to Martha's house this morning and she's gone."

"Any idea where she is?"

"No. Yes. I have a theory."

Culverson raises his eyebrows, twiddles with his cigar.

"Okay," he says. "Lay it on me."

"Martha's cheating on Brett with someone she calls N."

"Right."

"N. dies on the Fourth—at least, Martha thinks he dies. She writes of his death in her diary, but then Brett finds the diary, Brett decides this means his marriage is over, he's free to go."

"On his mission."

"Crusade."

"Crusade."

"So he leaves. Martha's confused and upset; she asks me to go out and find Brett. But while I'm out looking for him, the lover turns out not to be dead after all. They reunite, hit Cortez with a shovel, and leave town together."

"Riding on a dragon," says Culverson.

"You're teasing me."

"I am."

Culverson widens his grin and drains the tea. In the silence I picture Alyssa and Micah. Where could they have gone? Where's Martha? Where's my sister?

It's too quiet in here, unnervingly quiet: no radio playing from the kitchen, as there used to be, the cook Maurice singing along with a deep cut from *Planet Waves*. No muted clang of cutlery and murmured conversation from other tables, no humming ceiling fans. It occurs to me that this institution is in its twilight, not just the Somerset but this whole setup: young Palace putting the case to sage Culverson; Culverson pushing back, finding flaws. It's untenable. It's like the hospital, everybody doing their best on a project that is ultimately doomed.

"What I'm wondering about is that diary page," he says. "You're sure that diary page was the real McCoy?"

"Yes." I pause. I stare at him. "No. I don't know."

"I'm talking about the handwriting," he says. "You're sure it was the girl's handwriting?"

"No," I say. "Yes. Dammit."

I close my eyes and I can picture it, the block letters on the cinnamon-scented page: HE'S DEAD N. IS DEAD HE'S REALLY DEAD. I try then to hold it up next to the quote, transcribed from St. Catherine and taped up by Martha's bathroom mirror: IF YOU ARE WHAT YOU SHOULD BE . . . but I'm uncertain, I can't tell, and I don't have that pink page anymore. It's somewhere in the blockhouse, it's drowning in the mud of Fort Riley or fluttering out over the ocean like a bird.

"I just didn't think of it," I say, appalled that I could have overlooked something so obvious.

"It's okay," says Culverson, signaling to Ruth-Ann with two fingers for more hot water.

It's not okay. Nothing is okay. I toy with the mostly empty condiment jars: ketchup, mustard, salt. A plastic vase sits among them, bits of stem floating in a quarter inch of water at the bottom. It's hot and dark in here, a couple stray beams of weak sunlight filtering through the dusty blinds. So simple. So obvious. The handwriting.

"I suppose it would be useless to note," says Culverson, "that there is no point in investigating anything. It's not like, you find this killer, and he's locked up and you get a promotion. The office of the attorney general is shuttered. There are literally raccoons living in there."

"Yeah," I say. "Yeah, I know all that."

"And if your babysitter has really been kidnapped, what are you going to do? Rescue her with that cute little gun that McConnell gave you?"

"No." I scratch my head. "Actually, I lost it."

Culverson looks at me for a second, and then he bursts out laughing, and I do, too, and we both sit there cracking up for a second, Houdini staring at me with questioning eyes from where he's stationed himself under the table. Ruth-Ann comes over to pour our hot water—that's about all she's got left, hot water, and there's something funny about that, too, there really is. And I'm really dying now, pounding the table, making the condiment containers dance and slide around the surface.

"You guys are a couple of lunatics, you know that, right?" says Ruth-Ann.

We both look down, and then up at her. Culverson's shirt billows around my slender frame like a nightdress. Tufts of graying chest hair poke out over the V-neck of his undershirt. We laugh all over again, about our own ridiculousness, and then Culverson remembers he wanted to tell me about poor Sergeant Thunder, the weatherman, who has been waiting outside on his porch since six this morning, apparently, waiting for the convoy that's supposedly coming to escort him to the World of Tomorrow.

"I just know the dumb S.O.B.'s going to come over tonight," says Culverson, "wanting to borrow a cup of *everything*."

We collapse in fresh giggles, and Ruth-Ann shakes her head, over at her counter, turns back to the same issue of the *Monitor* everyone has been reading for a month.

"All right," I say to Culverson at last, pushing the last small teardrops from the corner of my eyes with the back of my working hand. "I'm going."

"Home?"

"Not yet. I've got a quick idea I want to follow up on, on the

Martha thing."

"Of course you do."

I smile. "I'll let you know what happens."

Houdini gets up as I get up, looks sharply into the corners of the room, stands stiff and straight with head cocked to one side.

"Oh, wait," says Culverson. "Hold on. Sit. Don't you wanna see it?"

"See what?"

"The samurai sword, man."

I sit. The dog sits.

"You said not to ask you about it."

"Well, yeah, you know. People say all kinds of stuff." He takes it out from under the table, slowly, one curved inch at a time: a real weapon, glinting in the pale light.

"Holy moly."

"I know."

"I said a toy sword."

"I couldn't find a toy one." He tugs the sweaty undershirt forward off his chest. "Listen, Stretch. You go solve your case. I'll find the kids."

I try and fail to hide the pleasure that this announcement brings me. I bite my lip, employ the dry and sarcastic voice I have learned, over many years, from Detective Culverson. "I thought you said there was no point in investigating anything."

"Yeah," he says, and stands, lifting the sword. "I know what I said."

4.

"No way," says Nico's awful friend Jordan, staring at me in the doorway of the vintage clothing store. "You're *kidding* me."

He's wearing jean shorts, the Ray-Bans, no shirt, no shoes. His hair is a slovenly mess. A blonde is passed out in a sleeping bag on the shop floor behind him, fast asleep, cheek pressed against the one slim bare arm thrown out from the bag.

"Jordan," I say, peering behind him into the store, the cluttered bins, big black garbage bags overflowing with wool socks and winter hats. "What are you doing here?"

"What am *I* doing here?" he says, pressing a hand into his bare chest. "*Ésta es mi casa, señor.* What are *you* doing here?" He looks at me in Culverson's oversized shirt. "Are you here for some clothes?"

"Nico said you were all going to the Midwest." I can't bring myself to say "to recon with the team." It's too ridiculous. "For the next phase of your plan."

We're still standing on the threshold of the store, desolate Wilson Avenue behind me. "These sorts of plans are changing all the time." Jordan lifts one foot to scratch the opposite calf. "I've been reassigned. This is team holding-down-the-fort."

The blonde girl makes a sleepy mew and stretches, rolls over. Jordan sees me watching her and grins wolfishly.

"Do you need something?"

"Yes," I say. "I do."

I step past him, into the shop, and Jordan makes a light *tsk-tsk*.

"Hey, that's trespassing, dude. Don't make me call the police."

I know this tone of voice, it's one of Nico's favorites, glib and self-satisfied; it was her tone at UNH when she told me what was in the duffel bag: guns, maple syrup, human skulls.

Jordan stoops to tug a ratty yellow T-shirt from one of the disheveled piles on the ground and pull it on over his head. The room smells like mildew or mold. I look around at the clustered mannequins, some dressed and some undressed, some raising hands in greeting, some staring into the room's dusty corners. Two of them have been arranged to shake hands, like one is welcoming the other to a board meeting.

"Jordan," I say, "Is it possible . . ."

"Yes?"

He stretches out the word, simpering, like an obsequious butler. The shirt Jordan has selected has Super Mario on it, mustachioed and hydrocephalic and mock heroic. If I am remembering this incorrectly, or imagining it, what Nico told me on the helicopter, I am going to sound like a moron—I am aware of that. On the other hand, this man, of all the people in the world, already finds me ridiculous: my aesthetic, my attitude, my existence.

"Is it possible that you have an Internet connection in here?"

"Oh, sure," he says, unhesitating, grinning, proud. "Why? You want to check your e-mail?"

"No," I say. In my chest there is a starburst of excitement, possibilities sparkling to life like fireworks. "I need to do a search."

* * *

We tiptoe past Sleeping Beauty to a door marked MANAGER'S OFFICE, where Jordan asks me to stare at the floor while he runs the numbers on a combination lock and lets us in. And there it is, in the tiny claustrophobic office space, jammed between a three-drawer filing cabinet and a small unplugged break-room refrigerator with a missing door: a desk of particleboard and glass, with a big ugly Dell computer, the tall processor tower listing alarmingly. Jordan sees my skeptical expression and brays laughter as he plops into the spinning office chair behind the desk.

"Oh, ye of little faith," he says, leaning forward to depress the power button. "Do you think the head of the National Security Administration is offline right now? What about His Honor the President?"

"I can't say I've really thought about it," I say.

"Maybe you should," he says, swiveling in the chair to wink at me. "You heard of sipper?"

"No."

"No?" He spells it, S-I-P-R. "Never heard of that?"

"No."

"What about nipper?"

"No."

He cranes his head around, chuckles. "God. Wow. You've heard of Google, right? It starts with a G."

I ignore him. I squint hopefully at the screen, feeling like I'm in the middle of some kind of elaborate practical joke. Indeed, in that long uncertain moment, waiting to see if the monitor's black screen will come to life, I suddenly feel like maybe the whole *thing* is a practical joke, that this whole final year of human history is just a prank that's been played on me, on gullible ol' Hank Palace, and that all the world is going to jump out of the closet here in the manager's office at Next Time Around and say "*Surprise!*" and all the lights will come on and all the world go back to how it was.

"Ah, come on, Scott," says Jordan idly, interrupting my reverie. He's staring at the still-blank screen, playing drums on his thighs.

"What's wrong?"

"There's this jackoff in Toledo who's never up and running when he says he's going to be."

"I don't know what you're talking about."

"That's because of your limited policeman's mind." Again, I don't take the bait; again, I remain impassive, waiting to get what I need. "The Internet isn't one big thing hovering in the sky. It's a bunch of networks, and people can't get to the networks anymore because the devices that got them there are powered by lots and lots of electricity. So we built new networks. I got this shitty computer and three landlines and a 12.8 modem and a gas tank's worth of juice, and I can connect to some dudes I know in Pittsburgh with the same setup, who can connect to Toledo, and so on into the beautiful forever. It's like a super-old-school mesh network. Do you know what a mesh network is? Wait, lemme guess."

He blows a bubble, pops it with one dirty fingernail. It's maddening; he's like an obnoxious seven-year-old that someone has installed at the helm of a vast international conspiracy.

"Of course, all the sites are mirrors, so a lot of stuff is missing or corrupted or what have you. But still impressive, right?"

"I would be a lot more impressed," I say, "if we weren't still staring at a blank screen."

But even as I say it, the screen glows to life with the shimmering variegated panes of the Windows 98 logo, flickering ghostly like a hieroglyph on a cave wall.

"Oo," says Jordan, leaning forward. "That kind of made you look like an asshole, the way that played out."

I listen to the familiar *hiss* then *click* then *beep* of a dial-up modem making its connection. There's a prickling sensation from deep somewhere in the nerves of my injured arm. I reach over with my left hand and squeeze the right biceps in its sling, massaging it with two fingers. Jordan clicks on the Start menu and calls up a blank screen, cursor blinking. He cracks his knuckles ostentatiously, like a maestro, while my mind buzzes and flits. I'm suddenly deep back into my casework, trying to decide what information I need most, what's worth trying for. Jordan, however, makes no move to cede me the chair.

"You tell me what you're looking for, and I find it for you."

"No," I say. "Absolutely not."

"Okay, so we move to option B, which is you fucking yourself." He grins at me. "The way this thing works, you can't just type in what you want. I gotta run code for every search."

"Fine," I say. "Fine."

"And just so you know, in general the more trivial the information that you're looking for, the less likely you'll find it on our server. But of course, we all have different definitions of *trivial*, don't we?"

Behind us we hear a rustling and Jordan yells, "Abigail? You're awake?"

"Yes," the girl calls back. "And not happy about it."

"Can we get started?" I say, and Jordan tells me to fire away and I fire away. "I need to search something called the NCIC."

"National Crime Information Center," says Jordan, already typing.

"How did you know that?"

"I know everything. I thought you had that figured out?" he says, fingers still dancing across the keys. "Hey, you don't need to access the Pentagon by any chance, do you?"

"No."

"Oh well."

I give him the details: Rocky Milano. White male, age approximately fifty-five to sixty. No known aliases.

He types. We wait. It works slowly, streams of text flutter past,
the monitor flickers from gray screen to gray screen. All of the familiar soothing icons of human–machine interaction are absent: the
hourglass, the whirling circles of light. Finally Jordan squints at the
screen, shrugs his shoulders, and turns around.

"Nope."

"Nope, what? It's not working?"

"It's working. I'm in there. But there's no listing."

"Is it possible you don't have the whole thing?"

"The whole database?"

"Yes. That this is an incomplete—what did you call it?"

"Mirror," he says. "An incomplete mirror of the original
archives."

"Yeah," I say. "Is it possible?"

"Oh, sure," he says. "Very possible. Probable, in fact."

I grimace. Of course. Nothing for good. Nothing for certain. I
direct Jordan to get out of the FBI database and execute a simple
Web search for Rocky's name, setting us up for a fruitless fifteen minutes of scrolling through hundreds of hits—on the real Rocky and
on dozens of other Rocky Milanos.

"Dude," says Jordan at last. "What exactly are you looking for?"

I don't answer. What *am* I looking for? The same rap sheet I was looking for when I was ten years old and "everybody knew" that Martha's dad was a crook—that he had knocked over a liquor store, killed a guy with his bare hands. I'm looking for anything that would confirm my indistinct and ill-formed hypothesis that Rocky Milano had the wickedness of character and/or talent at long-distance riflery to gun down his son-in-law in cold blood to prevent him from reporting Rocky on IPSS violations and leave him counting down the earth from a jail cell.

"Okey-doke, darling," says Jordan, spinning in the chair. "Time's up."

"Give me five seconds, okay?"

He rolls his eyes, counts: "One . . ."

I pace behind Jordan in the small room, trying to gather my thoughts and move on, push past the disappointment and irritation of this—of the whole thing. There's no way to know anything anymore, is what it feels like. It's started early, the era of terrible ambiguity scheduled to begin when Maia smashes into the Gulf of Boni and causes something terrible to happen but nobody knows exactly what. This age of uncertain terrors is metastasizing, growing backward, destroying not just the future but the present, poisoning everything: relationships, investigations, society, making it impossible for anyone to know anything or do anything at all.

"Hello? Nico's brother?" Jordan is saying. "I got shit to do. Important shit."

"Hang on. Wait."

"Can't."

"Nils Ryan," I say. "A state trooper."

"Spells Nils."

"No. Wait—Canliss. Can you look up the last name Canliss?"

Jordan sighs elaborately and then slowly turns back to the keyboard, letting me know one last time who is in charge of this operation. I spell the name for him and lean over his shoulder while he rattles the keys. First he checks the NCIC and there are no matches, which I did not think there would be, and then he executes a simple search. I lean farther forward, bent practically horizontal across his desk and watching the words flash to life, the lines of text roll up onto the screen, green on black.

"There," says Jordan, launching backward from the desk on his rolling office chair, banging against my legs. "Does that help?"

I don't answer. I'm off in the distance somewhere, I'm racing through the wilderness, I'm standing in a storm with my hands raised, reaching out for bits and flakes of ideas like falling snow. First I thought that Brett had been untrue to Martha, and then I thought that it was Martha who been untrue, but I had it wrong the whole time. All the wickedness lay somewhere else.

I know the name Canliss from Canliss & Sons, a vendor that had contracts with the Concord Police Department. When I was fresh on the force, three months in, Sergeant Belroy had the flu and I got stuck for three shifts doing accounts-receivable paperwork, and I remember the name. Canliss & Sons was a local concern, a New England outfit that sold the CPD specialized gear: night-vision goggles, Tasers, bipods. Ghillie suits.

Canliss & Sons of New England. I knew it. I knew that name.

"Hello? Nico's brother?" says Jordan, waving his hands over his head like semaphore. "Are we done?"

"We are, yes," I say. "We are done, and I'm going."

"Wow," he says, leaning forward to click off the monitor. "It's like you're allergic to it."

"To what?"

"To saying thank you."

"Thank you, Jordan," I say, and I mean it, I do. "Thank you very much."

He only turned off the monitor, I notice in passing, not the hard drive, meaning that my search is still sitting there, and my search history, a fact that does not make me wild with excitement. But I don't have any more time to mess around. I have to go—I have to go right now.

So of course Jordan leaps up out of his office chair and stands in the doorway. He leans against the lintel; this is his default position, loafing light-heartedly in a doorway, malevolence and aggression teasing out from behind his child's smile. As for me, I now have a clear and distinct mental image of Martha Cavatone, and she might be in Jeremy Canliss's basement or she might be in the trunk of a car or under a patch of floorboard, and I must get to her and I must get to her now.

"Jordan, I have to go."

"Yes, I know that," he says, thumbs looped in the belt loops of his jeans, just hanging out. "You said. But I just wanted to ask. Do you believe us now?"

"Do I believe what?"

"Well, it's just that Nico, you know, your sister, she was really hurt that you didn't believe her. About everything. Our group, our plans, our future."

He's speaking in a leisurely adagio, doing it on purpose, absorbing my sudden desperate impatience and feeding it back to me as a taunting molasses rhythm. "You probably don't realize how much you mean to her."

I calculate my odds of just busting past the man and running out of here. He is small but compact, energetic, and though I am much taller I am also exhausted, I have been on my feet all day after a night in the hospital, and I have one arm that is useless to me.

"To be honest with you, I had forgotten all about it."

"Oh, well," he says, and shrugs. "I'm reminding you."

I switch modes, drop into rapid-fire cop talk, keeping my voice even and open and honest. "Jordan, listen to me. There is a woman whom I believe to have been abducted and I need to help her right now."

"Seriously?" he says, eyes bulging. "Are you serious? Gee, you better go! Are you going to stop at a phone booth on the way, Nico's brother? Put on your cape?"

"Jordan," I say. I think maybe I could take him, actually. I don't care how many arms I have. "Move."

"Take it easy, dude." He blows a bubble, pops it with one finger. "All I asked is whether you believe us yet."

"Do I believe that because you have a helicopter and Internet access, that means you have the capability to alter the path of an asteroid? No. I don't."

"Well, see, that's your problem. Limited imagination."

I barrel forward and roll my shoulder into him, but he just steps out of the way, sending me stumbling wildly out of the manager's office. I straighten up and walk quickly toward the front of the shop, Jordan laughing behind me, and I've got the front door open and Houdini is waiting for me as instructed on the curb.

"It's Nico's problem, too, you know," he says, and I stop with my hand on the door and turn back around. Such an innocuous comment, nothing to it at all, but something in the way he said it—or is it just that there's something in the way he says everything?—I turn.

"What do you mean, it's Nico's problem, too? What is?"

"Nothing," he says, and smiles wickedly, delighted, a fisherman hauling in a live one.

Jordan's friend Abigail comes out of the bathroom, dressed in a flowery skirt and a tank top, her hair pulled back in a ponytail. "Jordan, did you know the water's out?" she says.

"I did, actually," he says. "I did. And I think we should probably stay in tonight."

He's talking to her but his gaze is locked on mine, and all the funny ha-ha clown nonsense is drained from his eyes and suddenly he's all low-down nasty menace. "All I was pointing out, Mr. Palace, is that your sister suffers from a similarly limited imagination. Haven't you ever felt that?"

I'm across the room in two long strides staring intently in his eyes and holding on to his arm with my one good hand. Abigail says "hey" but Jordan doesn't flinch.

"What do you mean?"

"Nothing," he says, and the clown's grin is back. "I'm just talking."

I tighten my grip on his arm. When I first heard about this elusive organization of Nico's was when she explained to me that her husband, Derek—who had thought he was on the inside, thought he understood it all—had been unknowingly sacrificed to a greater goal that he had no idea about.

"Where's that helicopter going, Jordan?"

There is, then, a massive explosion. It sounds close—loud—like the stumbling tread of a dinosaur.

"Uh-oh," says Jordan. "Looks like one of the rez associations is breaking out the big guns."

"South Pill Hill," Abigail says.

"You think?"

She nods and looks at him like, *duh, of course.*

"This is going to be some night," says Jordan. "Like the Fourth."

"Worse," she says, gives him the look again. I'm standing here looking back and forth between the two of them. "Way worse."

"What?" I ask angrily, even though I know exactly what they're talking about: it's what McGully said, exactly what he warned, shouting in the Somerset, *just wait until the water goes out.* "What do you know?"

"I know everything, man, remember?"

"It'll be a kind of war," says Abigail simply, talking softly from the doorway. "There's one residents association that's been hoarding Poland Spring bottles in the gym at the YMCA. Thousands of them. Another group has got a ton in the basement of the science center. Everybody's been hearing the rumors, everyone's got a plan to protect their own stash and go after the other stashes."

"Or make a go at the reservoir," says Jordan, peeling my fingers off his arm, one by one.

Abigail nods. "Well, yeah, the reservoir goes without saying."

"It's going to be like capture the flag, except with guns," says Jordan, and Abigail nods again. "*Lots* of guns."

As if to underscore the point there's a second reverberating explosion, and it's hard to say whether it was closer or farther than the first, but it definitely sounded louder. A pause, and then the chilling multilayered sound of a lot of people screaming at once, followed by the unmistakable typewriter rattle of machine-gun fire.

I'm listening to all this, breathing heavily, my head tilted to one side. It's the overwhelming police presence that's been keeping the fragile peace, everybody knows that, the DOJ cruisers, a cop on every block, that's what's prevented the wariness and anxiety of the population from bubbling over and bursting out like underground steam. I haven't seen a single policeman today. Not a single car.

"Hey, Henry? You better get going. It's going to be a busy night."

5.

It's the one asset I have left, the one piece of law-enforcement equipment that I still carry with me, my bone-deep knowledge of the streets of Concord. I biked them as a kid and drove them as an adult, and now I walk swiftly and unerringly, from Wilson Avenue back up toward Main Street.

My house is back to the west, past Clinton Street, but I'm headed the other way. I just have to—I just have to get this done. That's all.

Jordan was right: It's going to be a busy night. I can hear gunfire coming from a dozen different directions and see smoke rising from a dozen distant fires. I pass a mob of people, thirty at least, walking down the street all together in a tight quasimilitary formation, dragging a trail of shopping carts lashed together with ropes and dog leashes. A family of five hightailing it on foot down the center of the road, dad carrying two kids to his chest, mom carrying one, looking back anxiously the way they came.

Detective McGully, glowering again in my memory, red faced and jabbing his finger: *You just wait until there's no water, you just fucking wait.*

Houdini is scouting ahead of me with his mottled-fur flanks and predator's sneer, lips pulled back over yellow canines. I bend forward, hastening my stride to keep up with him as we pass the Water West building, pass the statehouse, pass the McDonald's where once upon a time I found the corpse of a suicide named Peter Zell hanging in the bathroom.

On Phenix Street, where the movie theater still stands, the marquee still advertising the final installment of *Distant Pale Glimmers* from two months ago, a guy wearing a baseball cap backward is rolling by on a skateboard, clutching what looks like a five-liter drum of spring water, trying to get somewhere fast. A young woman in flat black shoes and a housewife's apron appears out of the doorway of the theater with a shotgun and shoots him in the side, and he topples off the board and into the street.

I keep going, faster and faster. I shake it off, shake it all away—the fleeing family, the woman with the shotgun, Jordan's leering insinuation, Nico on her helicopter, Alyssa and Micah Rose at the Quincy Street playground—everything everything everything—I keep my head down and my mind focused on the case because I'm sick of wondering why I'm doing this, why I care. This is just what I have, it's what I do.

I take the left off Route 1 before I get to the Hood Factory, then a sharp right into the little tangle of streets behind the prison.

It's dusk now. The sun is pinking on the horizon line, getting ready to sink.

I drifted away from my family, kind of, was what Jeremy Canliss told me—drifted away, but not before he inherited some sniper equipment from Canliss & Sons, not before he learned how to use it. Spent some time on the rifle range, not a converted bowling alley but a real range, learned to take a crack shot from three hundred yards. The murder weapon might even have been a sniper rifle from Dad's old supply. Unless he picked it up along the way, an unexpected piece of good fortune, fate smiling on his plan. After he followed me to UNH, after he made his own way past the unevenly attentive perimeter guards—suddenly here's Julia Stone's miniature armory, and Jeremy helps himself to a weapon from the same stash where Brett got his.

Because it's clear now what happened: Jeremy wanted Brett gone, and then he followed me to make sure he stayed gone.

I'm running now. I'm almost there.

Canliss told me where he lives without intending to. At the other side of my kitchen table, sweating and stammering through his story, he said how he and Brett would sit on his porch, watching the thugs go in and out of the state pen, Brett saying "there but for the grace of God." There's only one short street that runs directly behind the New Hampshire State Prison for Men, and that's Delaney Street, and when I get there my watch says it's 8:45—Tuesday, I think, somehow it is still Tuesday, and darkness has drawn down along this short crooked street.

Normally it would take me an hour to work my way down a street of nineteen homes. But nine out of the nineteen are abandoned, front doors caved in, windows smashed or papered over. At one house, number six, on the north side, the tile of the roof has peeled off like skin, revealing the bent beams of the attic. Of the remaining ten houses, two have lit torches in the windows, and I decide to start with one of those, number sixteen Delaney Street. I rush across the darkness of its weedy lawn.

The prison is directly behind the house and it's on fire, bright walls of flame coming up out of the building's old western wing.

I raise my left fist and bang on the door, shouting "Martha!" and the door is answered by an elderly couple, cowering, hands in the air, the woman in a nightgown and the man in slippers and pajama bottoms, pleading with me to leave them be. I exhale, step back from the door frame.

"Sorry to bother you," I say. I take a step down the porch, then turn back before they've closed the door.

"I'm a policeman," I say. "Do you have food?"

They nod.

"How much?"

"A lot," says the woman.

"Enough," says the man.

"Okay," I say. Our bones are rattled by a reverberant boom from the southwest, the area of Little Pond Road and the reservoir.

"Do me a favor, folks: Don't answer your door anymore."

They nod, wide eyed. "You mean, tonight?"

"Just don't answer your door anymore."

The wind is picking up, summer breezes transforming into a panicky wind, sending leaves skittering down the street and banging garbage cans together and fanning the flames jumping up off the roof of the prison.

Houdini bounds down the porch ahead of me and we go to the other torch-lit house, number nine Delaney Street. As we cross the lawn, Houdini barks at the ground and some nocturnal creature leaps away from him, rustling a row of bushes. Even in the darkness the heat is unrelenting. My arm sweats in the sling. It's a rickety wooden porch, cluttered with old junk. The door is unpainted and there's a big New England Patriots beach towel strung across the front windows. This is right—it seems right—like just the sort of house where a quasi-employed twenty-year-old jack-of-all-trades would be crashing with assorted friends and acquaintances. I take the steps, two at a time, my heart beating fast for Martha.

Cortez was hit on the head this morning, he said, three hours before I got there. I got there at around 11:30. That means Martha was taken twelve hours ago. I bang on the door and call out "Jeremy—" the story alive and clear in my head.

Jeremy loved Martha. Martha loved her husband.

But canny young Jeremy had seen into the husband's secret heart, and he knew that what Brett wanted was to leave. He knew from long talks over grocery runs and late nights at the pizza joint that Brett's heart was straining at the leash: Here was a strange and high-minded man who wanted to use the last months to do some furious good in the world—who felt sure, in fact, that God was calling him to do so. But he was trapped by another kind of goodness, bound by his marriage vows.

And so Jeremy's plan, the forged diary page, the deceit, like something out of Shakespeare, something from the opera: exile the man by guile, take the woman by force.

"Jeremy?" I call again, rattle the handle.

Fresh gunfire rends the air like distant thunder, and I hear indiscriminate screaming and then, by some trick of the wind, snatches from a desperate conversation—"no, come on—no . . ." "shut up, you shut your mouth"—from some other crisis, some other corner of the city.

No one answers the door. The wind is rifling my hair, raising hackles on my neck. Time to get in there.

"Stay," I tell the dog. "Stand guard." He looks up at me, his head at a tilt, his teeth bared. "Anybody comes up the steps, bark. Anybody comes out but me, attack. Okay?"

Houdini settles on his haunches at the top of the stairs, silent and purposeful. I haul back and kick, hard, with my right foot. The thin wood splinters; my body explodes in pain. The tissue shrieks in my sewn-up arm. I scream and double over and scream again, hold my head down until the pain concludes its route along the lines of my leg into the arm and back down to the ground. Houdini stands there, eyes wide with sympathy and wonder, but keeping in position as I have instructed.

"Good boy," I mutter, breathing in and out, in and out. "Good boy."

When I can move I go inside, into a dark and cluttered living room, one flickering torch burning down in a vase. A suitcase is propped against the back wall, half open, a few T-shirts spilling out like clustered snakes. An unplugged refrigerator lies on its side in the front room like a beached whale; someone has spray painted DOES NOT WORK across the top of it.

"Martha?" I call, and again, shouting, stepping carefully forward, no gun, hands raised before me. "Martha?

To the right is an arched doorway leading to a kitchen, to the left a long hallway. I head to the hallway and trip on something—a pair of sneakers, tongues lolling out obscenely, no laces. Once, I bet, this house was littered with pizza boxes, beer cans; once the TV was always on, someone was always on the sofa getting high, people were stumbling into and out of the bathroom getting dressed for small-time retail gigs. It's dark now; now all these young men are gone, wandering around the world. I imagine them, one gone home to be with mom and dad, one coupled off in an asteroid marriage, one to New Orleans, off and running.

And one still here. One a kidnapper, a murderer.

I hear him just at the moment I see him, slumped on a landing at the top of the stairs, moaning.

"Hey," he says dimly, his voice thick. "Someone there?"

Jeremy Canliss is collapsed with his back against the bannister, hovering above me on the stair landing, the outline of a man against the darkness like a ghost caught halfway to heaven. The little ponytail is undone, and his hair is greasy and lank, framing the small scared face. His eyes are twitching and sorrowful, his cheeks red and flushed, like he's nothing but a kid with a crush, a kid with a crush on Martha Milano.

A long-barreled rifle with a mounted scope, the gun he used to shoot Brett Cavatone, lies next to him on the floor, the barrel facing the wall, the handle jammed awkwardly under his left buttock.

"It's Detective Palace, Jeremy." I say it strong, barreling my voice up the stairs. It feels good, just the action of raising my voice, dipping into that powerful tough-policeman register. "Stay right where you are."

"You're like a monster, dude," he says, light amusement coloring his strained voice. "From a monster movie. The man who would not fucking quit."

"I need you to stand up, please, and put your hands in the air."

He laughs and mutters, "Cool, man," but stays where he is, his head rolling a little on his neck. It's like he's the last man at the frat party, abandoned by his brothers to sleep it off on the landing, maybe tumble down the steps.

I have no authority. I have no gun. I take a step up, toward the killer.

"Where's Martha, Jeremy?"

"I do not know."

"Where is she?"

"I wish I knew."

I take another step.

"Who's N.?"

"Nobody," he whispers, laughs. "It stands for 'nobody.' Funny, right?"

I'm not laughing. I take another step, getting closer. He's still not moving.

"Why did you do it?" he asks me, petulant, childish.

"Why did I do what, Jeremy?"

"Go and get him. I *told* you not to do that. I *told* you." He looks at me with genuine bafflement, puzzled and sorrowful. "I just wanted my chance, you know? I just wanted a chance with her. I just needed her to be alone, so I could talk to her, so I could make her understand."

All this I already know. After he created his forgery, tore out a page from Martha's hot-pink cinnamon-scented diary and crafted the incriminating passage, he "discovered" it and passed it on to Brett.

Jeez, man, I don't know how to tell you this . . . this was just, like, lying open . . . in your house . . . I'm sorry . . . I'm really sorry.

Any husband would have been skeptical, would have confronted his wife, demanded an explanation, hoped for a misunderstanding. Except for Brett: the husband who *wanted* to go, who wanted his marriage to be over, for the contract to be abrogated so he could go off and do God's work in the woods.

"He didn't even love her," Jeremy says, shaking his head, looking up at the ceiling. "You know? He didn't even love her. *I* love her."

"Where is she?" I ask him again, and he doesn't answer.

Another step and now I'm halfway up the flight of steps, almost within lunging distance of that damn rifle. I picture the physical motions—one last quick leap upward, push the suspect to the left with the force of my body, grab the rifle from under his body with my right hand. I don't have a right hand.

"Where is she, Jeremy?"

"I told you. I told you I don't know."

"That's not true."

I'm trying to keep my voice even, be calm, be cool, let him know that he can trust me, but inside I am exploding with anger at this foolish child and his stupid useless violent love. A year and a half ago all of this would have been a postadolescent crush, a daydream about a buddy's wife. But in Maia's shadow it's blossomed like nightshade, become a crazed obsession, a murderous plot.

He licks his lips, brings a hand up and rubs his face. I'm starting to get the very strong impression that the kid is high as a satellite, that he's drifting somewhere out of radio's reach.

"Martha?" I shout, loud, and get no reaction—not from Jeremy and not from some distant corner of the house, not from any closet or crawl space. "Martha, it's Henry. I need you to yell if you can hear me."

"Shut up," Jeremy says sharply, suddenly, anger clouding his voice. He shifts on the steps and grabs the butt of the rifle. The scruff of a beard, the sad little-boy face. "She's not *here*. I wish she was here, but she's not."

He says the words so quiet and soft, *I wish she was here, but she's not*, and I get very cold, like my insides are an underwater cavern suddenly flooded with frozen sea.

"Is she dead now? Did you kill her, Jeremy?"

"No. I just wanted to talk to her."

"You went to get her. This morning?"

"Yes." He nods, mouth slack and open.

"What happened, Jeremy?"

"Nothing. She was gone." He looks at me, helpless, confused. "There was some man there, I saw him—"

"Cortez. You attacked him. On the porch."

"No . . . no, he was inside. Martha was gone. I didn't understand. I left."

"That's not true, Jeremy." I shake my head, speak gently, coaxing. "What did you do to her?"

"I told you, she wasn't there." He twitches and yelps, rising quickly, improbably, to his feet. "I told you. I love her."

He stumbles toward me, the gun raised, and I take a step back on the stairs, putting up my one good hand in front of my face as if I could catch a bullet, like Superman, pluck it from the air and throw it back at him. A year and a half ago, I would have been a detective, interviewing suspects—except not even. I still would have been a patrolman, looping Loudon Road, picking up shoplifters and litterbugs.

"Jeremy—"

"No more," he says, and I say, "No, please—" and he's waving the thing in a wide arc as he comes down the steps, now the barrel is aimed at the wall, now at the floor, and then at me, right at my face.

My heart flutters and dives. I don't want to die—I don't—even now, I want to keep living.

"Wait, Jeremy," I say. "Please."

There's a bang at the bottom of the stairs, as loud as a firework, and Jeremy's eyes go wide and I whip around to see what he sees. The wind carried open the splintered door, flung it aside to reveal Houdini on the porch, staring stone-faced into the house, silent and cruel, eyes unwavering and teeth bared, sides flecked with ash and mud. The dog is lit from behind by the roaring furnace of the prison. Jeremy shrieks as the dog glares up at us, yellowed and ferocious and strange, and I leap up the three steps remaining and press my left forearm into Jeremy's throat to pin him to the wall.

"Where is she?"

"I swear—" He's struggling to breathe. Staring goggle eyed over my shoulder at the dog. "I swear, I don't know."

"Not true." I tower over the kid. I'm leaning into his throat with the blunt object of my arm, and it's killing him and I don't care. "You saw Cortez coming and you smashed him with a shovel."

He gasps, squeezes out words. "I don't know who that is." He struggles, breathes. "I would not hurt her."

I stare at his terror-stricken eyes and try to think. She waved me away, Cortez had said, she treated him like a Jehovah's Witness. Why did she do that, dismiss her protector? And she had a suitcase, he said, she was waiting for someone. Not Jeremy, surely—but who? I'm thinking about the timing of this—what day was Brett shot and when did Jeremy get back from shooting him and what time this

morning did Martha tell Cortez to leave her be? The world is spinning, days and events spilling over one another like loose marbles in
a bag.

"I'll die," Jeremy gasps, and I recover myself and I let him loose.

"No, you won't."

"You don't understand," he says. "I'm already dead."

I can see it now, in his eyes, the welling sickness, the pupils
tightening. *Dammit*.

"Come on," I say, crouching, pulling on his left arm with my
left arm. "Let's get to the bathroom."

He waves me off, slumps back against the bannister.

I roll him down the stairs, drag him to the bathroom, watching
the black bruise take shape across his Adam's apple where I attacked
him. I don't know when he took the pills, I don't know how long
he was sitting there before I showed up. If I can get him to the john
I can bend him over the toilet, get those pills up. Clear whatever it is
from his system. I can do that. His body can't have metabolized much
of the poison, not yet, it's too soon.

"Jeremy?"

Laboriously I settle him on his knees in front of the toilet and
he wobbles, body rolling forward and back. I clap my hands in front
of his face. His head lists on his neck and his torso slides forward.

"Jeremy!" I throw the taps so I can splash cold water on his
face, and of course nothing comes out. The flesh of his body is getting strangely warm, like he might begin to melt like a wax candle,
turn from solid to liquid and drip away from my grasp.

I try one more time: "Where's Martha, Jeremy?"

"You'll find her," he says, almost gently, encouragingly, like a coach—and you can really see it, with an overdose, you can watch the light dripping out of someone's eyes. "I bet you can find anyone."

* * *

Houdini and I look in every corner of that house. In every corner and under every bed and mattress, in the cheap wood pantry, overrun with roaches and water bugs, in the dark spiderwebbed corners of the basement.

My arm swells and radiates heat and pain. Sweat runs down my forehead and into my eyes. We look and look.

But it's not that big a house, and I'm not looking for misplaced keys or a wayward pair of glasses. It's a human being. My terrified friend, bound and trembling, or her body, hollow and staring. But we keep looking. There's no attic; the second-floor bedrooms are arched and peaked, but I get up on a chair and bang on the plaster of the ceiling to eliminate the possibility of a hidey-hole or secret room where Martha might have been shoved, duct-taped and struggling. The closets, the kitchen, the closets again, tearing everything out, kicking against the beadboard for a false back or hidden chamber.

Houdini yelps and sniffs at the floorboards. I find a claw hammer in a tool chest in the pantry, and I use the claw to pry up the floor in the living room, board by board, my back aching against the strain of it. I ignore the stabs of pain and the waves of nausea, drag up the boards one at a time like peeling open a stubborn fruit, but beneath the floor is insulation and pipes and the view of the basement.

I check it again, the basement, but she's not there—she's not here—she's nowhere.

I keep looking. The noise of the guns and the screaming outside, the windows lit up with the fire across the street, I keep looking, long after even the most diligent investigator would be forced to conclude that Martha Milano is not inside this house.

I look and look and scream her name until I'm hoarse.

* * *

Jeremy's body I leave in the bathtub. There is no other option that makes sense. I happen to know that the Willard Street Funeral Parlor is home now to a clutch of doomsday prophets, just as I happen to know that the morgue in the basement of Concord Hospital is abandoned, Dr. Fenton now upstairs doing furious triage along with whoever else is around.

There is nowhere to report this death or deliver this corpse, because suddenly the streets are on fire and ours is a savage land. I lay the man out more neatly in his claw-footed bathtub, push his eyelids shut with my forefingers, and go.

6.

My house is gone.

When at last the dog and I get back to my address on Clinton Street, we find just the bones of a house, just the beams, leaning precariously in the summer darkness among the shadowy silver maples. It was stripped for the metal and the siding and the bricks and then burned; or possibly it burned first, and then the looters came and carried away the remains. Grim drifting heaps of ash and stray pieces of furniture. My hoard of goods, my jars of peanut butter and my gas mask and my jugs of water, these were beneath the floorboards under the sofa in the back end of the living room. The hoard is gone. The floorboards are gone. The sofa is gone. The living room is gone.

Houdini and I wander slowly through the ruins like we're walking on the moon. The cement foundation is still in place, and I can trace the rough outlines of where the rooms used to be: the living room, the bathroom, the kitchen. Disintegrating plasterboard piles that used to be walls. Houdini noses at the wreckage and comes up with a table leg, clutched in his jaws like a shankbone. I find my copy of Farley and Leonard's *Criminal Investigation*, charred, recognizable by the pattern of colors on the cover. Piano keys like teeth. A scattering of old Polaroids: my parents mugging at a holiday party, Dad in a mistletoe cap, Mom's lips brushing his cheek.

I am aware, in an abstract way, that this is a catastrophe. The countdown has begun, and all the haphazard arrangements—the rummages and the ersatz restaurants and the bartering and the residents associations—all of the vestigial institutions are crumbling into the past, and it's every man for himself from now on, and here I am with no house, no gun, no possessions of any kind. I'm down one arm. I'm wearing a borrowed shirt and torn suit pants.

But what I feel is nothing. Numbness and cold. I'm a house full of burned-out rooms.

I told Martha I would make every effort to find her husband and bring him home. I told her I could do it. I promised.

The man she longed for is dead. And now she, too, is dead, or somewhere dying, somewhere alone, and the only person who knows her whereabouts is yet another dead man. The world collapsing, turning into death, disappearing before my eyes.

I sat at her kitchen table, smiled to see her again after all these years, looked into her worried eyes, and made a promise.

Houdini hunts around me in a circle, nose down, lifting and then dropping bits of plaster with his sharp teeth.

There is a bright and beautiful glow in the direction of downtown, a radiant bulb, pulsing with light. I stare at it until I understand that this is the capitol dome of the statehouse of New Hampshire, and that it is on fire.

The practicalities of my situation are hard to grasp. I will need help, but from whom? Dr. Fenton? Culverson?

I sink down cross-legged in the dirt and Houdini takes a position next to me, erect and watchful, panting. I lift a photograph from the mud, Nico and me with arms wrapped around each other at her high-school graduation. My expression is adult, serious, self-congratulatory, quietly proud for having seen to it that she made it to that day. Nico for her part is grinning, ear to ear, because she was high as a satellite.

I could have stayed on that helicopter. Could be in Idaho or Illinois right now, reconning with the team. Saving the world.

The thought of Nico is suddenly devastating, and I can't pretend to be cynical about it, not even to myself—the idea that I'm sitting here, and she is there. What have I done? *What have I done?* I should have stayed on that helicopter. I never should have let her go. I lie in the rutted crater that was my home and consider my choices: calling my sister a fool for pursuing a one-in-a-million chance at survival while I'm the one who's accepted a hundred percent chance of death.

A screech of tires and the slam of a car door, ancient and familiar sounds, and I sit upright and jerk my head around and Houdini takes a stance and barks. Parked diagonally across my yard is a

Chevrolet Impala, the standard Concord Police Department vehicle, a glimmer of moonlight dancing across the hood.

Footsteps, getting closer. I struggle to my feet. Houdini barks louder.

"Let's go, Henry."

Trish McConnell. I gape at her, and she grins like a naughty kid.

"What are you *doing* here?"

"Saving your life, Skinny." Officer McConnell somehow looks more like a cop when she's out of uniform: short and tough in blue jeans and a black T-shirt. "What happened to your arm?"

"Oh—" I wiggle the thick limb. It hurts. "It's fine. What's happening?"

"I'll tell you in the car. Come on."

I look at Trish and then toward downtown, toward the fires and the wildness. The city smells like smoke. "Shouldn't you be on patrol?"

"No one's on patrol. Our orders were to stand down, let this shit burn itself out. Risk no department resources. The rest of the force is at School Street, drinking beer and looking at dirty magazines."

"So, why aren't you there?

"I don't like dirty magazines." She laughs. McConnell is all fired up, that much is clear, this is her play, she's ready to roll. "I am away without leave, Officer Palace, and I ain't going back. I borrowed the Chevy from the Justice Department and I am taking off, right now, very quickly, and you're coming, too."

"Why me?"

She smiles cryptically. "Come on, you dummy."

The vehicle is on and purring, the exhaust from some real genuine DOJ regular unleaded gasoline pouring out of the tailpipe. It's a beautiful thing, a Chevrolet Impala, it really is, clean lines, efficient: a pure police car. Houdini is over there, peering up at its tinted windows. I'm trying to think quickly and smartly, trying to process everything. The statehouse is blazing ferociously in the distance, a Roman candle burning down in the heart of our little skyline.

"Come on, Palace," says McConnell, standing at the driver's side door. "The worst of the chaos is up by the reservoir, but we're going exactly the other way." She pounds on the hood of the car. "You ready to rock?"

"Yeah," I say. "Let me just . . ." I look around. I have no suitcase. No clothes to pack. Someone took my house. I tug Culverson's dress shirt closer around me and walk toward the car. "Okay," I say. "Let's go."

The shotgun seat is stuffed with suitcases and cardboard cartons of food and bottles of Gatorade. So I slide into the backseat next to McConnell's children, and Houdini takes a position between us.

"Hi," I say to Kelli and Robbie, as McConnell guns it and screeches out onto Clinton Street. Robbie has his thumb in his mouth, a ragged blue teddy bear tucked against his chin. Kelli looks solemn and scared.

"What kind of dog is that?" she asks me.

"A bichon frisé," I say. "He's tougher than he looks."

"Really?" says Kelli. "He actually looks pretty tough."

* * *

McConnell takes the Chevy down Clinton Street, away from downtown, toward the highway, and while Houdini consents for Robbie to tickle his neck scruff, I lean forward into the mesh grate and ask McConnell where we're going.

"The mansion."

"What mansion?

"I told you, Palace." She laughs. "Me and some of the others, the old-timers—Michelson, Capshaw, Rodriguez—we blocked this all out months ago.

"Oh, yeah," I say. "Oh right."

"It's in Western Mass., a little town called Furman, near the New York border. We got the place all set up. Plenty of water, plenty of food. Cooking oil. Necessary precautions." She raises her voice, glances in the rearview mirror. "And there are even some kids there, other kids. Officer Rogers has twin boys."

"Those guys are assholes," says Kelli, and McConnell says, "Language, honey," and leans on the gas, hits ninety miles an hour, sure and straight, barreling over back roads on the way out of town.

"I thought you were kidding about all that. The mansion in the country. The whole thing."

"I never kid."

McConnell smiles, sly, elusive, proud, the Impala whooshing along Highway 1, the Merrimack a brown ribbon to our left. Holy moly, I think, holy cow, easing back into my seat. Western Mass.

Kelli asks for a bottle of water so Houdini can have a drink, and Mc-Connell pushes two bottles through the seat-grate opening, not without a small wince of anxiety—nothing as precious as a bottle of water. I say thanks on the dog's behalf, and McConnell says, "Sure," says "Drink one yourself, you damn scarecrow."

McConnell, I like—I always have.

The moon glimmers through the tinted backseat windows of the Impala as we rattle over untended roads, out across the bridge, toward the junction with 89 South, the city in flames all around us. Robbie falls asleep. We roar past a long line of people, a block and a half long, lugging backpacks and duffel bags and pulling rolling suitcases, a residents' association heading together into exile by some prearrangement, headed out of town but God knows to where.

Despite everything, I lean back and let the exhaustion overtake me, let my eyelids drift and flutter, Houdini safe in Kelli's lap beside me, and I start to feel that kind of dreamy magic that comes with car rides late at night.

There's a word my mind is looking for.

I said, *McConnell, what are you doing here?* and she said, *Saving your life, Skinny*.

What's the word I'm looking for?

I lay in the dirt patch that had been my house, and the Impala came and what did she offer me?

Tell him he has to come home, Martha said, urgent and imploring. *Tell him his salvation depends on it.*

My eyes shoot open.

Kelli and Houdini are both snoring gently; we're way on the outskirts of the city by now, coming up on its limits and the westward highway.

Salvation.

All these people braving the terrible seas, getting shot or dragged out of the water in nets, casting themselves upon unfamiliar shores in search of what—the same thing my sister is chasing across the country in a stolen helicopter.

Salvation. And not in some glorious tomorrow, not in the majestic heights of heaven. Salvation *here*.

I've got no notebook. No pencil. I squeeze my eyes shut, try to do the timeline work, put it together, see if this makes sense.

Sergeant Thunder got that stupid brochure last week and bartered away his worldly goods last week, but evacuation day was *today*—Culverson saw him today, out on his porch, waiting and waiting, miserable and forlorn. That was *today*.

"McConnell?"

"Yeah, buddy."

Cortez saw her waiting on her porch at let's call it 8:30 this morning, waiting for someone. Jeremy got there at nine or ten, desperate and excited, ready to make his lovesick plea, but Martha was gone. Long gone.

"McConnell, I need to make just one quick stop."

"*What?*"

"Or—it's okay—you can drop me off."

"Palace."

"I'll catch up with you. Leave me the address. I need to get to this pizza place."

"A pizza place?"

"It's called Rocky's. Up by Steeplegate Mall."

Officer McConnell is not slowing down.

"One quick stop, Trish." I lean forward and plead into the mesh, like a criminal, desperate, like a sinner to his confessor. "Please. One stop."

7.

McConnell growls and goes full code, kicks on the lights and screamers and throws the Impala into a fishtailing U-turn, takes us a thousand miles an hour toward Rocky's Rock 'n' Bowl up by the mall. She veers onto the sidewalk to get around a thick mob milling about at the intersection of Loudon Road and Herndon Street. Half of them have big flashlights, most of them have handguns, and they're circled around a cluttered herd of shopping carts. One man in a leather jacket and motorcycle helmet is hanging from the top of a lamppost, shouting at them, instructions or warnings. I squint at the man as we race past—when I was a kid, he was our dentist.

As we slam to a stop outside Rocky's, I can see two distinct pyres radiating up from the different wings of the Steeplegate Mall.

"Minutes," says McConnell angrily. "This block will be on fire within five minutes."

"I know."

Kelli is waking, looking around, as I jump out of the car.

"I'm serious, McConnell," I call. "Go if you have to."

"I will," she says, shouting after me as I run toward the pizza place. "I'm *going* to."

The doors are closed and looped with chains. I'm wondering if it's too late, but I don't think it is. I think they're still in there, Martha and her father, Rocky. The city is on fire and they're huddled and waiting like Sergeant Thunder for salvation that is not coming. Huddled together in the center of that giant room, the vast space emptied of its valuables, everything turned over to the con: the wood-burning oven, the paintball guns and targets, the heavy appliances with their yards of copper and coolant and gas tanks.

I bang again, kick at the glass. Rocky and Martha in there, sitting, going crazy. They've been in there since this morning, since Rocky showed up to get her, today's the day, no more waiting around for your stupid runaway husband. Bad luck for Cortez that he happened to be there when Rocky arrived, time ticking away, in no mood to discuss a damn thing with anyone. He just needed his daughter, and he needed her now. Today was the big day—not a moment to waste.

I move to the left, along the wall of the building, occasionally pounding on one of the windows with the heel of my good hand. No chance of kicking open this door; it's thick Plexiglas. If Jeremy stopped by here after Martha's house, and I bet he did, he would have found another dead end, another place his true love had disappeared from. No wonder he went home and ate poison.

But they're in there. Waiting. I know they are. The world collapsing all around them and still waiting for the men who promised
they would come.

"Hey?" I shout, slamming against the window. "Hey!"

I shield my eyes and try to peer through the tinted glass, but I
can't see anything, and maybe they're not in here, maybe I've got it
wrong. Martha's not here to be rescued and I'm risking my life and
McConnell's and the kids', too, for nothing. I glance back over my
shoulder and I can see Trish glaring from the driver's seat. I hope she
does, I hope she goes, takes her children and my dog and abandons
me for safety.

It's hot, it's so hot, even in the middle of the night, the black
summer night tinted by the crazy oranges and yellows of the fires.

I yell their names again—*Rocky! Martha!*—but there must be
one more code word, a shibboleth they memorized at the behest of
the smooth-talking salesmen from the World Beyond, something
they're expecting to hear when the nice men from the rescue convoy
roll up in their black cars and jumpsuits. I turn around. McConnell
is still sitting there. I jab one finger in the air and I whirl it around, a
little piece of police sign language, and in case she can't see me or
doesn't understand, I yell it: "Lights, McConnell," I holler. "Turn on
the lights."

McConnell turns on the lights. They spin on the top of the car,
the classic cop-show colors, blue reflecting on black. It's a cruel trick,
but I need Martha out here. I need her to come out and you can't

tell a trooper car from a CPD Impala, not from inside a dark restaurant. And it works. She sees what she wants to see, just like she did in her dream. The door slams open and she races out, flies toward the car.

"Martha."

But she doesn't wait; she races past me to the police car, stares into the windows. I see McConnell up front and Kelli in the backseat, jerking backward, away from the desperate phantom at the window. He's not in there and she spins around as Rocky Milano comes lumbering out to retrieve her. He's out of his apron, in a sweat suit, his bald forehead red and dripping with sweat.

Martha runs back toward me, whipping her head one way and another, her cheeks flushed. Her pale eyes are wide with need. "Where is—where is he?"

"Martha—"

"*Where is he?*" cries Martha, lunging at me across the lot.

I don't know what to say, how much of the story is worth telling. A kid was obsessed with you. He tricked your husband into leaving. Your husband went on a madman's crusade. He was shot and he died in a field by a beach.

"Where is he?"

"Martha, get inside," says Rocky. "It's dangerous out here."

"That's right," I say. "Time to go."

Rocky peers at me like a stranger. Barely recognizes me. He's focused on the next step of his life, on cashing in the promise of escape he's been given—for himself and his daughter and for his

son-in-law, too, until Brett's mysterious disappearance. I wonder if
he asked the World Beyond people for that special: "Hey can this guy
get in there, too? My daughter won't come without him." I wonder
if the hucksters hemmed and hawed and finally agreed, no skin off
their backs, peddling one more nonexistent spot in their nonexistent
underground compound.

"Where's Brett, Henry?" says poor Martha, and I just tell her, I
say, "He's dead," and she collapses to the ground on her knees, buries
her face in her hands and wails, one long keening senseless syllable.
That's the end of the world right there for Martha Milano.

"Sweetheart?" Rocky is all business, heaving her up by the
armpits and clasping her with his big hands. "It's okay. We're going
to mourn him, but we're going to move on. Come on. We're moving on."

He's dragging her back toward the building, which will be on
fire any minute now. McConnell honks the horn. But I can't leave. I
can't leave her here. I can't let her die.

"Martha," I call. "You were right. There was no other woman.
He was—he was doing God's work."

Martha pulls away from her father. She looks at me, and then
up at the sky, at the asteroid, maybe, or at God. "He was?"

"He was." I take a step toward Martha, but Rocky grabs her
again.

"Enough," he says roughly. "We need to get inside and wait securely until they come."

"They're not coming," I say, to him, to her. "No one's coming."

"What? What the hell do you know?" Rocky steps toward me, veins bulging on his forehead.

But he understands—he's got to understand—some part of him must surely understand. Whatever time they told him the convoy would arrive, that time has long since passed. Even old Sergeant Thunder let himself admit it many hours ago.

I keep my voice calm and even, authoritative, as much for Martha's benefit as for Rocky's. "There is no such thing as the World Beyond. You've fallen prey to a con artist. No one is coming."

"Bullshit," says Rocky, pushing his hand into my chest, rolling me back on my heels. "Bull. *Shit*." He turns to Martha, grinning uneasily. "Don't worry, sweetheart. I did *everything* these people asked. Everything."

There's a rolling crash behind us, and everybody turns: it's the roof of the Steeplegate Mall, just across the parking lot, caving in with a series of splintering cracks. McConnell leans on the horn and I wheel around and shout, "I'm coming, here I come," and then I reach for Martha again, hold open my hand to her.

"Martha."

"No," says Rocky. "They're coming. They're fucking coming. We have a contract."

A contract. This is what he's got and he's going to stand on it. No shaking him loose. No making him see sense, because now, at this pass, this *is* sense. This is what's left of sense. And the helicopter did come for Nico, that is true, that did happen, and maybe Jesus Man really went to Jesus, and maybe *this* convoy is different from the one that didn't come for Sergeant Thunder: Maybe it's just up the road, maybe it's a con and maybe it's not. Nothing—nothing—nothing can be counted on, nothing is certain.

"Stay," I say to Rocky. "But let Martha go."

He shakes his head, starts to speak, but Martha interrupts him, suddenly composed, calm, clear as daylight. "Go?" she says. "Go *where?*"

That I cannot answer. The woman is waiting in a burning parking lot for an imaginary line of cars, and I have no better option for her. McConnell's country cop shop is not mine to offer. My own house was stripped from boards to beams. The world is running out of safe places.

"Thank you, Henry," says Martha Milano, and leans forward and kisses me gently, leaving the barest trace of lip gloss on my cheek. I raise one hand to touch the spot with two fingers. She's gone already, clutching her father's solid arm as he leads her back inside to wait for doomsday.

"I'm so sorry, McConnell," I say, as I dive back into the Impala. "Let's go."

EPILOGUE

....

Sunday, August 12

....

Right Ascension 19 03 39.1
Declination -68 41 32
Elongation 122.0
Delta 0.677 AU

We all hear it at the same time. It's the middle of the night and the house comes to life, cops rolling out of bed or leaping off mattresses, jamming guns into the waistbands of sweatpants; cops sticking their heads into the bedrooms crowded with kids, whispering "stay where you are, guys" and "everything's fine"; cops streaming outside to back up Officers Melwyn and Kelly, who are on porch duty tonight and are therefore the commanding officers on the scene, per our agreed-upon rules of engagement.

"Three sharp crashes," barks Officer Melwyn, holding his Beretta up against his chest, addressing the group. "On the property or just over the line."

"We need a team for the south lawn," says Officer Kelly, everybody nodding, weapons drawn. I'm carrying a SIG Sauer now, the same handgun I used to carry on patrol. We're breaking into clusters, getting ready to move, when we all hear the noise again: a loud crashing, like metal on metal, and everybody freezes.

"It's a bear," says Officer McConnell.

"What?" whispers Melwyn.

"Look. Bear."

We all look, the group of us, a crowd of cops on a porch in the western woods of Massachusetts at two, maybe three o'clock in the morning, flooded with adrenaline and staring at the massive lumbering figure of a brown bear pawing at the door of the shed. It's one of our several outbuildings, and it houses blocks of ice, barrels of raw sugar and salt and dried oats, boxes full of iodine tablets and bleach, stores of ammunition and a few pounds of explosives. For a second we are all paralyzed, awed by the burly majesty of the bear. It gives up on the padlocked shed and lopes across the lawn, making its shaggy way back toward the surrounding brush.

"Beautiful," whispers McConnell.

"Yeah," I say.

"We should shoot it," says Capshaw.

No one objects. Officer Capshaw steps down off the porch, a big man with a moon of a head and a buzzed scalp. He aims a rifle in the moonlight and brings down the bear with two quick shots, *pop, pop.*

Volunteers are asked for to skin and dress the bear, and the rest of us go back to bed.

* * *

What the children decided, after much debate and discussion, was that the big converted-barn country house in Furman, almost at the New York state line, should just be called Police House. Some of the younger kids spent a whole afternoon in secret, in the area of the barn designed for arts and crafts, painting an elaborate sign for Police House, with golden badges, arcing rainbows, peace signs, and sparkling silver stars. Among the adults there was intense debate, much to the children's consternation, about the wisdom of hanging such a colorful display above the eaves of what is, after all, a hideout. I was among the most skeptical. Trish, however, took the kids' side: "It's not like we're inconspicuous anyway, right?"

We are nineteen adults and thirteen kids altogether: all policemen and policewomen and police spouses and the children of police, plus three members of the support staff, including Rod Duncan, the saturnine but beloved ex-con who served as the CPD janitor for twenty-nine years. The children range in age from four to fifteen. Houdini is not the only pet: there are two cats, one rabbit, and a goldfish bowl that was transported effortfully by Officer Rogers' nine-year-old twins, balanced on laps for two hundred forty miles at ninety miles an hour. There is also a massive sheepdog named Alexander, the property of a patrolwoman named Rhonda Carstairs. Alexander is a shambling old creature with watery eyes and a befuddled expression who, despite being ten times Houdini's size, follows my dog around like an aide-de-camp.

Despite the size of the house and its attendant outbuildings, sleeping space is limited, and at some point Officer McConnell and

I made the mutual decision, with very little discussion, to share a bedroom. I asked her if she felt it was important to have a conversation with Kelli and Robbie about this, maybe offer some delicate explanation of the change, but Officer McConnell said no.

"They like you," she says. "They're happy."

"Are you happy?" I say.

"Well, shit." She leans against my torso. "As happy as it's gonna get. How's the arm?"

"I can feel it. When I poke it, it hurts."

"So stop poking it."

This was a Saturday morning, last Saturday—we were standing on the porch watching Kelli and two of the other kids on an improvised parade, with Houdini yipping along beside them like he was Secret Service protection, Alexander shambling behind.

* * *

Officer Capshaw and I are the guards on duty, and he is in the woods just past the property line, urinating against a tree, when a slow-moving vehicle appears in the distance, a dim bobbling light a hundred yards or so down the one narrow lane that approaches the house.

I stand up. Houdini stands up, too, tail at a sharp angle, snout pointed out toward the road, toward the strange noise we're hearing now: the unmistakable clip-clop of hooves along the roadway.

Houdini barks. "I know," I say. "I know."

It's a horse and carriage, appearing out of the darkness as if from the pages of a fairy tale, rattling along the graveled county road toward the house. Perched on the seat is Cortez, grinning, in a top hat, holding the reins of a speckled mare with comical gentility.

"Oh, hello," he says, reins in the horse and tips his hat. He's wearing his hair in a loose ponytail, like Thomas Jefferson.

I keep the gun raised. "How did you find me here?"

"You don't want to know how I got the carriage and the horse?"

"I want to know how you found me."

"Fine." Cortez climbs out of his gig and tosses the top hat onto the porch, as if he's been living here all along and is very happy to be home. "But the horse story is better."

"Keep your hands where I can see them, please."

He sighs and obeys, and I ask him again for the story. Turns out there's a young officer named Martin Porter who was part of the original Furman-house plan but dropped out when he met a girl in Concord who wanted to go to Atlantic City because she'd heard about a countdown party getting going down there. Cortez knew Porter because Porter had a bunch of crystal meth he'd gotten from the evidence room before it was sealed, and Cortez had been selling it for him, fifty-fifty split, to some beach junkies on the Seacoast.

"Anyway, last week Ellen and I had a bit of a disagreement." Cortez waggles his left hand, and I see in the dim light of our outside torches that the tip of his pointer finger has been shot off. "And she got custody of our Office Depot. Porter tells me about this crazy hideaway in the woods, for policemen only! And I thought to myself: Hey, I know a policeman."

I am trying to formulate a reaction to some part of this story when Capshaw returns dramatically, bursting out of the woods with his gun drawn and aimed at Cortez.

"Put your hands in the air," he barks.

"My hands are already in the air."

"Who the fuck are you?"

"It's okay, Capshaw," I say. "I know him."

"I didn't ask if you know him, I said who *is* he?"

Capshaw is all keyed up, ready to make an arrest, build a jail and toss this guy in it. He's red faced, stormy eyed, brow furrowed under his crew cut. His T-shirt says Señor Frog's Spring Break Fiesta Cancun 1997.

"Hey, you know what you should do?" says Cortez mildly. "Search the carriage."

Capshaw looks at me and I shrug. He does it, stomps down the porch steps and begins rifling through the carriage while the horse shivers and tosses his head in the darkness. I keep the SIG Sauer pointed at Cortez as he leans against the rail of the porch stair, hands still in the air, unconcerned, humming. "Golden Years." David Bowie.

"Clothing. Personal effects," reports Capshaw, zipping closed a small black toiletries bag and tossing it in the dirt.

"There're Ecstasy pills there, too," says Cortez, to me, confidentially. "He missed the Ecstasy pills."

"Cooking oil," says Capshaw, taking out two big plastic drums.

"A box full of magazines."

"Mostly that is pornography."

"Knives," says Capshaw. "More knives."

Cortez looks at me, winks. "He'll find it in a second. Don't worry."

And then I hear it, a thick rustling sound like quarters in a casino cup. Or beans. My God. Beans tumbling over one another in a foil package. My heart catches in my throat, and Cortez grins. Capshaw looks up in amazement, tosses the bag back and forth in his hands, feeling its weight like recovered pirate treasure.

"Coffee beans," he says, gaping up at Cortez, who takes his hands down from the air.

"Many hundred pounds of them. You want to know where I got them? It's a great story."

* * *

Most days, as we get closer to the end, I am content to just be, to wait, to enjoy the company of McConnell and the others, to conscientiously perform the share of tasks that fall to me. And I am usually successful in my efforts to keep my mind focused on the immediate present, on whatever event or requirement comes next— to see not too far into the future, nor too far back into the past.

We tend to get up early, McConnell and I, and it's morning now, and we're drinking coffee in the kitchen and looking out the window at the lawn, the sheds, and past that the wooded expanse of the world. The very beginnings of autumn in western Massachusetts, the green trees goldening at their edges. Trish is across the table, telling me about an irritating conversation she had last night with Officer Michelson.

"I'm serious, I was about to fucking strangle the guy," she says. "Because basically what he was saying is, at this point if it *didn't* hit— if there was some last-minute thing, you know, some crazy scenario, like they can blow it up after all, or deflect it, or the religious people pray it out of the sky—Michelson says maybe that would be *worse*, at this point. You know how he is, sort of smirking, so you don't know if he's being serious or not, but he goes, at this point, imagine winding it back. With everything that's gotten f'ed up, imagine starting over? And I just said, 'Man, anything is better than death. *Anything.*'"

"Yeah," I say, "of course," and I'm nodding, trying to pay attention, but the moment Trish said the word *deflect*, my mind exploded with thoughts of Nico: memories of my vanished sister are suddenly everywhere in my head, like invaders pouring across a border. She is four years old and toppling off her bicycle; she is six and staring in confusion at the crowds during the funerals; she is ten and drunk and I am telling her that I will never let her go. The helicopter swoops down to lift me up from blockhouse at Fort Riley, and Nico presses masses of white washcloths into my mess of an arm, tells me it's going to be okay.

"Hank?"

"Yeah?" I say, blinking.

"You all right?"

In five minutes of talking I tell Trish the whole thing. About Next Time Around, about Jordan and the blonde girl and the computer, about the helicopter. She asks, so I give her what details I remember about the plan itself: the nuclear-standoff blast and the "back reaction"; a sufficient change in velocity with a minimum of ejecta; the secret scientist moldering in the military prison.

"Jesus H. Christ," says Trish.

"I know." My coffee is cold. I get up to refill it.

"If the government is so determined to keep this from happening, why didn't they kill the scientist?"

"Oh, hey," I say. "Great question. I didn't even ask that one."

"Listen, you can't beat yourself up about it," murmurs Trish. "If she was going to go, she was going to go." She had met Nico a couple times over the years—at cop parties, at the station, at my house once or twice.

"Go where?" says Kelli, wandering in in her Sleeping Beauty nightgown.

"Nowhere, honey."

Kelli is holding hands with her brother, and she opens the pantry to get them snack cakes. Police House follows a strict "kids can eat whatever they want" policy.

"You should go and find her."

We hadn't seen Cortez come in. He is standing in the doorway, his expression unusually serious.

"Why?" says McConnell, looking at him. They have yet to make up their minds about each other, these two.

"She's his sister," says Cortez. "Can I have one of those, please?"

Kelli hands him a snack cake, and he unwraps it while he talks.

"She is family. She matters to him. Look at him. Everything is different. The asteroid will strike in one and a half months. What if she's in trouble? What if she needs help?"

Cortez studies me while he bites into the snack cake. Mc-Connell is looking at me, too, her hand on my forearm while I watch the steam rise off my cup.

Yeah, is what I'm thinking. *What if?*

THANK YOU

Dr. Timothy Spahr, director of the Minor Planet Center at the Harvard-Smithsonian Center for Astrophysics; Officer Joseph Wright and everyone at the Concord Police Department in New Hampshire; Andrew Winters

My family at Quirk Books: Jason, Nicole, Eric, Doogie, Mary Ellen, Jane, Dave, Brett, and—seriously—everyone else they got over there

My family at my house: Diana, Rosalie, Ike, and Milly

My agent, Joelle Delbourgo

Smart people: business and economics author Eduardo Porter; Mitch Renkow, professor of agriculture and resource economics, North Carolina State University; Christopher Rudolph at the School of International Service at American University; Joe Loughmiller at Indiana American Water; Dr. Zara Cooper; Dr. Nora Osman; Dr. Gerardo Gomez and his colleagues at Wishard Hospital, Indianapolis; Dani Sher, PA-C, and her colleagues at Mount Sinai Hospital in Chicago; Lieutenant Colonel Eric Stewart of the Green Berets; the folks at Snipercraft, Inc., Sebring, Florida

Early readers: Kevin Maher, Laura Gutin, Erik Jackson, and especially Nick Tamarkin, my own personal Detective Culverson

Colleagues, students, and friends at Butler University, Indianapolis

Colleagues, students, and friends at Grub Street, Boston

And a special thank you to everyone who submitted a "What Would You Do?" essay at TheLastPoliceman.com. Keep 'em coming.

WHAT WOULD YOU DO …

… with just 77 days until the
end of the world?

Author Ben H. Winters posed this question to a variety
of writers, artists, and notable figures.

Visit QuirkBooks.com/TheLastPoliceman to:
- Read their answers
- Share your own responses
- Watch the book trailer
- Read a Q&A with Ben H. Winters
- Discover the science behind the science fiction

And much more!

•